Acts of the Women

By Patrick W. Andersen

Acts of the Women

Second Born Series, Volume 2

Patrick W. Andersen

Published by Patrick W. Andersen, 2023.

ACTS OF THE WOMEN

First edition. November 1, 2023.

Copyright © 2023 Patrick W. Andersen.

ISBN: 979-8230479772

Written by Patrick W. Andersen.

What others are saying

"An inventive and gripping work of historical fiction focusing on Jesus."

Kirkus Reviews

(Regarding *Second Born*)

Patrick W. Andersen's thrilling new novel, *Acts of the Women*, is a celebration of the women of the New Testament. Beautifully written in a humorous tone, the author seamlessly weaves together vivid prose with intelligent but surprising conclusions based on years of biblical studies. His women are wise, courageous leaders who rule the men as the risen Jesus and his disciples spread out across the world: France, India, and beyond. This excellent novel is a must-read for anyone interested in exploring the non-traditional stories around Jesus. It is an ode to women and a spiritual gift that should be savored with an open mind.

Kristi Saare Duarte,

Author, *Holy Conspiracy*, and *The Transmigrant*

A fascinating, refreshing, well-crafted, and unique interpretation (or perhaps a new telling) of those women in the Bible who were not only instrumental in the development of early Christianity, but powerful in their roles of protecting—and influencing—the man known as Jesus. The women in this book are not subservient or meek but strong, brave, and radiate such inner beauty that their stories will undoubtedly inspire readers. I was also struck that Jesus, the second-born son of Joseph and Miriam, is portrayed as an entirely relatable human being. This compelling tale is a must-read for Biblical scholars, theologians, open-minded and open-hearted Christians, and open-minded, open-hearted non-Christians alike. *Acts of the Women* is extraordinary. I consider this book a must-read.

Peggy A. Wheeler,

Author, *The Raven's Daughter*, and *The Desert Raven*

Andersen once again gives a fresh, plausible life to the greatest story ever told, the story of Christ and the young church. Rather than unraveling and spinning the same story, we get a new look at the disciples, the women, who played a large role in the beginning of Christianity, and the faith that sustained them.

Ellen L. Ekstrom,
Author, *Tallis' Third Tune*, and *Scarborough*

Cast of Characters

Abban — Son of Amrit. Due to an accident that broke his arm, he stayed in Galilee for several months as a boy and became friends with Judas when they were both young.

Alexander — The governor of Judeans in Alexandria, Egypt, and brother of Philo.

Amrit — A trader from the East. While his injured son Abban stayed in Galilee under Mother Miriam's care, Amrit took Jesus with him on the Silk Road.

Aquila — Husband of Priscilla.

Benjamin — Uncle to Jesus and his siblings. He and his wife Leah allowed James to stay at their estate in Bethany from the time he was young and began studying at the Temple.

Chuza — Also known as Joses, the husband of Joanna and the steward of Herod Antipas.

Gamaliel — One of the greatest scholars at the Temple in Jerusalem, and the tutor of many young men studying for the priesthood.

James — The first-born son of Joseph and Miriam. After studying at the Temple since his childhood, as a man he has become renowned as the Righteous One. Gamaliel has made James the steward of his own household in David's City, below the Temple in Jerusalem.

Jesus — The second-born son of Joseph and Miriam. Following his revelation upon his baptism by John, he became known as the King and was crucified by the Romans following a riot at the Temple. Unlike most members of his family, his skin was dark.

Joanna — The oldest daughter of Joseph and Miriam, she is a year younger than Judas.

Judas — The third-born son of Joseph and Miriam, he is one year younger than Jesus and shares his dark complexion. Because they look so much alike, he has grown up with the nickname Thomas, which means the Twin.

Judith — Wife of Simon.

Leah — Wife of Benjamin.

Mark — Son of Alexander.

Martha — Mother of Andrew and Simon Peter.

Mary — Daughter of Benjamin and Leah and sister of Lazarus. Jesus called her the Migdal, the name of the tall fish tower in Magdala, which stood as a landmark for fishermen on the Sea of Galilee. Conflating the honorific title with the village where the tower stood, some later followers referred to her as Mary Magdalen.

Miriam — Wife of the late Joseph and mother of James, Jesus, Judas, Joanna, Simon, and Susanna.

Philo — Brother of Alexander and the spiritual leader of Judeans in Egypt.

Priscilla — Wife of Aquila and companion to Paul.

Rachel — House servant for Gamaliel and James.

Rebecca — Young servant woman assisting Rachel.

Sarah — Daughter of Judas and Mary.

Saul (Paul) — A man born in Tarsus. Like James, his parents sent him at a young age to study with Gamaliel (and later James) in Jerusalem.

Stephen — A young man who studied under Gamaliel and James.

Symmachus — A rabbi in Pella.

Susanna — The youngest child of Joseph and Miriam.

MARY, THE MIGDAL

I saw the look of condescension in their eyes, and I was not going to stand for it.

"I tell you, I saw him. He's still alive."

The men didn't say anything, but they all exchanged looks silently among themselves, as if to say I was crazy. Even Judas, my own husband, treated me as if I'd been hit on the head with a large object and was babbling groggily. It made me so mad that I wanted to scream. What right did they have to doubt?

"Look, while the rest of you ran and hid, I stood there and watched when they beat your brother Jesus with whips. I followed along as they made him carry a beam of wood out to the hill among the olive trees across the Kidron Valley. I stood there with Mother Miriam and we watched as they strung him up on the cross. As he hung there gasping for breath, he called me his beloved disciple and entrusted his own mother to my care."

I turned and glared at each of them in turn, daring them to deny it.

"I watched him die. I watched them take his body down and put it in a cave nearby. I'm the one who held Mother Miriam in my arms while she wailed. Where were you? And where were you? And you?" I asked, pointing at each of them. "I tell you, when Lazarus and I returned to the cave this morning, my brother went inside and brought Jesus out. He was alive."

My beloved husband seemed almost too embarrassed to speak. "That's just it, Dear." Ooh! He called me *Dear*! If I'd been close enough, I'd have hit him in the head with something that would make *him* groggy! "You witnessed the tragedy, and it's shaken you up quite a bit. Maybe, just maybe, you were seeing things this morning that you wish were true but weren't really there?"

Miriam had stayed behind in Bethany while I came into the city this morning, so I did not have her here to back me up. When I married her son Judas, she taught me how to hold my own against men. "Look them straight in the eye and never waver," she had told me. "No matter what they say or how loudly they yell, never lower your eyes." I know Judas and the men in the family all called it the Stare, and they felt helpless against it. I had not yet attained Mother Miriam's level of skill. Nevertheless, I locked my eyes onto

Judas's, squared myself in front of him, and slowly rested the knuckles of my cocked fists on my hips. I said nothing, and neither did he.

In the space of time it would take to gasp for breath twelve times, the small muscles around his eyes began to quiver. He opened his mouth once, then shut it, and then opened it again to speak in a pleading voice. "We all heard the Father's voice a moment ago."

I wouldn't release him, not yet. "Yes, we all heard his voice. And yet you still don't believe me?" I held his eyes for a moment longer, and then turned to his brothers James and Simon. James had been sheltered here at the Temple away from his mother Miriam, so he crumpled under my Stare almost instantly. Simon, the seasoned militia leader, immediately recognized a superior force and surrendered without resistance.

"Okay, okay, so he's alive," Judas muttered. "What do you want us to do?"

"Don't do anything yet," I said evenly. "We're hiding Jesus in a tent outside the city walls until he can recover, so we must not say a word outside this house. Simon, before your men flee the city for the road to Galilee, wait for word from me. James, you stay here and send word to the Temple that you're staying in seclusion. Ask the priests to keep secret that Jesus is your brother, or else the Romans may arrest you.

"Judas," I said over my shoulder as I started toward the stairs, "stay here with James and concoct some stories that will divert the Romans away from the family. Jesus survived the cross, but I don't want to take a chance on you three having to do the same."

I was just starting down the stairs when Judas blurted out, "But wait — where are you going?"

I turned my gaze back on the three of them and held them for a moment before speaking. "Many lives are at stake here, so I'm going to need people with common sense. I'm going to talk to the women."

I found Rachel in the kitchen, fussing over a large cake of bread she had just pulled out of the oven. She poked a small knife into the middle and examined inside to see if the dough was cooked all the way through. Apparently satisfied with what she found, she set the knife down and turned to me.

"I was sorry to hear of your family's loss," she said with a slight bow of her head. "The Rabbi Gamaliel was so sad when he told me. I'm sure the Rabbi James must be grievin' terribly, it bein' his brother and all."

I clutched her forearms in greeting the way the men did, and locked eyes with her. "Rachel, he's alive. I saw him this morning. I need you to gather some women that you can trust to help me take care of him."

Rachel's eyes widened in a mixture of shock, disbelief and wild joy. "Alive? But we heard the Romans killed him. They said the King is dead."

"No, they failed to kill him, or at least they can't keep him dead. But we have to hide him and care for him or else he may die. He's badly wounded. And then we have to smuggle him away."

She looked off vacantly for a moment as if consulting a list that hung in the air before her, then snapped back into focus. "I know some people who can help. We'll go to them." Then she looked at my belly. "You look like your baby's gonna pop out any minute. Why don't you rest here while I go take care o' things?"

I tilted my head as if I were looking at a teenager who had just uttered a mouthful of nonsense. "Rachel, we are women. Who do you think actually gets things done in this world — the men?"

She ducked her head in momentary shame. "You're right, no offense intended, my lady. Speakin' o' which, just let me tell the Rabbi James and his brothers upstairs that their bread is baked. If I leave the house without tellin' him where to find it, he'll starve."

I laughed and hugged her. I went upstairs with her and had a brief shouting match with Judas that yes, I damn well *was* strong enough to go out, and that he'd better stay where he was to avoid capture by the soldiers. James saw the glare in Rachel's eye and apparently knew well enough to keep his mouth shut. Simon stayed out of it too. I agreed that I would accompany Judas to Bethlehem where I could safely give birth, but not until we had found a safe place for Jesus to rest and heal. Stay out of it, I warned all three of them. The women will handle it.

"I need to ask one favor," Judas interjected. "For our safety, please call me Thomas from now on. Even if Jesus is still alive, Judas will be a hunted man."

Good idea, I thought to myself as I went down the stairs. That showed some foresight. There's hope for him yet.

JOANNA

Sometimes, no matter how anxious you are to move forward, the best you can do is offer comfort to one who is grieving. For the past three days, I seemed to have no other purpose than to hold Mom and let her weep, sometimes in silence, sometimes in loud wails. Mary and Lazarus had left us here at Uncle Benjamin's house in Bethany early this morning while they went to anoint Jesus's body. I had expected them to return much earlier in the day, but the afternoon was wearing on already.

Susanna, sitting on the other side of Mom, made eye contact with me and gave a minute tilt of her head slightly toward the door. I responded with a small nod and gently disengaged Mom's arms clutched about me. She continued crying as Susanna and I slipped out of the room.

"We have to get her to eat something," my sister said in an urgent whisper. "She's losing strength, and I'm afraid she'll get very sick."

I nodded in agreement. Mom had always stood like a rock for us. Seeing her in this state had immobilized us ever since we heard of the crucifixion, and we'd let her down. It was up to us to nurse her to recovery. "Mary and Lazarus's servants left out bread, cheese and figs a few hours ago. Do you think we could get her to nibble on some of that? At the very least, we've got to get her to drink some water."

We cut off a piece of bread and a sliver of cheese and poured a cup of water and took it in to her. Against my worst fears, she actually took a few bites of the food. But she refused the water, instead asking for wine. I went back to the kitchen and filled a cup with wine and brought it to her.

She took a long sip and raised her eyes to look at us both. Turning up the corner of her mouth, she muttered, "Jesus's Nectar of Nazareth is far superior."

I couldn't hold it back. I laughed long and hard, tears rolling freely down my cheeks. Susanna joined in, and the three of us hugged amid our shared gloom, gleefully recalling the wine my brother produced that was the talk of southern Galilee.

"Do you remember the time he gave Dad a drink of his wine as he lay on his deathbed?" Susanna howled. "In that moment I thought Dad was going to get up and dance."

"Hah!" I giggled. "I believed he and Jesus were really going to get on their donkeys and ride into town together."

Mom didn't say anything, but a small smile crept over her face as she recalled that day. The household had been wrapped in a cloud of gloom as Dad's death approached. Then Jesus came home and there was life again, even if it only lasted for a few more days. He'd pulled the family together and gave us hope, just as he pulled the people of the countryside together and gave them all hope too.

Maybe we all had put too much hope on his shoulders alone. He was just a man, after all, and he never pretended to be a savior for all the people. In fact, Jesus was trying to bring the people to James, who might really be a savior. The Righteous One, many people called him. James the Just.

Mom finally stirred herself and spoke. "There is no shame in his crucifixion. He brought us hope and faith in the Father, who is mightier than the Romans with their swords and chariots. You girls and I — we must carry on so James can lead the nation."

In the silence that followed, I heard the creaking of wagon wheels outside. I glanced out the door expecting to see Mary and Lazarus but was surprised to see a crowd of women.

"What's this?" I asked aloud, turning to Susanna and Mom and pointing outside.

The three of us went outside to find Rachel, the servant at the house of Gamaliel, where James lived, with seven or eight other women. They all wore aprons over their robes, as if they'd been cooking or cleaning house before suddenly deciding to leave the city to walk here to Bethany. They had been chattering among themselves, but all fell silent as we came out of the house.

"It's her," Rachel called out to the other women. "It's the mother of the Righteous One and the King." They all bowed their heads in respect, and two made a clumsy attempt at curtsying.

Mom looked surprised at their deference but recovered quickly. "Greetings, and thank you for visiting me in my grief. The mistress of this house is not here, but please come in and we'll get water and towels for you to wash your feet."

"Ah, no, my lady, the mistress is here, and she's the one who asked us to come. Plenty o' time later for washin' feet," Rachel said. With that the group of women parted, and we saw Mary and Lazarus standing near the back of the cart. It was covered with a tarp of tent-like material, and I could not see what was underneath.

"Joanna, Susanna," Mary called. "Are all the servants out of the house? Is there anyone nearby who will see us here?"

I didn't understand this concern for secrecy. "Yes, we've been alone here for a few hours. They left us some food before they went out to do their work."

"Then come help us," she said. "And even if no one is nearby, keep quiet at what you're going to see."

They pulled the tarp back, and there in the back of wagon lay Jesus. Dried blood covered most of his body, and I could see welts where the whips had lashed his skin. Bruises shadowed the cheeks beneath his eyes, but those eyes were open! His chest rose and fell with breathing — rough, perhaps, but steady. When he saw Mom, he grinned and muttered, "Woman, behold your son."

Mom started to squeal but, at a sharp rebuke from Mary, silenced her delight immediately. She surged forward and wrapped her arms around Jesus but flinched backward when he gasped in pain. "Careful," he muttered as he sucked air through his clenched teeth. "The spirit is willing but the flesh is weak."

When we had moved him into the barn and laid him on hay on a pallet and wrapped him in blankets, all of us women moved into the central courtyard. Rachel and the other women from the city all turned their eyes reverently to Mom, waiting for her to tell them what to do.

But it was Mary who held up the palm of her hand to call for silence. Before we made our fateful trip to Jerusalem several weeks earlier, before the riot and Jesus's crucifixion, he had referred to Mary as the Migdal, named for the fish tower in Magdala. He considered her a beacon, just as the tower is a landmark for fishermen on the lake in Galilee.

"Many thanks to all of you for helping us get the King out of the city," Mary said. "But he is not safe yet, and I need your help. We must keep the Romans from finding him, and we also have to protect the men and women who were following him. The Romans will kill us all if they identify and capture us."

One of the women appeared shaken but resolute. "I can't fight those men with their swords. But tell me what I can do, and I'll do it." The others around her nodded in agreement.

Mary looked at each face in the courtyard, measuring the strength she could see in each of our eyes. "Joanna," she said to me, "stand across from me there near the wall. Susanna, you stand to the right, and Mother Miriam, to the left.

"The rest of you," Mary said to the women wearing their aprons and work clothes, "fill in the gaps between us and form one large circle. And then I want you to hold hands with the women on either side of you."

When all of us had positioned ourselves and joined hands as she requested, we turned to Mary. After a moment's smile, Mary bowed her head and closed her eyes. Following her lead, I closed mine too. I assume everyone else in the circle did so as well.

As we stood in silence, I felt a calm come over me. I became intensely focused on my breathing, filling my lungs with air easily, and then letting it ease back out through my mouth quietly. Inhale luxuriantly through my nostrils, exhale from my mouth any sort of stress that may have been lingering within me. Inhale. Exhale. And repeat the cycle, slipping into a sense of peace that had already been present there in the courtyard but of which we were just now becoming aware. Inhale. Exhale.

"Our Father in heaven, we revere your name," Mary intoned. "Your ways in heaven are just. Help us to realize that your kingdom is among us now, here on this earth. Help us sustain ourselves this day so we can do your work, and help us resist the evil that would assail us. You are the God of Abraham and Isaac and Leah and Rachel and us all. Amen."

In that moment I felt a presence, and I dared not move. The women on either side of me suddenly clenched their hands in mine — whether in fear or joy, I could not tell.

You are all my daughters, with whom I am well pleased, said a voice. Except it wasn't really a voice. I heard it in my mind, but I don't know if it was aloud in the air. Apparently, the others heard it or felt it too, because one gasped and I could feel movement in the circle through the hands I held on either side as if someone had yanked a pair of chains. Whether in awe or terror, we all kept our silence.

"Father," Mary said softly, "thank you for your presence among us. We ask your help in protecting your son Jesus from the Romans. They will kill him if they find him, and they will certainly kill us for hiding him. If we must die, so be it. But we could provide you better service if we lived."

The voice didn't really laugh, but the effect was the same. We all felt an air of lightness around us.

Yes, I think it would be better if you kept yourselves alive. Do not fear. I will be with you — always.

The moment passed, and we all exhaled loudly as if we had been holding our breath. Rachel's friends all turned and hugged each other, giggling nervously, before catching themselves and turning reverently to Mary.

She slowly turned her gaze upon each of us in turn. When she looked at me, I felt lost in the depth of her eyes, and I was sure she could see directly into my mind and heart. In that moment I would have obeyed whatever command she might give. Judging from the stillness in the courtyard, I think all the women felt the same. I wasn't sure what had happened moments ago, but I know that it was Mary who brought it to us and shared the experience with us. I wasn't sure whether to hug her or kneel at her feet.

"You have heard the voice of God, and you are all blessed among women," she said. "I will tell you what we must do. The King will be sheltered here until he is strong enough to travel. But we have dozens of men who must also be hidden. Joanna," she said, turning to me, "you and Susanna must take charge of concealing Simon's men, and Jesus's followers. You must do this under Herod's very nose — your husband Chuza cannot breathe a word that will make Antipas suspicious."

I shared a knowing glance with Mary and Susanna. The corners of all of our mouths curled upward, and we included the Jerusalem women in our joke as I said, "Husbands will do as they are told. It is the way of the Lord."

Amid the gleeful outburst of chuckles that followed, Mom reached out to Rachel and held both of her hands. Shocked at the intimacy, Rachel's mouth gaped open as she looked into Mom's eyes. She could say nothing.

"Hear me, all of you," Mom said. "Rachel here has cared for God's Righteous One in her household for many years, and I believe she will have to continue in this task for many years to come. Heaven knows James can't take care of himself," she said jokingly, drawing more chuckles. "But now the Romans may seek to kill him, so I must call on you and all your friends to protect him. Stand in the way of those who would hurt him. When you see soldiers coming to silence him, move him to a place of safety and cover the signs of his path from those who would pursue him. And when he speaks, spread his message to those who were not present to hear it with their own ears."

Rachel's face turned red with embarrassment but glowed at the words of praise. She clutched Mom's hands and shook them up and down as if nodding. "Yes, my lady. The Righteous One'll suffer no evil at the hands of the Romans, of that you can be sure. We'll make sure all the women of the city stand as one to protect him. And we'll make sure the men do their part too, such as they're capable." More twitters erupted.

"And what of the King, my lady?" Rachel asked Mom. "Do you need us to find some healer who can be trusted?"

Mom smiled. "We shall see. I may need for all of you to find me some herbs to soothe his wounds. I am grateful to all of you for your help."

Rachel beamed as she looked around at the other women. Then, drawing herself up to leave, she said, "Well, let's not just stand around like a bunch of men. It's time to get to work."

SUSANNA

Mary and Judas — oops, I have to get used to calling him just Thomas — Mary and Thomas slipped out of the city to the road south. Her plan was to give birth to her baby in a safe location, somewhere obscure where no prying eyes would reveal them. We had received word that the Romans were hunting for a tax rebel named Judas. It was one thing for a man to be seen as a prophet or even a would-be king, but far more serious for the Romans to suspect he was telling the masses to refuse to pay their taxes! The soldiers had beaten Jesus and hung him up on a cross to die, but they wouldn't be so lenient with Judas. They would cut his head off in a public square and mount it on a stake for all to see. We spread a rumor that Judas had killed himself out of remorse, hoping that would convince the Romans to quit searching.

So Mary asked Rachel to find a tattered robe that a peasant would wear, with a hood to hide the fugitive's face. Thomas looked uncomfortable when he first put it on, but we assured him it was for the best. We watched as they left, from a distance of course, so we wouldn't draw attention to them. Pregnant as she was, Mary rode on an ass led by Thomas, his back hunched over as if he were carrying a burden, his face turned toward the ground before his feet. If I didn't already know who they were, I would never have noticed them among the hundreds of peasants making their way into and out of the city. After a few minutes, we couldn't see any more of them and could only pray for their safety.

But we had no time to waste. Rachel had gathered us together the previous night for planning, and we each had our assignments. Joanna, acting as the wife of a visiting officer of Herod Antipas' court, led what would appear to casual observers to be her household slaves behind her as she went with another of the women to escort Simon's men to homes where they could hide. They could only take a pair of men at a time, so the task consumed an entire day. My job was to collect all of their and the other men's swords into a cart, hidden under a blanket, of course, and return them to Gamaliel's house until the men were ready to take the road back to Galilee. Mom would care for Jesus at Uncle Benjamin's, nursing him back to health so he could travel.

Our tasks became all the more dangerous because, as much as we emphasized the need for secrecy, the word was seeping out throughout the city. The King was alive! Jesus had survived the cross and still walked the earth. The news thrilled so many people in the narrow lanes as we tried to move about the city. It seemed everyone was talking about it. Did you hear? one peasant would ask. Yes, and I heard he is amassing an army of rebels outside the gates to drive the Romans out, the other would answer. Hah, shouted yet another, I heard he needs no army, that God raised him up in the air and he will merely point his finger at the Antonia and cause the Romans' fortress to crumble. And one more would join the conversation saying the Romans with their swords and whips and crosses cannot kill our King, nor can they touch the Righteous One.

I wanted to scream at them, Shut up! By mocking Rome, you'll only bring its wrath down on us all. You'll provoke them to prove that yes, they really can kill James if they want to. And they really can conduct a house-to-house search to root out Jesus's followers and slit their throats, and they really can track down Jesus and kill him for good this time. Just shut up, will you all?

But I couldn't say a thing. Mom had warned us all not to draw any attention to ourselves. One word of anger might get us all arrested or attract spies who would follow us. And though I think Jesus had taught Lazarus how to go into a death-like trance, none of the rest of us could do that. Those of us whom the Romans chose to execute would surely die, because the soldiers would leave nothing to chance this time. We women would probably be sold as slaves, and forced to work for cruel masters or, worse yet, submit our bodies to them. No, I would ignore my fears and keep my mouth shut as the peasants in the city cheered Jesus's survival.

The men were reluctant to give up their swords. Even that big oaf Simon, the one Jesus nicknamed Peter the Rock, thought he could protect himself against the foreigners' army if he kept his blade. I had to tell a fib — I told him the order came directly from the King, that Jesus himself had demanded the men give up their weapons for as long as they remained in the city. I even made up a slogan and attributed it to my brother, "He who lives by the sword will die by the sword." Peter repeated it several times reverently as if the words had come from God himself, and then he gently placed his sword in my hands. I wrapped it in a cloak and returned it to Gamaliel's house, where I stacked it in the upper room with the others.

After covering the pile of swords, I stopped downstairs in the kitchen to see Rachel. She had three big baskets of fruits sitting against one wall, and five large loaves of bread on the table. When she noticed me, she straightened up and brushed off her hands against her apron. "Miss Susanna, you'll be gettin' hungry soon, I'll guess?"

My eyes took in the sight of all the food, and it reminded me of the community kitchen in Sepphoris where Mom, Joanna and I would go years ago to buy bread and other victuals from the women in town. "Rachel, are you cooking for a banquet?"

She looked to the loaves and fruit as if counting them for the first time. "No, just for a few dozen men we're hidin' in houses around the city. My friends were able to find places for them to stay out of sight, but they don't all have enough food to keep 'em fed. So I'm doin' as much as I can."

Her devotion touched me. "I can help you carry food to these houses," I offered.

"Nah, Miss, you got your own job to do. I can handle this."

"But Rachel," I persisted, "I have to go see the men to collect their swords. I would need you to show me where they are hiding anyway, so let me help you."

She nodded agreement as she realized the sense of what I was saying. We sorted some bread, fruit and cheeses into separate piles and wrapped them in sackcloth bundles. We slung them over our shoulders and set off into the narrow street outside Gamaliel's door.

Here in David's City, the area beneath the highland that held the Temple complex, the people worked hard for every meal. Much of the farming that fed the city was done in the lands outside the city walls, so many men made their living working the fields for the landowners, leaving their homes before the sun rose and not returning until late afternoon. Others drove oxen to pull wagons of produce into the city to sell in the marketplace.

We carried our parcels of food into the lower city, down toward the Siloam Pool. I remembered when I was a girl, hearing my father speak about how King Hezekiah in ancient times had built a long tunnel to divert water from the Gihon Spring to this pool, giving the city drinking water while denying it to the invading army outside the walls in the Kidron Valley. Many people to this day considered the digging of the tunnel to be more important than the old Herod's building of the Temple about fifty years ago. While the Temple had restored God's house — destroyed by invaders hundreds of years earlier — the much older tunnel gave water to quench our thirst and purify us before God. And just as the Pool of Siloam helped sustain us, so Rachel's bread and fruit would sustain the men who were trying to restore righteousness to the Temple. My part in the scheme of it all — hiding their weapons to protect them — seemed tiny in comparison. So I was proud to walk the streets with Rachel and be seen by the other women as her assistant.

And Rachel, bless her, raised me up even higher! She introduced me as the youngest sister of the King and the Righteous One, as if our shared bloodline in itself made me holy. I had no words I could say when the servant women of the city bowed their heads to me. But it frightened me to realize that the Romans, if they saw the attention paid to me, might start asking questions. So I begged them to treat me like one of their own.

MIRIAM

"Mom, let me get up and help them. I feel terrible laying here doing nothing."

I swatted at him as Jesus made a motion to lift himself up to stand. Weeks ago, the women and I had placed a pallet in the barn and covered it with a layer of hay, then we covered the hay with a blanket, and put a second blanket over Jesus's body to keep him warm. We put a few things around for his comfort — a pitcher of water and a cup, and a few scrolls of the Law and Prophets along with a lantern to read by. I shuddered to think of my son sleeping in a manger, but it was for his own safety. Besides, I told myself, he had probably lived in much worse conditions in all his years on the road, at the vineyard, and at the River Jordan.

"Mom, the Festival of Weeks is coming. They have to harvest all of Benjamin's wheat and take it to market. I can help"

I swung the palm of my hand at him again, not close enough to actually hit him but to shoo him back onto his pallet. "Benjamin's people have harvested their wheat for many long years without your supervision, thank you, and I'm sure they can manage it again this year," I said. "You settle down. You don't want to find out how much you could hurt yourself by trying to move around before your body is healed. Now, a lot of people have gone to a lot of trouble and put their own lives at risk to keep you safe. I'm not going to let you put their work to waste."

He grinned that grin of his at me, and I half expected him to leap off his bed and lift me off my feet. But he lay back. "Ah yes, how many are the ways I could hurt myself. Judas and Simon and I learned many of those ways when we were boys. Speaking of my brothers, where are they?"

I stood ready to smack him in the head if he tried to get up again, but it looked like he had decided to stay put. "Thomas — nobody calls him Judas anymore, because the Romans want his hide almost as much as yours — Thomas took Mary out of the city to give birth to my grandchild. Simon and some of his men are still in the city, hiding from the soldiers until they think it's safe to travel."

He seemed to take a moment to absorb the news. "Joanna and Susanna?"

"The girls are helping the women in the city take care of Simon and his men. Joanna's instructed Chuza keep an ear open to Herod Antipas's plans. Susanna is making the rounds with the serving woman Rachel to make sure all the men are cared for and are keeping quiet. And of course, Rachel is taking care of James, who has been laying low since the riot at the Temple."

His eyebrow jumped at the mention of the riot. "Did everyone escape?

I folded my arms across my chest. "The Romans only captured one man, the notorious rebel who masterminded the uprising. The people called him the King, but the soldiers hung him on a cross and killed him. Mary and I were there, and we saw him breathe his last."

"Too bad — he sounds like a wonderful man," he said with mock innocence. "In fact, he sounds brilliant. I would have liked to meet him."

"He was reckless and arrogant and I'm sure he caused his mother enough grief to last two lifetimes," I said, and this time I really did smack him on the side of the head.

He rubbed the spot I had hit as if he were severely wounded, but I knew better. "Like I said," he hissed between clenched teeth, "this king of yours sounds brilliant. We have a lot on common, him and I."

MARY

Thank God we found a midwife, because if Thomas were in here assisting me, I would have strangled him by now. The baby inside me had apparently changed its mind several times about entering the world but thrashed violently against itself every time it decided to switch directions. A war raged in my loins, and it seemed that the little monster would win. The midwife coaxed me to take short breaths and push downward rhythmically with the muscles of my stomach. But every push brought its own punishment — the baby wanted to split me apart!

I screamed. I screamed again as I pushed. And a third scream, and it felt like something broke. The pressure seemed to lighten, and then a gush of water splashed on the ground. I was spent. As I took a deep breath, I heard a light slap and then a light, screeching cry. My baby!

"Hello little one," cooed the midwife. After she wiped away some goo from the child's face and body, she turned to me and held the bundle out to my outstretched arms. "Here is your daughter, my lady."

"My daughter?" I almost shouted. "Oh, thank the Lord! She will do great things in this world."

The midwife chuckled. "Most women pray for a son to take care of them in their old age."

"Yes," I breathed, exhausted, "I will need someone to take care of me. That's why I need a daughter."

JOANNA

"You told me yourself that Herod wants to use me as a hostage against Judas," I said. "I don't think I should travel with you and Herod's entourage back to Galilee."

Chuza's expression clearly showed that he was torn. "But he knows you're here in the city. Won't he get suspicious if you don't return with us?"

I looked up from the table where I had been sorting packets of food to be delivered to Simon's men. Here at Uncle Benjamin's home, we had plenty of cheese, fruit, and grain to make bread, which took pressure off of Rachel and the women in the city. Although Benjamin had resisted supporting men whom the Romans branded as rebels, Aunt Leah laid down the law on her husband. "My granddaughter Sarah is one of the central fugitives in this so-called rebellion," she had said, poking her finger toward his normally staid face. "You are not only going to provide food for Simon's men. You're going to do everything necessary to keep them safe and make sure they succeed."

As I looked at Chuza, the memory of Leah's fierce but firm handling of her husband put steel in my resolve. As I started to fix my eyes on his, the way Mom had taught Susanna and me, he saw what was coming and surrendered immediately.

"Okay, I'll make up some excuse. I'll tell him you're traveling with your mother to keep her safe. I'll tell him you're helping care for your newborn niece. I'll say you're working with your brother to bring more merchants to Sepphoris and Tiberius." He was desperate to come up with an alibi that would rescue him from the Stare. "I'll think of something."

"You do that." I held his eyes a moment more and then released him. "I think you need to rejoin Herod now so he can get out on the road. I will see you back in Sepphoris in about two weeks." I embraced him and kissed him long and deeply. "And then you and I will have a lot to catch up on," I added, playfully tweaking his manhood.

He grinned at the intimacy and started to reach for my breast, but I swatted his hand away. "Off with you now! We'll save up all that for our reunion in two weeks."

Chuza's face looked like he was in actual physical pain. Good — that would remind him who's in charge.

RACHEL

The rabbi told me to do whatever the Righteous One asked, but he worried me. This newest idea seemed reckless after all the trouble the other women and I took to keep them safe. He wanted to bring all of Simon's men together for a meeting in the upper room here at the house ten days before the Festival of Weeks. I told him it was too dangerous. The Rabbi Gamaliel said even now, five weeks after the riot at the Temple, the soldiers were still looking out for anyone who might have been involved.

We had been storing their swords upstairs in James's meetin' room where he tutored the Temple students, hidden under thick piles of blankets so none of his students would see them. Some of Simon's men had hired themselves out as farmhands outside the city, partly to pay for their hosts' hospitality but also because they were going stir-crazy, sittin' around with nothin' to do. Who knew what mischief they might stir up if they came here and got reunited with their swords?

"This year, the Lord our God has again spoken to us as he did to Moses at Mt. Horeb. First through my brother Jesus, the King, and then through my sister-in-law Mary, and finally through my brothers and me. Now is the time for us to meet and discern what God wants us to do."

I couldn't argue with that, but I sure let him know that he'd better be careful about organizin' this here meetin'. All this talk about Moses when the Romans were patrolling outside our front door sounded like he thought a pillar of fire was going to keep the soldiers away. I preferred to just avoid givin' 'em any reason to be suspicious in the first place. I had to ask him every night for details about how the plans were coming, because I didn't trust him to protect us. Men get good ideas sometimes, but you've got to keep an eye on them or else it'll go to their heads and they'll get sloppy.

So today was the big day. We had already moved all the furniture out of the upper room to clear some space. Susanna said she would bring food from Bethany. Some of the women had drawn extra pails of water for me so I wouldn't have to go out while the men were talkin' upstairs.

One by one, my women friends started showing up at the door with the fellows they'd been hiding. The men all wore their hoods over their heads to hide their faces. They went upstairs to wait for James to come home from the Temple, and I warned them to keep their voices down.

When almost two dozen of 'em had crowded into the room, James finally came in the front door. He clasped my forearms as if he was greeting one of his fellow priests, and then he went upstairs. Things quieted down then, and I set about my chores. Even though I didn't have to do all the cookin' this day, just havin' that many people in the house created a lot of extra work. I got down to it.

After a time I heard three light knocks at the door. That would be Miss Susanna, bringin' the food from Bethany. I opened the door and saw she had a small cart outside, narrow enough to pull through the alley. A man held the ox that was yoked to the cart, and another man was unloadin' stuff. I waved him on inside. His hood hid his face too, but I was getting pretty used to that. After the other man led the oxcart away, I closed the door and went back to my kitchen.

The supplies had been stacked on my table. Susanna was talkin' to the man when I walked in. "So what sort of food do we have for all these men?" I asked to no one in particular.

The man turned toward me. "Rachel, when you bless the food, anything we give them will be more than they could wish for," he said, pulling back his hood.

It was Jesus! "The King! What are you doin' here? The soldiers have heard all the rumors that you're still alive, and they're searchin' everywhere for you." I didn't know whether to bow to one knee in respect or swat him on the side of his head for bein' so reckless, so I did both.

He flinched when I smacked him, but I didn't really hit him hard enough to hurt. "You too?" he said, rubbing his temple. "So far on this trip I've been hit in the same spot by my host's wife, by my mother, and by both my sisters. If Mary were still here, she'd probably hit me too. I need some of Simon's men to protect me from all you women. Are they here yet?"

I wrapped both my arms around him in a hug. I'd never hugged his brother or the rabbi in all my years here, but I was so glad to see the King alive that there were tears on my cheeks. "Susanna and I were going to take some bread and water upstairs to them now anyway. Why don't you follow up behind us and you can show yourself after we've gone in."

The King had a twinkle in his eye. "We also brought some skins of Nazareth wine. I'll carry that."

I gave him a stern eye. "Be careful about givin' wine to that bunch. They've just been given back their swords."

The men barely noticed when Susanna and I came into the room with several large loaves of bread. The buzz of conversation continued as if we were just part of the group. But then I heard every one of 'em gasp when they saw who was coming in after us. The room went suddenly silent. And then, just like I had downstairs, they all dropped to one knee in respect, and then got up hissing at him. "What are you doing here? The Romans are looking for you."

The King made eye contact with me — with me! And then he smiled at the men and said, "My peace I bring to you." He went around the room, touching and blessing each of the men. He said a few extra words to Simon Peter and the Jericho brothers, John and James. And finally, he met in the middle of the room with his own brothers, James and Simon, and his sister Susanna. The four of them said no words but merely closed their eyes and grasped hands in a small circle. A hush fell on the whole room, and I felt a presence like the time Mary spoke to the Father in front of all us women out in Bethany. We didn't hear any words this time, or at least I didn't. But I *knew*, and I'm pretty sure everyone else in the room knew too. No words were needed.

"Thank you, Father," was all the King said.

Then everybody stirred, as if waking up from a daydream. Jesus held his hands up for silence. "My friends, thank you for all you have done. I have come to ask you to let the Father guide you in all you do. Most of all, I want you to do everything you can to support James. He is bringing the poor to the Temple, restoring them to their rightful place. Many will oppose him, so he needs your help."

Andrew raised his hand to catch attention. "What of you, Jesus. What will you do?"

Some of the men buzzed in agreement with the question. "My presence here is no longer needed, because you have the Father. In fact, as long as I am here, the Romans will continue searching for me and disrupting what you are trying to accomplish for the Righteous One. It would be better if I remove myself from the scene, perhaps go back to Galilee. I don't know what the Father has in mind for me after that."

Simon spoke up. "My men and I will escort you on the road, of course."

Andrew and several of the others voiced agreement, but his brother Simon Peter grasped his own elbow with one hand as he stroked his beard with the other. "I'm not sure if there's anything for me to do in Galilee anymore," he said. "You go along and protect the King, but I think I should protect the Righteous One. You tell Ma that I'll come see her when I get a chance, but I think my place is here for now."

The Jericho brothers sided with Peter. "We have nothing in Galilee, but we can help here in Judea," said John.

As if an unseen hand were sorting them into two groups, the men divided between those who would stay and those who'd accompany the King. They divided more or less evenly, almost like it was planned that way.

I was just watchin' it all from my corner. But then the King called out, "Where is the lady Rachel?" The men parted to make a clear path aimed directly at me. Jesus smiled and walked across the room, his arms stretched out. When he reached me, he wrapped me in a hug that made me glow inside. I coulda died right then and gone to meet my maker with a smile on my face.

"Listen, all of you," he called out. "All of you have important work to do, but Rachel here has one of the most important jobs of all. She not only has to take care of James and the Rabbi Gamaliel, but she also has to keep control over all of you men. This house is now God the Father's headquarters in Jerusalem and all of Israel, and Rachel is the boss here. So I want you to treat her with as much respect as you would give me. If you don't, you'll have to answer to the Father."

Yes, he said those exact words about me. About *me*! I burst into tears every time I remember it. In fact, I'm bawlin' like a baby as I tell you about it right now. The *King* said that about *me*!

MARY

I found another world in Alexandria. It was a world of huge Greek buildings, statues of philosophers and pagan idols, well-ordered streets that seemed to go on forever, and beautiful women who reclined on canopied litters carried through the streets by whole teams of slaves. My home at Bethany was close enough to Jerusalem and the road to Jericho for me to have seen countless wealthy foreigners, but nothing like this. I felt like a country peasant girl as Thomas led the ass I rode, with baby Sarah in my arms in swaddling cloths. My heart leapt to my throat every time I looked at her round, chubby face. Her skin looked a bit lighter than Thomas's dark, almost brown complexion but her face was certainly much darker than mine.

Thomas seemed awed by the sights in Alexandria as well. He no longer stayed hidden under the hood of his robe, and I saw his head swivel from side to side at the sights. He would point at a building or some beautiful fountain and utter, "Did you see that?" Well, of course I had seen it, and usually even before he did. But I kept quiet and let him take it in.

And then we found ourselves amid not just one building, but what seemed like an extended family of buildings. The parents of this family were clearly ahead of us, two massive structures to the left and right, but their children seemed to spread out in all directions. Some of the buildings in the distance were probably nieces and nephews, and it looked like many grandchildren were off in the distance. All of the structures were so grand and elegant that our great Temple in Jerusalem seemed almost quaint in comparison, it being an only child in comparison to this huge clan.

"This is it," Thomas said as he gazed at an inscription written on a large stone wall. "This is the library of Alexandria, the greatest center of learning in the world."

It was hard for me to imagine such a large space devoted to teaching. "There is so much here!" I said in wonder. "How many scrolls do you think they have here?"

Thomas turned, his eyes wide with excitement. "Not just scrolls. I've been told by some of the merchants who used to trade with us in Galilee that the scribes here have copied all the great scrolls into books as well."

Seeing a question on my face, he explained, "Books are flat pieces of paper collected into stacks and then bound together. Some of the scholars prefer them over scrolls, because they can find a passage in the middle of a great writing without unrolling the entire document."

He probably expected me to ask how this could be easier, but I didn't bother. It was obvious. No, I was more interested in seeing some of these books.

MIRIAM

"I don't care if you are strong enough to work. You stay hidden or else you could get all of us arrested." Jesus grinned at me, but I stood my ground. "Too many people have put themselves at risk. You stay here in the house or else I'll have the servants tie you hand and foot and stuff a rag in your mouth."

"Aw, Mom, you never let me have *any* fun." He was putting on the teenage act, behaving like the boy who caused me so much worry when I was raising my children. But his act wouldn't work this time. He had been agitating to get out and about ever since we returned home to Sepphoris, but I wouldn't let him.

"You stay where you are. Chuza tells Joanna that Herod Antipas has already been asking around about Judas. He might not have believed the story about your brother supposedly killing himself in remorse after your execution. If anyone sees you, they may mistake you for Judas and report you to Herod, and that would be the ruin of us all."

I considered locking my eyes on his in a Stare to make my point, but then I remembered that Jesus was immune to the Stare. He alone among all the males I knew could resist me. But I nevertheless stood as solidly as I could in front of him to let him know he wouldn't go anywhere without a fight.

He arched one eyebrow as if an idea had just sprung to mind. "If anyone sees me and says anything, you can just say I'm his twin. In fact, I think Judas had a good idea. I obviously can't go around Sepphoris introducing myself as Jesus. Maybe I should just say my name is Thomas. It was Judas's family nickname, but I don't think anyone in town ever knew it."

"Your brother had many great ideas," I answered, my eyes suddenly misting. "And he managed this household like he was born to the task. I'm not sure how we are going to continue."

Just then one of the servants knocked at the door and poked his head in. "Sorry to disturb you, ma'am, but that old friend of Judas's from years ago is here. Abban was his name."

"Abban!" both Jesus and I shouted simultaneously. This time I didn't try to stop him from going outside. We both ran to the front gate, where my former guest stood wrapped in a coat of bright silk.

Back when my boys were teenagers, Jesus had gone with Joseph and his men to barter with a trader from the east. That trader was named Amrit. The man's son, Abban, broke his arm in an accident, and Jesus offered himself as a hostage to travel with Amrit back to Malabar while Abban healed here in Sepphoris. Abban had taught mathematics to Judas, who in turn taught Abban about our faith in the one God. Meanwhile, traveling with Amrit, Jesus had learned many mystical practices that, to this day, I have never learned to understand. All I knew was that my boy returned home a changed person, and the boy who had remained at home changed too. Truth be told, I think my youngest daughter, Susanna, also changed. The mother-daughter talks we held in rooms where the males never entered took on a different tone after she met Abban.

And now, after all these years, Abban stood again at our gate.

He turned and smiled at us, his teeth a bright white against the dark skin of his face. But I could see that he was troubled, and I stopped short before I reached him. "What's wrong?"

Abban continued smiling but his brows squeezed toward each other in the ridge above his nose. He inhaled deeply and exhaled before speaking.

"It is my father," he almost choked. "We established a farm near the trade route north of the lake, near Bethsaida, and have settled into being an outpost rather than traveling the roads ourselves. It is a much quieter life but more stable. My lady, I remember all you did for me when I broke my arm and stayed with your family all those years ago. But now, in these past several weeks, my father seems to have lost the will to live. Is there anything you can do for him?'

Before answering, I placed my hands on his shoulders and looked deeply into his eyes. I could see that he had grown in years and experience. Those eyes carried anxiety for his father, yes, but also the wisdom gained after traveling many roads. He still dressed in silks, just as he had as a twelve-year-old boy.

"What has happened to your father? What brought on his illness?" I asked.

His face twisted in uncertainty. "That's just it. Nothing in particular happened to him. He does not seem to have any disease, or at least none that we are familiar with. He has not suffered any accident. But he has fallen into a state of malaise. He barely eats or drinks, and he sits and stares off into space. It's almost as if he is just waiting to die."

I was about to speak, maybe just to mumble words of encouragement while I searched my mind for a possible answer on how to treat this condition he described. Sometimes it doesn't matter what words you say, just that you coo some consoling tones of sympathy.

But at that moment Jesus placed his hand on my arm and gave a gentle squeeze. He fixed his eyes on mine, and for the first time I realized that he had true power. That was not just the Stare he fixed upon me! In an instant I was struck silent. Not violently or against my will. I felt strangely content to wait for him to speak. Or if he did not speak, I would still be content.

"Mom," he said, "I think I should accompany you for this healing."

His eyes still held me in thrall. Over the years since my own mother had taught it to me, I had exerted my will on others with my Stare, but never like this. "Of course, you should go," I muttered in awe. "In fact, I will probably not be needed at all."

Jesus smiled warmly. "Of course, you will be needed. And I think we should bring Susanna along too," he added with a wink at Abban.

Our visitor's skin was too dark to turn red. But he was clearly blushing, and he lowered his face as he peered up at both of us, a bashful smile curling the corners of his mouth.

RACHEL

I generally try to stay out of the Rabbi's way. He's got enough on his mind without me interferin', what with his surprise election to head of the Sanhedrin and all. I just make sure he's well fed and gets out of the house in time to go do whatever it is he does every day, and make sure he's comfortable and well fed when he comes home for the evening. I don't have a head for book learnin', and I most certainly could not care a bit about temple politics and the affairs of the city — so long as it don't interfere with food deliveries. He's pretty easy to care for, so I have time to talk to the other women in David's City here, below the Temple.

And I stay out of the Righteous One's business too, but not so much as with the Rabbi. For one thing, young James has still got his head in the sky and sometimes forgets to put his feet on the ground when he goes walkin'. I don't mean any disrespect, but I worry that he apparently isn't makin' any effort to find himself a wife. I'm not going to live forever, and somebody's got to be around to take care of him or else he won't survive. Sure, he's got God watchin' out for him, but God's got a lot of other responsibilities too and could be forgiven if he forgets to keep an eye out for one man out of all the thousands in this city. So I keep my eye on him like he was my own little boy.

And like all little boys, this one is sometimes likely to bring home "friends" who ain't worthy of the name, if you catch my meaning. Now, for years he's been bringin' home students from Gamaliel's class at the Temple, offering them special tutoring so they can become great priests themselves someday. And some of 'em have latched onto James even after their time in the classes is over. Most of these young men are okay, I suppose, but I need to keep my eye on some of 'em. There are those who think more of themselves than they ought to, and some who don't think as much of James as I think they ought to. It was this last group that bothered me the most. They come makin' airs like they was Moses himself, and arguing with James like he was the student and they were his teachers. Like I said, I don't know much about what's in those scrolls they read, but I trust the Rabbi, and the Rabbi says our James is the smartest one he's ever seen. So, if that's what Rabbi Gamaliel says, then that's good enough for me and none of these other pretenders better ever raise their voices against my boy or else I'll knock 'em flat. Forgive me for threatenin' violence — I know the Righteous One says there are better ways to settle differences — but I figure the Good Lord wouldn't have given them such soft butts if He didn't mean for me to kick 'em every now and then.

I 'specially got riled up at young Saul, the worst of the bunch. Why, you almost couldn't say good afternoon to him but what he's got to go into a long speech about whether it's really afternoon or early evening, and was it good or bad, and maybe old Rachel hasn't got enough wits about her to make such important judgments for the rest of us. The stories tell us Moses brought ten commandments down from the mountain, and I come close to breaking at least three or four of 'em every time I saw Saul's face coming through the front door. I hope the Lord doesn't really hold it against me when I take his name in vain, and I hope he gives me credit for only *thinkin'* about murder instead of actually doing the deed. I don't really covet anything that belongs to my neighbor. I just covet wrappin' my fingers around Saul's throat. And squeezin'. I covet squeezin' Saul's throat too.

Well, a bunch of them came to the house and were upstairs waitin' for James to come home. Young Stephen was goin' on about how the King was still alive and it was God's will and so forth, when I climbed the stairs to the upper room. I didn't mind this sort of talk, because after all, the King was James's own brother and he had come to this very house and told the others that they'd better mind ol' Rachel or else God himself would come kick those soft butts of theirs. I loved the King as much as our Righteous One, so Stephen could go on as much as he liked about him as far as I was concerned.

But Saul started arguing with Stephen about whether Jesus was really alive, or if he was ever really dead, and how maybe Stephen and James and all the rest of the men were lying when they said they saw the King alive.

That did it! Saul was accusing James of lying — and lying about the King! I stood square in front of him with my hands on my hips.

"Get out of this house. I won't be havin' you insult James and call him a liar, not while I'm still breathin'. Get out right now."

Saul pretended not to hear me and turned his back to me to continue with his arguing with Stephen and the others. When he turned and ignored me like that, I didn't hesitate for a second. I swung my foot up with all the strength my leg had in it. When my toe connected with his hind side, it felt like I'd kicked a rotting melon, the skin was so soft. These young men never did a lick of heavy work, so there wasn't much muscle to worry about. And this here Saul claimed to work as a tentmaker, but that didn't involve anything more than cuttin' the edges of the hides and sewing them together. I'd seen young rich girls who could lift burdens with more strength than he had in those skinny arms of his.

When I kicked his hind side, I'd almost swear I saw his whole body lift up off the floor. All the talkin' in the room suddenly stopped, and the other men sort of backed away into a circle, with just me and Saul in the middle. They all looked afraid, as well they should.

"How — how dare you lay a hand on one of your betters?" he sputtered.

"That wasn't my hand what hit you just now, but I can use my hands too if you want," I shouted at him. "Now, I can take these hands and throw you out that window right behind you, or you can get out right now and never come back. You're no longer welcome in this house."

He turned his nose up and started speaking over his shoulder to the others. "This woman thinks she can speak to me like she was my equal. Why, when James gets home, I shall have to tell him that she — "

Saul never finished sayin' whatever was on his mind, because I grabbed him by the collar of his fancy tunic and dragged him to the stairs. The other men scurried out of my path, because I guess they knew better than to get in my way. I stood Saul up straight and turned him toward the stairs.

"I don't have to do what you — " he started again, but his voice turned to a shriek like a little girl when I kicked him again and he almost tumbled down the stairs.

I followed him down the stairs, shoving him by the shoulders every time he tried to stop and say something. "Get out!" I shouted. "Get out."

"I'll tell James," he cried, sounding like a little boy who was going to tattle on a playmate.

"You won't have to because I'll tell him myself," I yelled back at him.

Saul hesitated when he got to the front door, so I reached around him and opened it. He stepped over the threshold, stopped, and made as if he was going to turn around to argue again. That's when I gave my strongest kick yet, and this time he really did fly off his feet and landed on his face on the wet mud in the street. I'd imagine his pretty Roman tunic got plenty dirty, but I didn't care.

"And don't come back, or else you'll find out what I'm like when I'm *really* mad," I yelled as I slammed the door.

I made my way back up the stairs to where the other men were huddling around the window, looking down at Saul in the street. One of 'em saw me comin' into the room and nudged the other fellows. They all turned and looked at me in silence, their eyes wide.

"Now, what I was going to ask when I came up here before," I started, "was whether you fine gentlemen would like some wine and bread while you're waitin' for James to get home."

In a flash they all rushed forward, surrounding me and each hugging me like I was their long-lost aunt or somethin', gushin' with words of praise and leadin' me over to the grandest chair that was normally reserved for the Rabbi or the Righteous One. "Here, you sit down and put your feet up, and we'll get the wine and bread for you," one of them called out in a voice I would have thought he reserved for his own mother. "Can we get anything else for you?"

I screwed up my eye at him and warned with my finger. "The bread and wine and the cups are sittin' out on the table. Don't you dare touch anything else in my kitchen or else you'll hear about it."

They all shook their heads from side to side. "No, we won't touch a thing if you tell us not to." They scurried down the stairs, chattering among themselves in excited voices like they'd just been invited to the King's table. I swear, I never heard them all sound so happy.

Then they came back upstairs and poured me a cup of wine and tore off a chunk of bread for me, and then they all sat on the floor in a half circle around the chair. They all looked up at me expectantly, as if I was supposed to start explainin' to them the meaning of what was written in the scrolls. I took a long sip of wine to settle myself down from all the excitement of the past few minutes, and one of them jumped up immediately to refill my cup.

I could get used to this, I could.

JOANNA

Chuza, I mean Joses — I keep forgetting to use the Greek name he adopted for his work at the palace — Joses accompanied me as we walked around the estate, checking in on the servants. I knew that this was the sort of thing he did every day at the palace for Herod Antipas, but these were *my* people and they didn't know my husband very well. I told him to just smile and say hello but let me do all the talking. In my mother's absence I was now the mistress of this estate, and I did not want him to cause any confusion.

"I hear you and obey. We who are about to die salute you." He slapped his fist to his heart as he mockingly called out the phrase the gladiators said to Caesar before they began battle.

"Good," I said without breaking stride. "Just remember your place or else I'll throw you to the lions."

First, we stopped at the house of Levi, the farm master. Years of sun had turned the skin on his face almost to leather and had given him wrinkles beyond his age. But his family had worked this land for my father and my father's father, and our family had given his family its own plot of land in payment. So, though Levi was a landowner and a freeman, he still considered himself beholden to my family. He worked his own land to support his family, but he also oversaw my family's farmland for a share of our crops. It was a partnership that profited us both, and I considered him like my own kinsman.

He wore a broad smile when he opened the door and recognized me. Levi nodded in acknowledgment to Joses but looked me in the eye as he said, "Happy to see you! Please come in."

I kissed him on both cheeks like an uncle, and then took a seat in his front room. Joses, taking my lead, clasped forearms with Levi and stood behind me. I glanced back and saw that he had his arms folded across his chest.

After offering us wine and exchanging pleasantries, Levi sat and held his palms out and facing upward in invitation. "What can I do for you, Daughter of Joseph?"

"No," I replied with a small laugh, "I have come to ask what I can do for *you*. Do you have enough strong animals to plow the land? Enough compost to enrich the soil, enough seed to sow and enough workers to sow the seed? Is there anything you need from me to help us make our harvest this year a rich one for us both?"

I heard a low cough behind me, as if Joses were clearing his throat. I ignored it and held eye contact with Levi.

"No, my lady," he said. "I have all that I need except for rain, so I can only ask you to pray that the Lord our God will send rain to us in abundance."

We continued our eye contact, both of us wearing broad smiles. And then I said, "If my brother the Righteous One were here, he would lead us in prayer for rain. Or if my other brother, the King, were here, he would speak to God directly. But even though they are both far away, I am sure they have asked the Father to watch over us. I am sure you will have your rain."

"Yes, I heard people say the King is still alive, that the Romans were unable to kill him. Then it's true — the Lord our God has blessed our nation and will stand with us," Levi said, his eyes shining.

"The Father is with us," I cautioned, "but I dare not predict what will happen to our nation." With that, I stood and indicated that I should take up no more of Levi's time. He graciously ushered us to the door, and he actually sang a psalm about the wonderful harvest we would have this year.

As we walked toward the next destination, Joses scolded me.

"You were too weak with that man. Now he thinks that you are indebted to him, that he has the upper hand whenever he deals with you. You should let me handle him from now on."

I stopped right there in my tracks, slowly turned toward my husband, and placed my cocked fists on my hips as Mom had taught me. After just a moment of holding his eye, to let him know what was coming if he didn't stay in his place, I said, "It's too bad you never got a chance to get to know my father. He would have told you that you can gain the fruits of a man's labors by exerting force against him, but you will never gain his loyalty. Rather, you ask what you can do for him and his family.

"Now," I continued, "I know that Levi is too proud to accept my offer of help. But he knows that I made the offer, and he will be forever grateful to me for that. And you heard him promise that we would have a rich harvest this year. Out of pride and loyalty — not to mention his own thirst for profit — he will work his hardest to make sure that this year we have the biggest harvest in memory. Just you watch and see."

I turned and continued on our path. After a moment of thoughtful silence, Joses hurried to catch up.

MARY

Judas Thomas seemed to know exactly where he wanted to go, or at least whom he wanted to see. When we got to a neighborhood of Alexandria where people recognized his shawl as that of the tribe of Judah, more words of greeting and offers of help came our way.

"Peace to you also," he would answer to each Shalom. "Tell me, do you know where I might find a man named Marcus Julius Alexander? He is the nephew of Philo."

The first few men he asked just smiled and pointed over their shoulders at the large group of buildings ahead of us. But the fourth man, after asking to hear the question again because he couldn't understand Thomas's foreign (!) accent, stopped and laughed heartily.

"Nephew of Philo," he scoffed. "You should identify him by his father, Alexander, the governor of all Judeans in this city. You will find him at the palace. But you may have difficulty seeing him. You have to get past his guards first, and you have to get past the palace guards before you get to his personal guards."

We bowed our heads in thanks and continued on our way. Our path ran parallel to the water for a bit. We went past a large shipbuilding yard, where we could see dozens of men at work on a boat that looked large enough to carry a hundred sailors. Thomas explained that Alexandria built the greatest ships of the eastern empire.

And rising toward the heavens on a small island across the water was a magnificent tower of light-colored stone, none other than the Lighthouse of Pharos. I had never seen any structure made by man that stood so high! Even the Temple in Jerusalem, as grand as it was, seemed almost like a small hut in comparison. And the Temple stood high because it was built atop a hill. The Lighthouse of Pharos stood high from the ground up. The furnace that the Egyptians kept burning at the top of the lighthouse gave guidance to sailors on their way to this busy port. As I gazed at the tower more than a hundred cubits above the water, I thought surely the helmsmen on those boats would deem it as important as the stars themselves.

Finally, we arrived at a majestic structure that exuded a sense of royalty. The wide stone steps, the columns on either side holding up the stunning Greek proscenium. I could see the similarity to the buildings that Herod Antipas had so proudly constructed back home, but nothing in Sepphoris compared to this either in size or beauty. Thomas led our ass to a pen where it could drink water and eat some dried grass, and my husband lifted his saddle bag off the animal's back and draped it over his own shoulder. We climbed the steps to the wide doors, where two armed soldiers with red plumes on their helmets stood at attention.

I was fussing with Sarah, who was squirming in her swaddling cloth as if she wanted to get on the ground and crawl on her own, so I could not hear what the soldiers said to Thomas nor his response. But out of the corner of my eye, I saw him slip a hand under the right side of his tunic and fish something out, which he handed to the two soldiers one at a time. After biting on the coins to test the metal, they stood aside and opened the door. I caught up with my husband and we passed into the dim light within.

When we were out of earshot from the guards, he muttered, "Back home it would only have taken coppers. Here they demanded silvers!"

As we continued through a wide hall, a number of people stood in small groups chatting together or poring over short scrolls of figures. Thomas apparently made a quick assessment of the layout and geography, because he set off at a firm pace toward a large door in the corner of the back wall.

"Don't you think we should ask for instructions? We've never been here before," I said as I hugged Sarah to my shoulder.

"Not necessary," Thomas replied briskly. "Besides," he hissed more quietly, "I don't want to betray that I don't know my way around. It would make me look weaker in front of the other men." I had heard him and other men spout this sort of nonsense countless times before, so I knew better than to object. Heaven forbid that they should ever ask for directions! I just hoped he had guessed his destination correctly. Perhaps his experience with navigating Herod's palace in Sepphoris would serve him here. In my opinion, he would look even more weak and foolish if he went the wrong way, but there was no use telling him. After all, he was a man.

As we had been warned, another pair of guards stood at the door we were approaching. Judas Thomas held his palm back toward me to halt me while he stepped forward to speak to the guards. After a brief discussion, this time he reached under the center of his tunic to extract a pair of coins. After they let us pass and we entered the next hall, he hissed angrily, "Gold! These thieves demanded gold."

Fortunately, Sarah had gone to sleep in my arms. I think that if she were awake and crying, her voice would have echoed mightily in this hall. As it was, I almost winced at the clatter of our sandals slapping the stone floor as we made our way toward a series of doors on either side of the hallway.

Thomas stopped at the second door on the right. "This looks like the one," he said confidently, and then he knocked. A voice from within made a noise of permission to enter, but it was too muffled for me to tell whether it was a spoken word or just a loud grunt.

When we entered the huge door, we found a man dressed elegantly, seated and waiting to greet us.

"Shalom," said Marcus Julius Alexander. These Egyptians seemed to pack both their lineage and their loyalties into their names. But I kept my thoughts to myself, waiting to see how Judas Thomas would conduct the talk. "How can I help you?" the man asked.

Thomas bowed his head in respect, as did I. "We have not met face-to-face, but we have conducted much commerce over the years. My name is Judas bar Joseph, of Sepphoris in the Galilee."

A beam of recognition suddenly lit up the Egyptian's face, and he rose quickly from his bench to clasp Thomas by the forearms in greeting, and then he kissed my husband on both cheeks. "I am so glad to finally meet you! Yes, we have traded a great deal these many years. You are one of my best customers for our cotton, and your saffron spices have kept my coffers full at the local markets here in Alexandria. What brings you here?"

Thomas, smart enough to avoid that question for the moment, diverted the talk to a more general topic. "Let me introduce my wife, Mary, and our daughter Sarah, who was born just a few weeks ago." He held his arm out to include us in the conversation, and the man bowed to us.

"Now, I learned something new from some men as we were entering the city," Thomas continued. "In our trading, your men have always identified you as the nephew of Philo, the man who writes so eloquently of our bonds to God and defends us before the Romans. But now I am told that you are the son of the governor."

The other man shrugged as if it were inconsequential. "Marcus Julius Alexander. The Alexander is for my father. The Julius is for the Caesar who established the Romans' dominance here. Marcus, my familiar name, gives the Greeks their due. But please, just call me Mark."

I watched Thomas's face, and his expression registered the proper amount of joy at being given this man's familiar nickname at their first introduction. After a few more pleasantries, Mark called for a small pail of water and a pair of towels for us to wash our feet, and he bade us sit and make ourselves comfortable.

"Yes, many people consider my father the governor of the Judeans in this city, and I am sure that I greatly disappointed him when I showed absolutely no interest in following in his footsteps. The administration of so many other people's affairs — and the headaches involved with settling their disputes — goes far outside my area of command."

"I quite understand," Judas Thomas responded. "My family is descended from David through Solomon's line, but I would never be able to settle a dispute between two women both claiming to be a baby's mother. I could never order the child cut in half."

Sarah began gurgling at just that moment, leading all three of us adults to punctuate the remark with laughter.

Mark leaned forward. "My uncle Philo interests me much more, though. He explores the meaning of the Law and the Prophets. He tries to teach us what lies behind and beneath the words in the scrolls. And more importantly in our current day, he represents our people before the emperor when the Greeks here oppress us. I wish I could become just a portion of the man he is."

Judas Thomas turned his face just slightly toward me, an eyebrow raised in question. I nodded. Mark was a man I felt we could trust.

"Again, we are so alike," Thomas said. "I will confide something to you that I hope will remain between just us. My name is Judas, but nowadays I am asking people to only call me Thomas."

"The Twin?" Mark asked.

"Yes. My brother Jesus and I were often mistaken for twins, we look so much alike. The people in Judea and Galilee called my brother the King, and the Romans crucified him."

Mark's eyebrows rose at this reference. "I heard about this king. But I heard the people say he is still alive, that he rose from the dead."

Now I spoke up, as Sarah murmured against my chest. "I was the first to see him, on the third day after they killed him on the cross. Then the men who had protected him all saw him, as well as the Righteous One."

Mark looked startled at the title. "The Righteous One? You have met him too?"

Thomas laughed. "James bar Joseph, whom the people now call the Righteous One, is the first-born son of our family. Jesus is the second-born, I am the third. My brother Simon, who leads a militia in the Galilee, is the fourth."

"I grew up with James in my father's household," I added. "He began studying at the Temple in Jerusalem when he was a young boy, and Joseph entrusted his care to my parents."

Mark bowed his head toward both of us. "This is very humbling. I feel that I am in the presence of members of the royal family."

I felt the time had come to push this conversation to another level. "Judas Thomas, will you balance Sarah on your lap for a moment? Thank you. Now, each of you take one of my hands, and hold each other's hand. This is something I learned when Jesus baptized me in the Jordan River. Please be quiet for a moment and focus on your breathing."

When our circle was complete, I closed my eyes and took several deep breaths. I assumed they closed their eyes too; I could hear them breathing.

"Father, thank you for your presence among us each moment of each day. And thank you for the path you have laid before us, and the good nourishment and good friends you have placed along the path for us."

The presence of God became palpable to us in an instant.

"You are my children, and I am well pleased with you all."

As before, the voice was not in the air like normal sounds. It touched our souls, our minds, and our hearts. I don't know if it was speaking in Hebrew, Aramaic, Greek or Latin, or all of those at once. I don't know if it was really a male voice or female, or both. All I know is that tears burst from my eyes and rolled happily down my cheeks. Even Sarah raised her dark little arms and began laughing.

The moment was over as fast as it had come.

"What was that?" Mark almost shouted.

"That," I said simply, "was God the Father. Jesus the King taught us how to speak to him, and James the Just is teaching us to live rightly in the world he has given us."

Mark sat in shock for a full minute, his mouth hanging open and his eyes staring into the space before him. Finally, his eyes came back into focus and he looked at my husband.

"I have a feeling you won't be sending me spices from Galilee anymore."

SUSANNA

I tried to conceal my joy at seeing Abban again, but I probably failed miserably. Mom had always taught us girls to remain aloof around men no matter how much we admired them, because that was the basis for our control of them later. Make them come begging, and then grant them only a fraction of what they want so they keep begging. And make them fear that you will take away even that small fraction if they don't submit to you. "The Stare," Mom told us so many times that it seemed like a tribal prayer from the scrolls, "has no power unless you maintain leverage. Never let on that you are vulnerable, that a man might have power over you. He is subject to your wishes, not the other way around."

That's what she taught us. It served Joanna well when Chuza was pining after her as a teenage boy. And now, even though he was her husband and served as the household steward to Herod himself, Chuza, now known by his Greek name Joses, knew better than to cross his wife's will. Joanna could make him crumble.

Truth be told, Mom (and when he was alive, Dad) had tried to marry me off a number of times since the days when I was still a girl. Tradition dictates that a girl should be betrothed before she starts to become a woman and should marry before her fifteenth or sixteenth year. Dad had suggested matches with various men whose fathers had large farms or vast networks of trading partners, but I detested them all! They treated women like dogs, or more like horses who were intended only to run when whipped and pull plows when shackled. Mom stood up to Dad for me, and I remained unwed. But now I was in my twenties and everyone assumed I was barren, or else why wouldn't a suitable man have taken me for his wife by now? No one else knew I remained a maid out of my own choice, because such a thing for a woman was unheard of.

But Abban bore no resemblance to the men in Galilee. The most obvious difference was his skin — he bore a dark complexion like my brothers Judas and Jesus. (Oops, I mean Judas Thomas and Jesus Thomas. Hmm, I wondered if I would have to just call them both Thomas now that we have to keep their identities secret. I supposed we'd sort that out eventually.)

But aside from the color of his skin, and of course his colorful silk clothing, Abban had always treated me as his equal. Even though Galileans all knew that women controlled their households and thus held substantial sway over the affairs of the entire community, if not the entire country, many of our men continued to pretend that they held us like pieces of property. That was true among the Greeks and the Romans, but the women of Israel and Judea stood tall! (In fact, I thought a day was coming when the Greeks and Romans would be forced to see reason. Because of their attitude toward women, they often left baby girls exposed to die. Baby boys would be nurtured enthusiastically, but the women of the empire raised very few daughters. The time had already come when our so-called conquerors would beg to take us as their brides. Hah — talk about leverage! The Romans' armies might overrun our men, but our women would someday bring the Empire to its knees!)

When Jesus Thomas told me to pack some belongings to go with him, Mom and Abban to his father's farm near Bethsaida, I struggled to hide my joy. For one thing, it meant I would get to spend days on the road with Abban. And although no one was saying anything about it openly (or at least not in front of me), I certainly understood the possible significance of introducing me to Abban's father.

Simon and his wife Judith would help Joanna manage the family estate in our absence. So, though Mom made a point of repeatedly reciting lists of chores and responsibilities to Judith and the servants (lists that they already knew by heart and had performed for years), we could leave confident that all would be well here at home. Judith had a good head on her shoulders, so she and Joanna would take care of everything.

Mom said we may have to stay in Bethsaida for a long time to nurse Amrit, Abban's father, back to health, so we should pack enough clothing and other belongings for an extended stay. Jesus Thomas took this to mean he should pack one extra robe in the leather bag he carried on his shoulder, but I understood that I would need at least seven changes of clothing and at least as many different types of sandals. (Certainly, one would not wear the same type of sandals for walking a dusty path as for sitting at table with one's host, would one? And there would of course be a different pair for walking into town to visit the farmers selling their produce in the open marketplace.

I would never understand men — Jesus Thomas owned only one pair of sandals, which he wore everywhere!)

Simon helped Jesus Thomas load several of my trunks onto our wagon, and then they shifted them round to make room for Mom's belongings. I noticed they grimaced and grunted as they hefted a relatively small chest onto the wagon and they were careful to place it in the center where our trunks would be stacked around and above it. I assumed this chest contained gold because of its obvious weight and the trouble they took to conceal it under the rest of the baggage. Eventually, everything was packed together on the wagon, stacked as high as my head would be if I were standing on the wagon myself.

Mom and I sat on the seat of the wagon where a driver would ordinarily hold reins on the oxen, but Jesus walked and kept his hand on the lead ox himself, and Abban walked at his side. Six of Simon's men accompanied us — two in front, two behind, and one on each side. My brothers said this number would be sufficient; any more than that would attract undue attention.

We encountered no bandits or soldiers on the trip around the western side of the lake, and very few of the other people walking on the road paid any attention to us. Jesus Thomas kept his face hidden under his hood, lest any passersby recognize him. Several people recognized a few of Simon's men, who were known to guard traveling parties for a fee. So, assuming that we were just travelers passing through, nobody paid us much mind.

That afternoon we passed the seaside town of Magdala, where so many fishermen took their catch to be smoked and dried. Jesus Thomas stopped the wagon for a moment, gazing at the migdal, the tower where the drying and smoking was done. Suddenly, he wondered aloud, "I wonder how Mary and Judas Thomas are doing?" He gave no explanation for his remarks, but then continued to lead to lead the oxen forward. But I remembered how, on that fateful journey through Samaria to Jerusalem for the Passover, he had compared Mary to the migdal and said she would be a beacon just as the tower was a beacon to the fishermen on the lake.

Much later, we approached the bustling town of Capernaum. Now Jesus Thomas not only covered his head with the hood of his robe but also stooped forward to completely hide his face. He gave Abban a drab shawl to cover his dark skin and bright silks. The foreigner objected at first, but my brother warned him that we must avoid drawing attention to ourselves. He said Roman soldiers watched the roads closely the last time he was here, and they monitored the goings-on in town. Abban acquiesced and wrapped a length of ugly cloth over his lovely garb.

As we entered the town, I did not see more than a few soldiers, and they did not seem to be paying much attention to anyone or anything. Maybe affairs had quieted down since the last time Jesus was here. Oh — of course! The Romans killed him on a cross, so he was no longer a threat. Why didn't I remember that sooner? But despite the lack of uniforms and swords visible on the street, my brother signaled to us to keep quiet. I guess enough of the townsfolk might remember him, and he did not want to draw attention.

He stopped in front of a stone house that looked not much different than any of the others around here. After unyoking the oxen and leading them to a small trough filled with water, he approached the door of the house and knocked on it. A man I had never seen opened it and, after a moment of astonishment, dropped to his knees and clutched my brother's hands. Jesus Thomas yanked him to his feet immediately and held his forefinger up to his lips, cautioning for silence. He pointed at one of Simon's men to keep watch on the wagon and motioned for the rest of us to come in.

"Jesus, you're alive!" cried the man after he had closed the door behind us.

My brother made a show of inspecting himself, patting his sides and shoulders to make sure before agreeing, "Why, so I am! I hadn't noticed it before, but I think I am alive, just as I was when you saw me in Jerusalem. I rather like it. But more important, how is your mother? I've worried about her since I saw her last. And by the way, I think everyone is calling me Thomas now. It seems the sound of my name attracts the ears of the wrong sort of people." Turning to the rest of us, he said to our host. "Andrew, let me introduce my own mother, Miriam. And this is my sister Susanna, and my dear friend Abban, whose father taught me much many years ago." He also introduced the men from Simon's militia who were accompanying us.

Andrew bowed in respect to Mom and me, and nodded acknowledgment to each of the men. "My ma is doing fine, thanks to you. She went to the market a little while ago and should be back in a few minutes."

Jesus Thomas laughed. "You're still making your elderly mother go to market to get food for you? Oh, she's going to pound you down to the ground for being such a terrible boy."

Andrew grinned but seemed to remember his manners. "Please, all of you sit down while I go get water and towels for you to wash your feet. Jesus — I mean Thomas — maybe you can come help me." The two of them left the room, chatting merrily.

A short while later, we were sitting and sipping wine when the door opened and an old woman hobbled in. Her eyes widened when she saw the number of people in the room. Then her eyes lit on Jesus Thomas, and she cried out. "It's true — the King is alive!"

"Martha," my brother said, getting up and hugging the woman, "I see the Father has given you strength to care for your son Andrew. I should tell you that your other son, Simon, whom I call Peter the Rock, is personally protecting the Righteous One in Jerusalem. You have raised your boys well."

The old lady looked into Jesus Thomas's eyes and smiled. "Then my work here is done? I can die and go to the Father?"

"Of course not," my brother said. "I said you have done well, but your work is not finished. This one, for instance," he pointed his thumb sideways toward Andrew, "looks like he is still a work in progress. You've got a lot more to do before he's ready to face the world. In fact, maybe you should find him a wife so you can pass the responsibility to her when the time comes."

The whole house rang with merriment. And no one laughed louder than Andrew and Martha.

RACHEL

I won't deny I heard a lot of squawkin' after I threw Saul out on his face. Rabbi Gamaliel worried about the politics at the Temple. He told me the Sanhedrin has always been known for polite debates, that men of opposin' views could speak their minds without fear of retaliation. I said I didn't know much about that, but from what I'd heard, it sounded like there was a whole lot of back-stabbin' meanness goin' on at that Sanhedrin of his. And the King himself put me in charge — *me!* — and I wasn't going to tolerate anyone comin' into this house and calling the Righteous One a liar. It was an insult against this entire household — the Rabbi Gamaliel included — and it was time for me to put a stop to it.

And James politely said maybe I could have remembered the rule from the ancient prophet, "Do not do to others what you would not want them to do to you." And I told him to his face that if I was bringing shame on my family by lyin' before God, I'd want somebody to come kick me in the butt like I did to Saul. I think both of them stiffened a bit when I mentioned where I'd kicked Saul, but then I think I saw the Rabbi hiding a grin behind his hand. As for James, I think he caught on when I mentioned bringing dishonor to one's parents and all. After all, that was going against one of the commandments Moses gave us.

"And you'd best be careful around that Saul if you see him out on the street," I warned them. "That man's dangerous. I wouldn't put it past him to kill you if he gets the chance. He's always been jealous of you, ever since he was sent to the Temple as a boy by his parents."

James looked shocked that I would say such a thing. "I'm sure Saul would never commit murder."

"No," I agreed, "he's not brave enough to do anything on his own. But he could rile up some other people to do the deed for him."

James and Gamaliel both shook their heads, convinced that I was exaggeratin'. A good man like Saul of Tarsus would never do that, they said.

They went on their way, talkin' between themselves. But I made a note to myself to tell the other women of the city. The Righteous One was in danger, and that danger's name was Saul. I decided then and there that I'd warn the other women to keep their eyes on him. If he ever lifted a hand against anyone, we'd throw him out of the city.

SUSANNA

Amrit, Abban's father, looked like he might have dozed off while sitting upright on the chair at his table. But, watching closely, I saw that his eyes tilted upward slightly at the sound of his son's voice. He still did not move, not even smile. He remained slouched over, his back curving forward to hang his shoulders limply above his chest. Unlike Abban in his bright silks, Amrit wore a drab tunic over drab pants, and they looked like they had not been washed for several weeks. In fact, it looked like the old man had slept in his clothes, perhaps in this very spot. When we arrived here, one of Amrit's men told Abban that his father had eaten only a few bites of each of his meals and sipped a bit of water when pressed to do so, but otherwise remained as we saw him now.

Abban turned a worried look to the rest of us. Jesus Thomas nodded first to Mom and then Abban, and stepped forward, knelt in front of the old man and clutched his forearms in greeting. The man still did not stir and his eyes remained unfocused.

"Amrit, my master, I have come to learn at your feet again. Come, let us chant together. You must lead me in meditation."

At the sound of my brother's voice, Amrit's eyes snapped open suddenly. They took on a look of wonderment, as if asking how Abban had suddenly turned into this man from his long-ago past. Certainly, Jesus Thomas's appearance had changed since he had traveled with Amrit's caravan as a boy, but the voice was the same.

Slowly, the arc of his back straightened a bit as he sat up, and the corners of his mouth stretched out and upward in the beginning of a smile. "Jesus," he whispered in a cracked voice, "I heard you were dead, that the Romans had killed you."

"They did kill me," he replied in a cheerful tone, still clutching Amrit's forearms. "But the Father led me to you many years ago so that you could teach me how to come back from the dead. And now the Father has brought me to you again, apparently to restore you to life also. Breathe, my teacher. There is much work to be done, and you are needed."

I don't think there was any change in the light in that dim room. But Mom and I clutched each other and lowered our eyes slightly as if there were a sudden bright glow. We felt that presence, just as we did when Mary had made us all hold hands in a circle back at Uncle Benjamin's house in Bethany. I don't have words to describe it — but I felt like a giant unseen beast had just brushed up against me. Not a frightening beast — dangerous, for sure, if not respected, but benevolent if held in friendship. But beast is the wrong sort of word, because that suggests a brute lack of intelligence. Just standing next to this presence, I felt I was gazing into a bottomless well of vast intelligence and compassion. I felt like this was my Father and Mother and all of my nation holding me. It sounds so huge, but like I said, even these words are inadequate. It was much bigger than that.

Apparently, Amrit felt it too. His chest rose and fell as he took in great breaths of air and then expelled them. The bent arc of his back completely disappeared as he first sat up straight and then, surprisingly, stood up and stretched his arms out to either side, palms facing up as if he were basking in the morning sun. He turned around slowly, arms still outstretched, his face turned upward.

His face beaming with vitality, Amrit gazed upon Thomas. "What is this that you have brought to me?"

My brother held his arms out to his sides, palms facing upward. "Amrit, the Father has healed you. He has much that he wants you to accomplish yet in your life, so you must stand strong."

"I will do whatever you ask." Amrit patted his own upper arms and chest as if checking whether they were intact. "I feel like I could do anything, anything at all. I have never felt like this in my entire life."

"Good." Thomas seemed to turn a pivot mentally. "Now, the first thing I want you to think about is this: Abban, your only begotten son, has grown to be an old man of about thirty winters and has not yet married. Despite his age, he appears to turn into a boy again whenever he is near my sister, Susanna," he said, indicating me. Abban blushed at this description of himself but said nothing.

Thomas continued, "Susanna, for her part, has refused to marry another man for all these years. I suspect she was hoping to be reunited with Abban."

He folded his arms across his chest and pretended to look like Daddy when he was negotiating prices for goods back so many years ago. "Now, I propose that you and I wed the fortunes of our families together with these two. But first we must come to agreement on her dowry. I must make sure that she brings enough wealth with her from her family to live comfortably, in case this son of yours fails to support her."

Abban started to gasp in protest, but I firmly clamped my right hand over his mouth. I wagged my left forefinger at him to signal to keep quiet. Jesus Thomas was now the eldest man of our household, and the traditions must be followed.

A light came into Amrit's eyes. I think he was secretly thrilled to be back in the position of negotiating what was essentially a business deal, but he did not let on what was going through his mind. The old man made a show of looking me over from head to foot, supposedly checking for defects as if I were a sheep or ox. I might really have protested if he had gone so far as to examine my teeth or test the strength of my legs, but he had the good sense not to do so.

"I don't know," Amrit murmured. "Her skin is so pale in comparison to ours, and even compared to you, her brother. And she is so slim — I shudder to think of the pain she will suffer giving birth to my grandchildren. Speaking of which, is she capable of giving birth? As you said, she has grown much older than the usual marrying age."

Thomas chuckled with a throwaway gesture at Abban. "If your son's seed has not lost its potency in his old age, I assure you my sister will produce strong, healthy babies. The women of our family produce only the finest sons, as you can see before you," he joked, indicating himself, "and the most beautiful daughters," he added, nodding toward me.

At the apparent questioning of his ability to produce potent seed, Abban shook with suppressed energy as if he were eager to leap at my brother's throat with both hands. But I continued to hold his mouth shut and keep him in his place.

Amrit stroked his chin and looked at me appraisingly again. "Yes, I see what you mean. Very well, I will agree to take your sister into my family. She will be my daughter, and Abban's wife."

With that, the two clutched their forearms together in the universally recognized symbol of agreement. Now I released my grip on Abban and took my hand off his mouth. "Father," he gasped, "I don't care if there is no dowry at all! I will make her as wealthy as a princess, and I will make you many grandchildren."

Silently, Amrit and Jesus Thomas exchanged glances. As if on cue, they each shook their heads as if in disappointment. "Don't worry," my brother said. "I'll negotiate for him when you're no longer here."

"But Abban," Jesus Thomas added, turning to my beloved, "there is more that will be required of you before I can allow you to marry into my family."

"I will do anything," Abban almost shouted. "Anything at all!"

My brother wore a grim look on his face as he wrapped a sympathetic arm over Abban's shoulder. "Yes, I see. Now, in all the years you knew my brother Judas, did he ever tell you about our people's customs? I'm speaking particularly of one of the most basic requirements for all our men. Did he ever tell you about circumcision?"

Mom and I left the room at that moment, so we did not hear any more of their discussion. However, as we settled into a room in the far corner of the house, I did hear an anguished cry, almost as if Abban was being beaten with a whip. Then Jesus Thomas's voice rang out, "Stop whining. You said you would do anything."

MARY

Mark had brought us to an amphitheater where a number of men and women were settling onto the stone benches to await a speaker. Judging by their complexions, most of them were Greek. But some were the darker-skinned native Egyptians whose ancestors lived in this land more than a thousand years ago when the Hebrew slaves fled. The men wore Judean prayer shawls. The women seemed much more assertive than others I had seen in this city, so I assumed they were Judean as well. The pagans oppressed their women, but Judean men knew better than to get in our way.

As more people entered the amphitheater and found places to sit, Mark turned to us excitedly. "My uncle is speaking today, but I hope to get him alone afterward so you can meet him."

Judas Thomas held the side of his hand against his brow to shade his eyes as he scanned the crowd. "So many people. I don't think we ever assembled this many at the synagogue in Sepphoris."

Mark's wife, Berenice, clutched my hand as she sat next to me. "I miss Judea and Galilee so much," she said, her eyes glistening. "My kinfolk almost never send me letters. You must tell me everything that has happened."

Thomas interjected, "Well, Antipas and Phillip do have large territories to reign over, so I could understand them not having time to write." I'm sure he said this for my benefit, to caution me against blurting out anything about his brothers in front of this Herodian princess. I thought to myself, yes, my husband, I am well aware that her father is Agrippa, who hopes to be the new Herod someday. No need to worry — I would tell her only superficial news until I could tell which way her loyalties lie.

At long last the seats had all filled. The audience cheered when a man with a gray beard stepped into the speaker's area. As he took his place midway between the wings of the semicircular rows of seats, I saw that he carried himself with the confidence that comes with deep knowledge tempered with a touch of humility. This famous man before us now, Philo, acknowledged the crowd as if they were his own children but, at the same time, seemed to scoff at himself as if he were not worthy of their attention. I liked him immediately, even though he had not yet said a word.

When Philo held out the palms of his hands to call for quiet, the cheering and chatter stilled in an instant. He bowed his head for a moment as if asking for strength, and then looked up with a great light in his eyes.

"In the beginning was the word, the logos, and the logos was with God. The logos was not God himself but rather a reflection. And whenever the mind of God created an idea, his word brought it into being."

After pausing for a moment to allow his words to resonate, Philo continued, "I begin to believe, in these my latter years, that the logos also found expression in humans. But we are still searching for one human who truly reveals the mind of God to the rest of us. For if we found one who could do so, then perhaps the rest of us would eventually find the mind of God that has already manifested itself within each of us."

He continued speaking, and the people around me continued to clap and cheer. But I heard almost none of it. I must meet this man, I told myself. I must show him what has been shown to me.

RACHEL

"He came to talk to my master," Ruth said in a low voice. "I couldn't hear who they were talking about, but that Saul said somethin' about makin' sure they had a lot of stones close by when the time came."

The other women in our circle all gasped. Stones — that could mean only one thing. They were plannin' to kill somebody. When the men couldn't figure out how to win an argument, they'd accuse their opponent of blasphemy and then stone him to death. It didn't make for exchangin' good ideas, like us women do, but it certainly gave a lot of power to whoever came out on top.

"You don't think they were talkin' 'bout the Righteous One, do you?" I asked.

The girls held their fists to their mouths, almost afraid of what the answer might be. They'd all promised me they'd help protect James. After all, the King himself had ordered us to do so. If it came right down to it, me and all my friends here would form a protective ring around James if he was bein' attacked. Whether it was the Romans or some jealous Judeans, they'd have to come through us first before they could ever lay a hand on him. And though we never let on so that an outsider would expect it and try to protect himself, we women know how to bring a man to his knees. Doesn't matter whether he's carrying a sword or a scroll, we can stop him good so he won't try to get past us again.

Ruth shook her head. "No, I've heard them talk about the Righteous One before, and they're always respectful when his name comes up in conversation. Nah, I think they're after one of his students. That Saul, he talks big when there's just other men around, but now he lowers his voice when I'm there."

I couldn't help it. I snorted with laughter.

"What is it?" Tamar asked. "What's so funny?"

I let my smile spread across my face. I told them about how I had thrown that little pipsqueak Saul down the stairs and out on his face in the mud when he dared to speak against James. The girls all giggled when I described it. We'd all had to put up with Saul at one time or another, with his superior airs and all. And he always bragged that he worked and paid his own way, but we knew that he was always comin' 'round to get free meals and wine whenever he could get away with it. The men in the homes we worked for didn't seem to notice he was leechin' from them, but we knew. So my ladies all got a kick out of hearing that I'd thrown him out the door and told him never to come back.

"He lowers his voice because he's finally figured out that the women of Jerusalem will kick his weak little butt if he steps out of line," I almost shouted with laughter.

The others chuckled, but Rahab spoke up. "But what if Saul really is after one of James's students? What can we do?"

The other looked at each other with the question in their eyes. But I slowly held out my hand in front of me and clenched it into a fist. "Saul doesn't strike me as a stupid man. But if he's stupid enough to do somethin' rash, then he'll have us to deal with. And we won't be gentle."

A dozen women's voices all rang out. "Aye!"

JOANNA

"Chuza, you just tell him you're taking off for two weeks," I said. "You don't make it sound like you are asking his permission, because then he'll think he has the power to say no."

My husband looked irritated but knew better than to raise his voice. "How many times have I told you to call me Joses? Even here at home. Look, one does not simply tell Herod Antipas what is or is not going to be. This must be done with finesse. Best of all, I should make him think it's his own idea to send me to Bethsaida to attend your sister's wedding. In fact, that might be best. That way, he'd have to pay me to go, rather than deduct wages for the time I am absent from work."

The messenger who had brought us word about the wedding had already left, so we were alone out in the yard between the main house and the gate. At this time of day, the servants would all be working at their jobs, so I had no fear that any of them would overhear our talk. Nevertheless, I avoided any gestures or body stances that would show an observer that I was giving orders to my husband. His authority at the palace depended on outsiders' perception of his strength, so appearances must be maintained just in case anyone was watching from afar.

But Chuza — Joses, I mean! — knew better than to cross me.

"Look," he pleaded, "just give me a day to set it up. I'll tell him I've heard word that some rebel is at large near the border with his half-brother Phillip's territory. I'll tell him I'd like to quietly look and learn, without any troops accompanying me or else the people will refuse to talk. I'll tell him the sight of military uniforms would cause concern. And also, if I need to slip over the border into Bethsaida, I can't have soldiers with me or else it would ignite a dispute with Phillip's forces. Yes," he said almost to himself, "that's what I'll do."

I gave him a moment to continue formulating the plan before breaking his concentration. "Just be sure not to say anything that would point to my brother, Jesus Thomas. I don't want Herod to launch another manhunt."

Joses nodded in agreement. "You're right. Antipas knows that Pilate had Jesus killed in Jerusalem months ago, but rumors coming into the palace from throughout the countryside are saying he's come back to life. In fact, it's not just an idle rumor. Every report is wilder than the last — not only saying that he's still alive but that God raised him up and gave him an army to drive out the Romans."

"Really?" I had not heard about this. "People in the countryside know that he's still alive? This is dangerous. Has Antipas started planning any military action?"

At that moment we both heard someone approaching the gate. "No," Joses said, lowering his voice. "Herod is quite confident of Pilate's ability to kill a prisoner. And he's much more relaxed now that the tax revolt seems to have died out. Yes, I'm aware that Judas Thomas led that revolt, but his name has been kept out of it."

With that, Joses went to the gate to see who was there, and I returned to the main house. While Mom was away, I occupied the main house instead of the structure Judas had given us a few years ago. Authority attached itself to the matron in the main house. So if Mom was gone, I must live there.

SUSANNA

In comparison to our usual flamboyance in regard to such affairs, we celebrated the wedding quietly and almost in secret. Our people, so long oppressed by foreign invaders like the Babylonians, the Persians, the Greeks and now the Romans, really let go of our inhibitions when it came to celebrating a marriage. In the countryside an entire village and all the surrounding farms would join the party. And since the country folks never had very much to talk about but the weather and the price of grain, a wedding would fill their gossip for months on end. Did you taste the stew they served? I wonder what that spice was. Did you see the bracelet the husband gave his bride? Did you see how drunk all the men got? I bet some of them woke up in the fields the next morning covered with dried mud. Even weddings in the city took on major importance in the people's lives. Did you hear what the rabbi said before he joined them together? Did you see how many of Herod's men attended the event? Did they look like they were enjoying themselves, or do you think they were spying?

For our people, weddings became major events because we seldom got the chance to celebrate anything at all in our lives. Even our worship on Saturdays remained subdued; the men would gather in the front of the synagogue, and the women sit quietly in the back. If a rabbi or some other man in the group could read, he might stand and unroll a scroll to share some sacred passage. If none of the men present had the ability to read, then one who had memorized an important passage from the Law or the Prophets would stand and recite it. After the prayer and comments ended, the people would greet each other and share pleasantries but would then return home for the day of rest. No work was permitted on the Sabbath, so a large communal meal or party would be out of the question.

That's why weddings became such huge events for us. We had a need to join together as a people, and weddings provided one of the few opportunities.

So I felt a huge stab of disappointment when I realized that the only people I would know at my own wedding in Bethsaida would be members of my family and Amrit's entourage. Local villagers and farmers would attend, of course, because Amrit's wealth would provide for a huge celebration with enough food and wine and music to provide gossip for a year. And the fact that a Judean woman was marrying outside her community — to a dark-skinned prince from beyond Persia, for that matter — would give enough additional fodder for the gossip to extend for years to come.

But I had always dreamed that my own people would be the ones talking about my wedding. Why, after my brother Simon married Judith in Cana, the talk never died down. Truth be told, the main reason for all the talk was that Jesus Thomas gave that wonderful speech when they ran out of wine, and the whole countryside started calling him the King. Of course, Jesus Thomas would attend my wedding, but he would keep as quiet as possible. Joses had brought word that Herod Antipas was keeping a close watch throughout the Galilee for any signs of trouble. He also told us that people from one end of the countryside to the other were gossiping about my brother. They all seemed to know he was still alive, and many of them thought he was bringing the Father's blessings back to Israel. Herod, of course, would interpret that as stirrings for an uprising to overthrow his rule, so we had to keep quiet.

But despite all that, the wedding did give the country folks plenty to talk about. Amrit called on his trading friends to bring foods that I had never tasted before, and spices that left a memory on the tongue of every guest. Simon and his men brought dozens of barrels of wine — the so-called Nectar of Nazareth that Jesus Thomas had made famous. Flutes played and people danced as if the Father himself was clapping the rhythm.

Well, now that I think of it, he probably was doing just that.

RACHEL

Rabbi Gamaliel looked devastated. He entered the front door in a daze and, without so much as a hello, turned and staggered up the steps to the upper room. I ordinarily wouldn't pay much mind, but this looked like someone had knocked him in the head and he hadn't fully recovered yet. I set down my pan and wiped my hands on my apron as I hurried up the stairs after him to find out what was wrong.

I arrived just in time to hear him say, "Stephen is dead!"

Stephen? Our young student? I wanted to shout but kept quiet to find out how it happened.

James looked like he had been hit in the gut too. He tried to speak but choked on his words. So he held his palms out to his side, facing forward, as if to ask. I held my breath so I wouldn't miss hearing anything.

"The mob stoned him," Rabbi Gamaliel said. "He was singing the praises of your brother, and some men started shouting at him. They yelled that we have no king but Caesar, that his blasphemy would bring the wrath of Rome down on us."

"Blasphemy?" James muttered. "How could this be blasphemy? He didn't call my brother God, did he?"

The Rabbi shook his head from side to side, as if he was still in a fog.

I finally spoke up. "Was Saul there?"

The Rabbi shook himself awake, as if he just now realized I was there. "Why yes, I heard that Saul was there. In fact, I was told he was holding the tunic of one of the men accusing Stephen and throwing the stones."

I didn't need to hear more. "There's bread and cheese on the table downstairs, and a fresh wineskin. Can you two feed yourselves?"

James finally seemed to snap out of his daze and turned to me. "I'm sure we're capable of feeding ourselves. Why — do you need to go somewhere?"

I was already startin' toward the stairs but stopped to tell them, "I need to go see some women I know. It's urgent, is why I have to go right away."

I didn't wait for an answer. The sun would go down in a few hours, so I needed to get a move on.

The plan came together fast. All the women had taken up their positions where they needed to be. They were just waitin' for my signal. I stood my ground, knowin' that what I was doin' was right.

Before long I heard his voice, boastin' as if he had done the deed himself. Saul laughed in that whiny voice of his and called goodbye to whoever it was that he was talkin' at. He turned to walk toward the house where he had a room.

Then he saw me.

Saul stopped sudden like, and he glanced this way and that lookin' for a way to escape. He backed up and turned down a narrow alley, and then started walkin' as fast as he could to get away from me.

Just like we planned.

A large, thick blanket fell over Saul's head. Before he could reach the edges to get out from under it, half a dozen women swarmed him from all sides. Two of my friends spun him around, the blanket still over the upper half of his body, and they looped some twine around him over the blanket as they turned him. The rest of the women had brooms in their hands, and they took to whackin' him over the head with the handles. The blanket softened the blows, but we servin' women are a strong lot and when we hit somebody with a broom handle, he feels it — blanket or no. He started cryin' out like a girl who was bein' chased by Roman soldiers, but I signaled one of the others to warn him.

"If you want to get through this alive, you'll keep your mouth shut," she said, leaning her mouth down to where his ear would have been. And just like so many of us had done when Roman soldiers had caught us back when we were just girls, his body went limp and he just nodded his head to make it clear that he understood.

We finished tying the twine around the blanket over his head and arms. We cut a small hole in the blanket near his mouth to give him fresh air, and then we tied his hands together behind his back. He started to protest and I personally whacked him over the head with a broomstick. I put a little effort into it too, and the woman who had warned him before said, "I told you to keep your mouth shut." He kept real quiet after that.

As we had arranged, a couple of men driving a wagon pulled by a pair of oxen stopped near us then. We hoisted Saul onto the back of the cart, none too gentle like, and then we covered him up with hay. Us women had pooled our copper pennies together and put them in a small bag. I handed the bag to one of the men on the wagon, and he grinned like a thief.

"You can give him food and water when you get down the hills toward the Jordan," I said in a low voice. "But don't untie his hands until you get to Galilee."

He waved to say he understood, and then shook the reins and the oxen set off toward the city gate.

MARY

The amphitheater appeared much different when I looked up at it from the stage. The stone benches ringed in a semicircle around from my left to right, rising in tiers above the ground. I estimated that three hundred people could sit on those benches without overly crowding each other. And with the outstanding acoustics of this place, those three hundred would have no problem hearing the speaker. Assuming, of course, that the speaker raised his voice.

Or, in my case, *her* voice.

Fortunately, I had no worry that I would have to speak to that many souls this day. Only twenty-five women of Alexandria had said they might attend, and several of them had said they would bring their husbands too. I figured maybe half of the women would not be able to come because of last-minute chores or pressing family matters, and others would decide, in the comfort of their kitchens, that they really had no interest and would stay home after all. So, I assured myself, I would probably have to speak to no more than a dozen people, fifteen at the most.

"Are you nervous?" a voice called out from behind me. Turning, I saw that the speaker was Mark, with Thomas beside him. A tile wall framed the back of the speaker's area, and behind the wall were a few rooms where people could meet before or after an oration. I had left Thomas and Mark there a few minutes earlier while I came out to survey the arena and try to calm myself.

"No, not nervous at all," I lied. "I think if the people all bunch together here in the center, maybe on just two or three tiers, then they shouldn't have any trouble hearing me." I looked at the seats and held my hands straight in front of my face, framing a narrow section of the benches immediately in front of me. Yes, if they sat together in three tiers of four or five each, they could all fit in this space right in front of me and I would not have to raise my voice too much above my normal conversational tone.

I turned just in time to see what might have been a smirk pass between the two men, but it was gone in an instant. I ignored it — whatever secret they were sharing was unimportant. They were probably continuing to smile about some jest one of them had spoken in the main room on the other side of the tile wall. I couldn't trouble myself over it, I needed to gather my thoughts for what lay ahead.

"Mary, come back here for a moment. I want to introduce you to someone," Mark said, holding his arm out toward the gap between the wall and the edge of the seating area. Taking one last look at the space where I expected my audience of fifteen to sit, maybe only twelve, I followed him and Judas around to the back and through the door.

Two men with white hair and beards, stood speaking to each other. One wore a white robe while the other had a tunic. The fabric of each garment looked so smooth and rich that I had to hold myself back from rushing to touch it. Their sandals barely had any dust on them. Both men had faces that seemed to radiate wisdom, but the man wearing the tunic had a creased brow that looked like it had born the weight of worry. I recognized the man in the robe as Philo, and he had a light in his eyes and a smile that immediately brought a smile to my own face. Despite the difference in their outlooks, they looked enough alike to be brothers.

"Father and Uncle, here is the woman I was telling you about," Mark said. Then I was correct, these two were in fact brothers. Facing me, Mark said, "Mary, allow me to introduce my uncle, whom you saw speak here the other day. This is Philo, the renowned teacher of our people."

I started to gush and curtsey, but Mark cut me off. "And this is my father, Alexander, the governor."

This time I had the sense not to act like a gushing girl. I dropped to my knee immediately and bowed my face in respect. "Your Highness! I am your servant." Glancing to my side, I saw that Thomas was still standing, so I elbowed him in the side of his leg and motioned with my head that he should kneel too.

But Alexander laughed merrily and reached out to take my hand. "Please stand," he said. "None of us here are servants to each other. In fact, let me pour you a cup of water. Your skin looks so soft that I'm sure the Egyptian sun would dry you out if we do not give you the greatest care." He poured from an elegant pitcher and extended the cup to me.

Sipping, I turned my eyes to Thomas for explanation. But he merely smiled and said nothing. Next, I glanced toward Mark. He, at least, broke into a wide grin and started to speak.

"I told my uncle and father about you, and they wanted to meet you. They have slightly different motives — one for God, one for country — but both want to hear more from you and Judas Thomas about your family."

We sat together, and Thomas explained the history that had led him and his brothers to their current situations: How the family was descended from King David through Joseph, and from Zadok, the high priest to David and Solomon, though Miriam. How these dual royal lineages placed James, the Righteous One, in a precarious position at the Temple and made him a target for the Romans whenever talk of rebellion circulated among the masses because they would see James as heir of both the king and high priest. How Simon had raised a militia to safeguard travelers from robbers and Romans in the Galilee and became hunted as a suspected guerilla fighter. How he himself, Judas Thomas, had organized a tax revolt to protest Herod Antipas's border war, which had been caused by his divorce of the Nabatean princess.

And, of course, Jesus. How he preached good news to the poor throughout the country, came to be known as the King, how he sacrificed himself for his brothers during the riot at the Temple. And how he had baptized me with the holy spirit of the Father when we saw him with John at the River Jordan.

We talked for a long time, and they asked many questions. Alexander seemed most interested in how all of the brothers navigated the intricacies of Rome's imperial occupation without actually breaking any laws and drawing the wrath of the Empire. Philo, on the other hand, sought to understand how Jesus had brought the people closer to God. What words did he use? How did he hold himself when he stood before a crowd? Did he leave any writings that Philo could study?

Thomas broke in at this point. "Perhaps rather than asking us to describe it, you would like to come out to the theater?"

"Yes," I chimed in. "A few women asked me to speak before them and their husbands. I'm only expecting ten or fifteen of them, and they should all have arrived by now. Please come and join us — there's plenty of room."

With that, we all stood up from the table and made our way to the door. Clouds scattered across the sky, and one particular cloud obscured the sun. But otherwise we had blue skies above us. As we walked toward the corner leading to the theater, I thought I heard more noise in the air than when we went into the room about a half hour earlier. Perhaps it was just the normal busy activity of the city, I thought to myself. Thomas walked between Philo and Alexander as they turned the corner around the wall to enter the theater.

But what was this? I heard a great cheer go up. I stopped and looked back over my shoulder to see if there was a crowd behind the building we had just exited, but I saw no one. I swiveled my head back and forth but could not discern where the cheers were coming from. But before I could give it any more thought, Thomas leaned back around the corner of the wall and beckoned me forward.

I turned the corner and had to catch my breath at the sight.

The seats of the theater were jammed with people, lining the benches from end to end, on every tier. They were cheering Alexander, their governor, and Philo, their spiritual leader. The two brothers held their arms up to acknowledge the crowd.

Just as I emerged into the theater, the sun peeked through a fold in that cloud and a single beam of light shone down. It seemed to focus directly on me, and the crowd suddenly hushed. Alexander and Philo turned toward me and held out their hands as if welcoming me. They each took one of my hands and escorted me to the center of the flat area facing the audience.

"My people," called out Alexander, "we have all heard of the many events in Israel these past few years. We have heard stories about a king who did not oppose the empire but rather led his followers to know God. We have heard stories about an army in the countryside that did not oppose the empire but rather existed only to protect poor people from danger. We have heard stories about a Righteous One who does not oppose the empire but rather seeks only to restore Israel to God's favor."

Now Philo stepped forward. "My friends," he called out, "here is Judas Thomas, so named because he so closely resembles his brother the king. Yes, this is the man who led the merchants of Galilee to oppose what they considered an unnecessary war. Yes, this is the brother of Jesus, who was called the King. He is also the brother of Simon, who raised a militia to protect his people in the countryside. And he is the brother of James, the Righteous One, who prays for all of us at the Temple even now."

The people oohed and aahed, and Thomas nodded his head silently in acknowledgment.

"But you did not come here today to listen to Judas Thomas. He is the brother of three great heroes, and he is a hero in his own right as well. But even more important, Judas Thomas is the husband of this lovely woman." He pointed to me and said, "My people, I give you Mary, whom the King named the Migdal."

My legs quivered — I had never stood before such a large crowd before. Did someone say the seats would contain three hundred people? I couldn't tell — the sight of so many simply overwhelmed me. It could have been three thousand, for all I knew. I handed Sarah to Thomas and took a deep breath as I faced the audience.

Then a sense of calm washed over me. In that moment I knew what to do.

"Dear people of Alexandria," I started. My voice surprised me; it sounded firm and confident. Where was this strength coming from?

"I am no one to command the attention of so many wonderful people as yourselves. It is true that the Righteous One grew up in my father's household, and I know him like a brother. It is true that I am the wife of Thomas here, the man who led a peaceful revolt to end an unjust war. It is true that I am sister-in-law to Simon, who has protected our people from the evil men who prey on the weak and vulnerable in the Galilee.

"And it is true that I am sister-in-law to Jesus the King. When he was with John at the River Jordan, Jesus baptized me with the holy spirit of God the Father. And so," I cried, raising my voice, "do not honor me. For I am a lowly maid. And though they are heroes, do not honor my husband and his brothers, for they are merely men. Rather, honor the Father, who works through us to gather you to himself."

I paused for a moment to collect myself.

"All of you, reach out to the man or woman next to you and hold hands together. Everyone in this arena, hold hands." I stepped between Philo and Alexander and grasped their hands in my own. I caught Thomas's eye and motioned for him to hold Alexander's other hand while cradling Sarah in his left arm.

When all the noise settled down to a murmur, I closed my eyes and tilted my face upward toward the sun. "Father, we thank you for your presence among us. Lead us this day and each day of our lives to more fully love you with all our hearts, with all our minds, and with all our strength."

A total hush of expectancy fell over the crowd. Even the sounds of the city vanished from our hearing in that moment. I felt that presence of the spirit (or should I say the Spirit?) within me and around me. Once again, I couldn't tell if it was a voice that spoke in the air or only within my heart, but the message was clear:

"I am with you every moment of every day. You may speak to me at any time, and I will listen."

Our sense of the presence was gone in an instant, but the crowd in the seats gasped aloud. They had felt it too! Men and women hugged each other and cried tears of glee. I saw one man sit down on the stone bench and lower his face down into his hands in his lap, his back heaving as he wept. Others held their hands up to the sky, some wailing while others shouted in joy.

But what happened next disturbed me to no end, and still bothers me now even as I remember it. Alexander and Philo nodded to each other as if some unspoken agreement had been reached between them. And then, at the same time, each of them dropped to one knee and bowed his head toward me, each still holding either of my hands. Seeing their leaders, the people in all the tiers also hushed and sank to their knees, bowing their heads. Even Judas Thomas bowed.

Sarah, bless her, would have none of it. She squealed with laughter.

"Please stand." I waved my arms upward for the people to rise. "Don't honor me. Honor the Father. Honor the king, who taught me how to speak to the Father. Honor the Righteous One, who prays for you daily. But not me. I am only a woman."

Some man on one of the upper tiers shouted, "But you brought us to God."

I had started to turn away but stopped and pointed up at the man. "Judas Thomas's brother Jesus, the King — he's the one who brought us to God. Ask

Thomas to tell you about Jesus. Write down the things he tells you so that you can tell your friends."

With that, I took Sarah from my husband's arms and walked back around the corner of the wall. I glanced over my shoulder at the last moment and saw a mob swarming around Judas, shouting questions and reaching over each other to touch him.

JUDITH

"Jesus Thomas, come quickly! This man is hurt." One of the workers (I still refused to call them servants) had called out to me that there was a body on the ground outside the estate wall. She was afraid to touch the body out of fear that, if the person was dead, she would be unclean for seven days as the Levites had warned since the writing of the Torah. When I saw the man, I knelt beside him and saw that he was still breathing. But I knew I did not have the skill to care for him. Simon and Jesus Thomas knew better than to ever tell me how to prepare food, and likewise I never told Simon how to lead his men nor Jesus Thomas how to ask the Father for healing. We had a clearly marked division of labor among us three.

My brother-in-law ran through the gate and hurried along the wall to where I knelt. Jesus Thomas turned the man over and studied the bruises on his face, arms and legs. His tunic was filthy and ripped in a few places, but the material looked rich. How did he get here? Had he been robbed? Perhaps I should tell Simon to patrol closer to home!

"I think I've seen this man before," Jesus Thomas muttered.

The man 's eyes fluttered slightly, and he mumbled a few words incoherently. His legs and arms twitched as though he were trying to flee, but his eyes remained closed. Jesus Thomas felt the man's forehead.

"He has a fever. We need to get him inside and under a blanket. I can carry him, if you'll run ahead and fetch water."

I was about to leave but the man started mumbling again, a bit more clearly this time. "Their so-called king is dead. When will the fools learn?" He wasn't awake; he seemed to be talking in his sleep. He rocked his head from side to side.

Jesus Thomas's head snapped upward when the man uttered the remark about the king being dead. "He must have come from Jerusalem. I'm sure I've seen this man before. I think he was one of James's students." He looked up for a moment, as if he were searching his memory, but I guess he could have been consulting the Father.

"Saul," he said suddenly, giving the man's shoulders a bit of a shake. "Saul of Tarsus. Why are you here?"

The man's eyelids fluttered again at the mention of his name. "Here I am, lord," he muttered. "They say Jesus is still alive. The Romans will crush Jerusalem if they think we have any king but Caesar. I must stop this blasphemy."

Simon arrived and placed his hand on my shoulder. I turned and held my finger to my lips, signaling him to remain quiet.

"Saul," our brother said again, "Stop kicking against the bricks. I am Jesus. And yes, I am alive."

Saul's eyes opened wide in shock, and he searched Jesus Thomas's face. "But you're dead. The Romans crucified you."

"Yes, they did," Jesus Thomas smiled. "And through the grace of the Father, I am alive again. Now, go to sleep and let these good people restore your health." With that he brushed his palms downward from the man's brows.

And Saul slept.

Jesus Thomas turned to Simon and me. "Let's get him inside before he wakes. He needs a blanket, plenty of water, food and rest to mend his injuries. But I cannot stay here while he is recovering. James told me about this man, and he must not learn where I am."

"But he has seen you," Simon said as he slipped one arm under Saul's back and the other under his knees. Saul was not a large or muscular man, so my Simon would be able to carry him alone.

"He was delirious," I suggested. "He might not even remember seeing Jesus Thomas. Or if he does remember, he might think it was a dream."

My brother-in-law looked downward for a moment in thought after my words. "You're right. And that brings up another thing. Even if I do happen to come up in conversation during my absence, make sure you refer to me only as Thomas. Jesus is the man he argued against in Jerusalem, and Jesus was the man he saw here a few minutes ago in his delirium. But your brother who is away taking care of chores in Bethsaida is Thomas. I don't want him making the connection."

RACHEL

The Rabbi Gamaliel and the Righteous One seemed genuinely confused. First, there was the tragic death of Stephen, the sweetest lad in the land. No one could understand how a mob could get so hot so suddenly that they would stone him to death without so much as a trial. Stephen might've gone a bit over the top sometimes in his praise of the King, but he never said a word that would hurt a soul.

And Saul had disappeared! Nobody had heard from him, and the master of the house where he stayed said Saul had not returned to the house in the month since Stephen's stoning. This surprised James the most, because he figured Saul would go about go about boastin' to anyone forced to listen that Stephen's death proved he was committin' blasphemy. That all this talk about the King returnin' to life after the crucifixion was an insult to God and was tellin' the Romans that we didn't think Caesar was the chief boss. Saul was always spoutin' nonsense like that, and Stephen's death should've given him the okay to say, I told you so! Anybody who had been forced to spend more than a few hours around Saul would know that he couldn't resist braggin' that he was smarter than the rest of us. It made no sense for him to just disappear.

Unless he was afraid, James wondered.

I saw my chance, so I jumped in with a few words as I was clearing the table. "Maybe that's it. Maybe it was Saul who whipped up the crowd. Maybe he was the one who caused young Stephen's death. Maybe he's the one who made sure there were stones up there by the Temple steps for the crowd to grab. You know as good as me that the Levites hire women to keep those steps swept clean every day. There aren't ever any big rocks up there unless somebody puts 'em there. So who arranged for the rocks? And everybody in the city is tellin' the tale that Saul was holding the coat for the man who threw the first stone. But after people of the city realized what had happened, maybe Saul got afraid he'd be accused of settin' the whole thing up. Maybe he decided he needed to run."

I told myself I wasn't really lyin' here. I was just suggestin' one possible explanation. I hoped the Father would forgive me. If he ever asked me about it when I was standin' before his throne in Heaven, I'd make a strong argument that Saul got what was comin' to him.

Rabbi Gamaliel stoked the beard on his chin, deep in thought. "We must be careful not to judge a man's guilt before we have all the facts of the case," he said. "But you are right, Rachel. From what we know so far, it would seem that Saul has fled the city. And yes, I too have heard that Saul was present at the mob's stoning of Stephen. If he has fled, that could certainly lead people to believe his guilt in the matter."

James spoke up. "You are correct, Rabbi, that we must reserve judgment until we know the full story. But I agree, I know he was generally disagreeable to everyone already, and Saul especially opposed Stephen for his devotion to my brother, Jesus. His disappearance immediately after the stoning would seem to point to his guilt. But I will not speak out against him when I am talking before others. What we said here should never leave this room, until we have proof."

"Agreed," the Rabbi said.

"As you wish, Rabbi. I won't say a thing," I said solemnly.

But I told myself to warn the women who helped me that we must never say a word.

SUSANNA

Since our move to Amrit's home at Bethsaida, I was still getting used to being the lady of the estate. Sure, Mom lived with us here, and she had lots of words of advice for every little thing that happened in the house or outside the house or in my relations with my husband or what I should name my baby if and when I had one and what color cloth I should wrap the baby in and... Well, Mom always had lots of opinions on everything, and she seemed to be in a hurry to pass them all on to me.

But even Mom acknowledged that this was *my* family. This was *my* house to rule. If anyone was going to use the Stare on Abban or his father Amrit, it was going to be *me*. The entire household and its servants might be almost all men, so I had a priority to let them all know who was in charge. *Me*. If it looked like the leadership was divided between Mom and me, that would undermine my authority. I could not stand for that, and Mom begrudgingly came to accept it. I may have had to bruise her ego a bit, but I bet she was secretly proud that her daughter had taken control so quickly.

Abban had also asserted authority. Amrit seemed more willing to accept his own demotion than Mom did hers. He sat and joked with visitors, or he wandered about the estate leaning on a cane, but he left all decisions to Abban and me. Which really meant he left them to me.

So when one of the men came to the house to report that a traveler was approaching on the road from the southwest, he came to me first. I immediately pressed him for details. Did this traveler walk or did he ride? Alone or with companions? Was he close enough to any trees or large rocks where companions might be hiding? Did he have any weapons visible?

Out of the corner of my eye, I saw Amrit nod approvingly at my questions.

"No, Madam. He walks alone and does not appear to be carrying anything except a pack strapped to his back. He has no weapons, no companions, no pack animals. And the land around him has no trees, no bushes, no large rocks." The man kept his eyes averted downward, not wishing to cause any offense.

"Very well," I said. "Send one man out to meet him, so that he does not feel threatened, but keep another man on alert to help if there is any mischief." I knew the best way to keep peace was to maintain a balance of forces but remain prepared just in case.

In the ten minutes that passed before the stranger reached the house with our escort, I sent Mom and Amrit inside where they could watch from a window. I placed a few of Abban's men inconspicuously near the barn on one side of the house and the grain silo on the other side. I called for Abban to come take a position in front of the house, but I stood squarely in the center of the porch facing the gate into the estate, my arms folded across my chest.

The man had a long cloth draped over the top of his head to protect against the sun, as would be expected. And to protect against the dust of the road occasionally whipped up by the wind, he had pulled the cloth across his mouth and nose. So I could see only his eyes gazing out from the folds of material, but only one man in the world could possess that pair of eyes!

"Jesus!" I shouted, and I ran down the steps of the porch and across the yard to where my brother stood. Abban's men seemed unaccustomed to any displays of affection, so I'm sure they averted their eyes when they saw their mistress brazenly run to this stranger and wrap her arms around him in glee. And kiss him on each cheek and hug him again. Other than Mom, I had not seen any members of my own kin for more than a year. Until this moment, I hadn't realized how much I missed them all. "What's been happening with Joanna and Joses? With Simon and Judith? Have you heard anything from James in Jerusalem? And have we gotten any news from Judas and Mary in Egypt?"

Jesus laughed. "Slow down, slow down. Yes, thank you for offering me water to drink and to wash my feet. Thank you for offering me shelter from the heat, inside that beautiful house I see behind you. And thank you so much for hospitably offering me a meal to give me strength after my long journey."

He was right, of course. I had forgotten my manners. But he was my brother, and he had to be taught a lesson. I wound up my arm and slugged him in his left shoulder, and while his attention was diverted to that direction, I used the other hand to slap the right side of his head. Not hard enough to cause pain — but quick enough to let him know he wasn't dealing with slow-poke softies like Judas or Simon.

"Now you march yourself into the house right this minute before I have to kick your skinny butt all the way up the path," I shouted loud enough for everyone in the yard to hear. I had my reputation to protect.

"Yes, Mom." Jesus grinned like he was a boy again. At that moment he looked almost like the teenage brother I remembered from my childhood, just at a moment when Mom was scolding him and our brothers. The moment almost brought tears to my eyes, but I covered it up by pushing him toward the house as if I really meant to kick him if he didn't move fast enough.

When we got inside away from the others' eyes, I again wrapped Jesus in a hug that was surely tight enough to restrict his breathing and then spun around with him in my arms. "What brings you to Bethsaida?" I asked when I had caught my breath.

He melodramatically fell away when I released him, pretending to be overwhelmed. He clutched his heart and gulped in deep, loud, wheezing breaths as if I had held him underwater. In fact, sniffing the air in the room, I made a mental note to hold him underwater this afternoon if he didn't go take a proper bath soon.

"Isn't it enough that I miss seeing the light of my life, my dear little sister?"

I knew better than to fall for that line. "Speak up, mister. Are you running from debt? Are the big estates after you because they paid you for fine wine but Nazareth didn't have enough barrels for you to deliver? Are the farmers chasing you because they want you to plow their fields in exchange for all the food you eat? Or did Herod find out your true identity and send Roman soldiers to hunt you down?" I was grinning as I said it, but inside I suspected there must really be something wrong.

Jesus raised one eyebrow, another reminder of our childhood. "That last one wasn't too far from the mark," he said. "A man who used to be James's student in Jerusalem was found beaten up and dumped outside our estate. He was delirious, but it was pretty clear he's one of the men who has been attacking the people who say that I am still alive, and also attacking the people who follow James. Judith and Simon are nursing him back to health, but I can't afford to let him see me again and inform the Romans."

I calculated the implications immediately. Herod Antipas probably didn't care one way or another if Jesus was alive. But if this person from Jerusalem alerted the Romans that he was alive and hiding under Herod's very nose, then the tetrarch would be forced to conduct exhaustive searches until he captured the fugitive, and then he would turn him over to executioners who would make sure they did their job thoroughly this time.

Worse, if Jesus was tied to our household in Sepphoris, Herod might seize the opportunity to arrest our family members and confiscate our land and money. He was always looking for ways to add to his treasury. And who knows? If his soldiers met even the slightest resistance when they attacked our estate, they might use it as an excuse to do worse than just arrest family members. Herod Antipas never shied away from ordering executions himself when the mood struck him. Remember John, our dear cousin who offered purification to travelers in the River Jordan. I instinctively put my hands up protectively to the sides of my neck, just thinking about them beheading John as he knelt in chains.

"We will keep you here as long as necessary. Fortunately, your skin is almost as dark as Abban and his men, so no one will notice you — as long as you don't go about curing lepers, raising the dead or feeding crowds of five thousand people."

When he raised his eyebrow again questioningly, I added, "You haven't heard the stories."

RACHEL

It had been several years now since the martyrdom of our dear Stephen. Folks around the Temple mostly accepted the followers of the Righteous One and his brother the King, as just another group of the faithful. There were the rich folks, the Sadducees. And then there were the Pharisees, like our Rabbi Gamaliel, mostly well-intentioned folks but I think some of 'em wore their codpieces a bit too tight, if you catch my meanin'. And of course the Essenes, who kept to themselves a lot and even maintained a monastery down the hills toward the Jordan.

Our folks just called the teachings by the King and the Righteous One "The Way." We didn't have no name for our folks yet. James and the Rabbi said we didn't need one, we were just doin' what was right in the eyes of the Father.

Gamaliel was no longer head of the Sanhedrin. That was just a temporary thing back when there was all that politics goin' on at the Temple. In fact, for the most part he had quit going to meetings and left that sort of stuff to James. And James, though he was rich, he spent most of his time with the poor people of the city and the farmlands outside the walls. Like the King used to do when he was here, James and his followers would have big meals that were open to everybody, and he would preach to them all about God's love.

That Galilean friend of the King's — his real name was Simon but everybody called him by the nickname the King gave him, Peter. Well, Peter was still in Jerusalem too, and he helped James lead the thousands of people who came to the meals to share food and hear the men preach.

Of course, it was us women who provided the food, and we were the ones who set up the meeting places and got the word out to all the faithful when and where they would be held. The men did most of the talkin' but the women did all of the work.

And we women were helpin' grow The Way by bringin' in more people. We already brought in a lot of the wives and their families. But the young women, the ones who weren't married yet, they were comin' too. And they were attracting some men we wouldn't ordinarily expect.

You see, the Romans and the Greeks liked to have sons. Didn't much care for daughters. So for more years than I'd been alive, they'd been forcing their women to nurse their male babies but to expose the baby girls — just leave 'em out in the wild to die. They thought the way to build an empire was to raise a whole bunch of strong, manly sons. Well, they did, but there weren't enough women for all them manly men when they were all grown up. As I might've mentioned before, a lot of the Roman soldiers, when they got lonely for a woman's charms and maybe had drunk enough wine to get brave, they'd try to chase down some of our virgins and have their ways. That pretty much stopped several years ago after that Roman governor, Pontius Pilate, was yanked out of Caesarea and sent back to Rome with his tail between his legs. The empire put that Marcellus in charge for a while, but he mostly stayed out of our affairs and the Temple leaders took measures to protect our girls. This Roman fella in charge now, Marullus, seems too scared to do much of anything. James says the latest emperor is crazier than a circus animal and would kill anybody just for the fun of watchin' 'em bleed. This emperor, this Caligula, even had a giant statue of himself built and wanted to bring it to Jerusalem and mount it in the Temple. One of our own, a fella named Agrippa who knows the emperor personally, had kept the statue out of the city so far.

So, back to my point, the Romans and Greeks don't get to catch and rape our girls so much like they used to. Nowadays they have to be polite and try to make friends with girls' fathers and try to convince the fathers to let them marry their daughters. The fathers have always demanded that the men get circumcised. That was always enough to scare away the fellers who weren't really serious. For a man to allow a rabbi to take a sharp knife to his privates — well, that takes commitment, and only the most committed would go through with it to marry any of our girls.

But now our young women have taken it a step further. Most of our girls are followers of The Way. And when these foreigners marry them, they're forcin' their new husbands to come to the meals and listen to James and Peter and all the others. So while James started out with a few dozen people all those years ago, every one of the meals nowadays had hundreds of people comin'. And a lot of them were giving money to help pay for the food or to support our people who were workin' at the Temple. And a lot of these Roman men were tellin' their friends about The Way too.

So now The Way was gettin' almost as big as the other groups. And our James was so popular that some of the new men were startin' a movement to have James appointed to a term as Head Priest. Of course, we'd have to raise money to pay the necessary bribes to the governor, but it was startin' to look like the Righteous One might be representin' all of us in the Holy of Holies up at the Temple someday soon.

My, the things I've seen in my lifetime!

MARY

"Mommy, can I go play with Anna next door?"

Sarah was eight now and clearly on her way to become a young woman in a few years. But I still considered her my little girl. Owing to Judas Thomas's lineage, her complexion was much darker than mine, almost the color of tree bark, and her hair was curly instead of straight. But she had my slender legs and would soon inherit my height. She certainly had my mouth.

"Have you finished your studies yet?" I asked. "You were supposed to write the first commandment in Hebrew, Greek, Aramaic, Demotic and Latin. Let me see your work."

She held out the crumpled piece of parchment I had given her to practice on. I retrieved used, discarded parchment wherever I could find it, due to the high cost of clean, unused sheets. The original owners usually only wrote on one side, so the back was available for Sara to practice her writing. I glanced over the sheet she had written on. She had drawn all the characters very neatly and arranged them in straight lines. But something wasn't right.

"What's this?" I pointed at one line of text.

"You said Demotic, but nobody uses that anymore," she whined. "The Egyptians are using Coptic now. If you're going to make me write Demotic, I might as well learn hieroglyphics too."

"Very well, then," I said, "you've written it in Coptic but I still want to see the Demotic as well. But because you're such a good student, I won't make you write in hieroglyphics. At least not for now, but that may change later."

Her face fell as she accepted the sheet back from me.

"And where is your mathematics work?" I demanded. She held out another sheet without enthusiasm. I studied her answers to the 10 problems I had set for her. She got all the answers correct. "Well done. Next time, I want you to make the columns of numbers a bit straighter."

She took back the sheet and made a mumbling noise.

"What's that? I couldn't hear you."

"I was saying that I saw Anna's brother's homework that the rabbi assigns him, and he doesn't have to write this many languages or do this much mathematics." She turned her face up toward me with a defiant glare in her eyes.

A learned rabbi taught all the boys in a group several days a week. Most girls never received any instruction beyond basic addition and subtraction. I taught Sarah on my own.

"I'm making you work harder than any rabbi would make the boys work for a reason. Listen," I added in a softer tone, placing my hands on her shoulders, "don't tell anybody that I said so — this is going to be our secret, just between you and me. You're smarter than Anna's brother, and you're smarter than any boy I've seen in all of Egypt. When you grow up, you're going to be the smartest person in the world. So I want you to know all the important languages so that everybody has to listen to you, and I want you to know mathematics better than even the scholars so that nobody can ever trick you. What your Daddy is teaching to the Egyptians about your uncles, the King and the Righteous One — someday you're going to take those teachings out to share them with the world. And no matter what country you go to, everybody will listen to you because you're the smartest person in the world. Do you understand what I'm telling you?"

Sarah still looked dejected. "Yes, Mommy."

"Okay." Now I really did soften. "So put your sheets back on your study table, and you can go play with Anna next door." Sarah's face lit up like a beacon, and her eyes and mouth went wide. "But don't you tell her what I said. And I want you home in time for dinner so that after you eat, you can write out the commandment in Demotic. You understand?"

"Yes, Mommy," she squealed as she ran out of the room.

SUSANNA

Amrit's latest illness seemed much more serious than the earlier attacks, and the old man recognized that his time might be coming soon. He called Abban, Jesus Thomas and me to his bed.

"My children, for years now I have loved this home we built together. The people of Bethsaida have treated us well, and I have been made to feel like one of them. I am happy.

"But I do not wish to have my bones buried in this foreign land," he said, wheezing a bit. "Though the journey is long, I wish to go home." Amrit did not bother to put a pleading look in his eyes as he gazed at each of us in turn, it was just a statement of fact.

The three of us glanced at each other's faces for only a moment to make sure there was no objection. Thomas spoke first. "We can travel that road. Amrit, I remember that you liked to lead the men in their defense of the caravan, but I would prefer that you stay on the wagon to protect Susanna. Abban and I will be too busy guarding your flanks to do so ourselves."

"Aye," agreed my husband. "And seeing that I will be marching on foot rather than riding, I might even exchange my beautiful silks for the drab clothing that the rest of our men wear. If there is a battle, I don't want to get stains or tears on my good clothing."

I made a show of looking shocked. "You would wear normal clothes? This must be really serious!"

Amrit reached out and patted my arm. Now I could see tears welling up in his eyes, so I spoke quickly to divert attention. I knew he would not want to shed tears in front of his son or my brother. "As for protecting me on the wagon, I will certainly need a strong man who has more wisdom than these two whelps. I would be honored if you would ride with me, Father Amrit."

With that, we sat together with the old man to begin discussions. We could not be sure if any of us would ever come this way again, so we must first decide whether to sell the house and farm here or leave a caretaker to keep it running until our return. Amrit said that if he were to sell it, he would feel obligated to stay here for several seasons to warn his trading partners from east and west that this post would shut down. That would probably delay our departure until next spring. Amrit made it plain that his ability to travel might not hold out that long.

Just then Mother Miriam entered the room. I had completely forgotten about her in our discussion! By the look on his face, Thomas also had let her slip from his mind.

"Mom," he called out. "We were just talking about you." I ignored the lie as he pulled Miriam into the room to sit. He told her Amrit's situation, slowly and painstakingly because in her old age her hearing had gotten worse. She barely moved a muscle during the explanation other than occasionally nodding slightly to signal her understanding.

Finally, she looked at us and said quite simply, "Then it sounds like you'd better take him home."

Abban spoke first. "Yes, Mother Miriam. But what about you? Will you stay here at the house, or will you go home to Sepphoris?"

Mom didn't do a full Stare, but she tilted her head slightly in that oh-you-silly-boy gesture that made men consider their words more carefully. "How do you know I won't accompany you home to Malabar?" After shock had registered on all three men's faces, she cracked a smile and added, "I don't know yet. I've grown accustomed to this place in the past several years, and I have some good friends among the traders who stop here each season. I may choose to stay. We will see."

All of us took seats around a table, where Amrit spread out a map he had carried for decades in his collection of traveling gear. He began to tell us of the potential obstacles, how long each leg of the trip might take, where we should beware of hostile forces.

"See here," the old man said, pointing at a spot to the east. "We will have to cross a wide wilderness, but we will pass a few villages along the way. And here we will meet the great River Euphrates and follow that south past ancient Baghdad. Here," he pointed further south, "we will reach the sea, where we must part with our wagons and board a ship. That will take us all the way down the coast to my homeland, Malabar."

Abban leaned forward and looked his father in the eye. "That is not the road we traveled in the past. We have always kept our wagons and stayed on land."

"That is true," Amrit said. "Our usual path is here," he pointed to a spot in the middle of intersecting lines, which I guessed were roads from several lands. "If we took that path, we would be able to trade gold for silk from the traders from the north, which we would then use to pay our way as we made the long trek south through the mountains to our homeland.

"But," he said sharply, "the pass through the mountains there is very high, and there is almost no water. When we passed that way years ago, my son, you were inside the wagon studying so you would not have seen all the bones alongside the road, the remains of so many animals that had been pulling other travelers' wagons. Thousands of animals have died on that pass, and many humans too who have become so desperate with thirst that they will attack other travelers. If we are to bring your wife Susanna with us, then we absolutely cannot take the pass. We must go by ship."

I started to protest that I could watch out for myself, but Amrit cut me off. "No, daughter, I do not wish to see you captured and sold into slavery. Nor do I wish to see any of my men killed trying to defend you. A beautiful woman, married or not, is worth more to the thieves in the hills than a box of silk, and they would mount a war against us."

When he spoke of the danger that I would bring upon his men, the sense of his words sank in.

Thomas raised an index finger into the air. "Amrit, my old friend, you bring up a topic that deserves our attention. It has been many years since most of your men protected your caravan on the roads where traders move their goods and thieves lie in wait to attack them. Do you think your men are still up to the task?"

Amrit smiled indulgently. "You remember the morning exercises we taught you when you were a boy? We will immediately begin doing these exercises daily. This trip cannot begin for several weeks yet, so we have time to prepare the men."

Thomas nodded. "It is good that we will wait. That will also give us time to collect as much saffron as we can from the famers throughout Israel. Just a few small boxes will be enough to pay for our entire trip. We can also collect supplies of spearmint and peppermint, mandrakes, and rock rose."

Amrit placed his hand on Thomas's shoulder. "I knew years ago that you would make a good trader. You'll find in my homeland in Malabar that there is a huge market for trading spices, and many Judeans have been sailing there for many, many years."

Mom cleared her throat, capturing our attention. "I believe I will stay here in this house and continue building my friendships with the traders who stop here in each season. Amrit, I will send for Simon to bring some of his men here to protect this outpost. I think we will carry on the outstanding work you have done."

Then Mom turned to me with solemn eyes. "I am old. It will be up to you to protect the King. Heaven knows, he can't do it himself."

Jesus Thomas started to open his mouth to say something in protest, but I turned my eye on him and shut him up. "I will, Mom. You can count on me."

JOANNA

"There is a bin for silks in the outbuilding over there. Put them in there but be very careful to handle them gently and don't tear them," I said to one of Simon's crew. He was a good man, but I knew that his usual job up until now had been protecting travelers through the wilderness, not loading and unloading valuable cargo. I needed to remind every one of them not to be rough.

The estate practically hummed, there was so much activity! Ever since Mom took over Amrit's trading post near Bethsaida on the north side of the lake, she had vastly increased the volume of goods going in and out of our home here in Sepphoris. Simon's men now protected shipments of merchandise to Capernaum and Sepphoris. In turn, we bought and bundled large amounts of grains and dried fruits from throughout Galilee and shipped it to Bethsaida for barter with the merchants going east on the great trade route. Although Mom spoke Greek reasonably well and could communicate with most of the traders, some of them spoke only their own languages and she was learning slowly how to speak with them.

And here at the estate! Farmers to the west and east all brought much of their crops to me, because I paid hard cash. They were hiring more workers to plant and harvest their grain, so everyone kept busy. And Nazareth — dear Nazareth! The village up on the hill where Jesus had worked on the vineyard in his youth had steady work for a crew that did nothing but make barrels, the demand for wine was so strong.

At times like this I missed having Judas Thomas at home, because he was so good with numbers and at keeping the accounts for our business. But since he and Mary had moved to Egypt all those years ago, I had learned to keep track of all our finances. And I had my husband Joses hire some of his friends to guard us against thieves who might rob us. He practically ran all of Herod's personal household now, but he still had plenty of pals from the days of his youth. They looked like ruffians, but they were good men.

SUSANNA

There was a lake! We were going to camp next to a lake! That meant, not only would we be able to water our animals and fill all our skins with enough liquid to sustain us for days on the road, but I would be able to bathe. Oh, dear Father in heaven, how I longed for a bath. I had felt filthy for days. And when I feel dirty, I lose strength. I don't want to touch the things I like. Yes, I perform whatever chores I have to, but with no energy at all. Life starts to feel like a chore itself. But now I would be able to wash off my depression. It would be almost like baptism, purifying myself of the sins that clung to me after traveling hundreds of miles through rocks and dust.

And Abban's men around me would bathe too! I would insist on it. The assault on my senses for these past several weeks had never relented. But now at least one sense — my sense of smell — would find some relief.

"Yes, Your Highness," Jesus Thomas said when I told him. During our short trip on the great trade route to the east and when we turned south to go past the lands of ancient Babylon, Amrit's and Abban's men had learned that having a woman in their entourage meant that they had to make some changes in their routines. For one thing, I now understood their home languages enough to know when they were not speaking decently, and I would make them grovel if they used disrespectful speech. And second, they could no longer lounge around our campsites wearing nothing more than a loincloth — or sometimes not even that — as they did in their previous travels together. And I insisted that we all sit down for meals together, and that they eat their food like civilized men and not like starving dogs. No more carrying a slab of food off to a corner to loudly devour it alone. They would all sit together in a circle and eat one morsel at a time. We would say a prayer to the Father before each meal. If in their culture they called God by another name, they could use that name if they wished, but everyone — and I meant everyone — would bow his head and give thanks to God before a single bit of food would pass his lips.

Mom would be proud of me. I never had to strike the cheek of any one of them. But every one of them knew he was powerless to the Stare.

So, a few of the men had taken to calling me Your Highness. Some of the men with darker complexions like Jesus Thomas's called me Rani instead, which I gathered meant some sort of princess in their homeland. I didn't care much what term they used as long as they remembered who was in charge here and jumped when I told them to jump.

One of Amrit's lieutenants stopped before me. "They have asked me," he said, motioning his head toward his crew, "if you want them to bathe in the lake as soon as they set up the camp and before our evening meal, or if we should wait until later."

I let him hang in silence for a moment before I answered. "Before they bathe, I would like," I said slowly, "for them to fill all our water skins and barrels with clean drinking water, and then to let our poor oxen drink as much as they need. Our traveling party is so dirty that I fear the water may be foul for some time when we have bathed. I will go first, shielded from others' eyes by a blanket that Abban will hold up for me. Then all of you will bathe. After that, we will eat without the stench of the road hovering over our meal."

I held his eyes with my own for a moment longer before releasing him.

"Yes, Rani. I will tell them." As he bowed, with one finger he touched his forehead and then his chest before swirling his hand toward the ground before his feet. I had grown so used to being treated like royalty that I knew it would be difficult to live among just normal people again. But I was enjoying this while I could.

Later, after we had eaten a meal of grain cakes and tangy fruits, I asked Amrit about our progress. Thomas and Abban were the actual leaders of our expedition, but the old man's mouth widened with a smile when I asked his opinion. He had traveled these roads for many years. Even if he was not on a horse at the head of the caravan, watching with his own eyes and personally receiving the reports from our forward scouts and those who guarded our rear and flanks, I knew that he could make a quick assessment based on what he heard my husband and brother discussing. I respected him for more than just his age; his wisdom helped lead us on a safer path.

Several of the men guarded the perimeters of the camp, as always, but the rest still sat in the circle where we had just eaten. Without anyone ever saying it out loud, a rule had developed that, unless they had to leave the "table" to perform a task, they all remained seated until I rose to signal the end of the meal. This evening I remained seated because I had a question for Amrit about our travel plans.

"We are about three days from the sea," the old man said, pointing to a roughly drawn map on an old roll of parchment. "When we reach there, we will sell our wagons and beasts and use the money to pay passage on a ship. We will sail far to the south to my homeland, Malabar, on the coast."

Even in the dimming light of the late afternoon, all of us could see on his map that the trip by sea would stretch far longer even than we had already come by land. "Is it safe?" I asked. I had never sailed on any trip farther than a short excursion on the lake in Galilee.

The whites of Amrit's eyes showed briefly as he looked up at me. "The sea is narrow in the first leg of our voyage," he said as he pointed again. "After we come through this narrow spot here, we will be on the open ocean and will find it much safer. But pirates may try to board our ship before we escape the narrow passage. We must choose a ship that can outrun them."

Abban nodded. "We must also display weapons openly so that any ship approaching us will fear us."

I looked across the circle at Thomas. I had grown so used to calling him The Twin by now that I seldom bothered to use his name Jesus anymore. He returned my gaze and nodded. "The Father will sail with us, so I will fear no pirates."

MARY

Philo seemed determined to transcribe as many of the King's sayings as possible. Judas Thomas and I had sat with him and a number of his followers on many days and evenings over the past few years, reminiscing about things Jesus had said, and also things that James had said and Jesus repeated. He eagerly latched onto some of the themes because they apparently agreed with some concepts that he himself had written about. He expanded on the ideas and used many of Jesus's pronouncements as building blocks for a much larger view of humans' relationship with the Father.

"I have long said that our universe began when God first uttered the Logos, the Word. But it was not just a word as you and I would speak, it was also the reason for existence, the logic behind everything that has come about in the world around us," the scholar said to us one day as we sat in a circle on cushions on the floor of his home. "It sounds like your brothers, both James and Jesus, came to embody the Logos. They showed us a path to understand the logic of the Father's creation."

"But they were just men, like yourself," I interjected.

"Yes," Philo's eyes sparkled. "But as you yourself have shown us, it is possible for us mere mortals to commune directly with the Father. And your brother Jesus has opened the path for the rest of us to do so. Before we were like children wandering in the dark, but now we can see a shaft of light and can work our way toward it on our own."

At that moment a friend of Thomas's walked into the room and knelt to whisper something into my husband's ear. His eyes widened in what I recognized as an expression of silent alarm. He raised one finger to signal that he would be back shortly, and he rose to leave the room with his friend.

Philo had kept talking as if he did not notice the interchange. "Yes, your brothers seem to have said to the rest of us, follow and we will show you what no eye has ever seen, what no ear has heard, what no hand has touched, and what has not entered into the heart of any man."

"You make it all sound so deep," I said. "At the times I was with them, they were just saying things that seemed logical in our discussions of the moment."

"It happens that way so often," he laughed.

Judas Thomas reentered the room, a worried look on his face. He stood behind his cushion, wavering between the desire to remain standing or sit and say his peace in a comfortable position. In the end he decided to sit.

"I've heard some disturbing news. Some Romans from Jerusalem have come here to the city. They say they heard that the infamous criminal Judas, the man who inspired the people of Galilee to stop paying their taxes, has taken refuge in Alexandria. They hope to capture and return him to Jerusalem to stand trial and face execution. Rome wants to make an example of Judas to remind the peasants what can happen if they disobey the emperor."

I clutched his arm. "Oh Judas Thomas, what are we going to do?"

"For one thing, we will not mention the name Judas at all," he reminded me. "Thomas only."

Philo did not seem to share our worry. "My friends, the Romans will first go to Julius, the governor. Then they will consult with my brother Alexander. I doubt that he would share any information with them, but I will warn him anyway that the Romans seek to extradite you for execution. He will keep them confused long enough for you to escape."

"But what if they ask people on the streets about me?"

"Fortunately," the old man chuckled, "it is your wife whom the people on the streets know of. Mary the Migdal is well known throughout the city. But Judas — not so much."

If he felt insulted, Thomas did not show it.

"That will help me temporarily, but what will I do after that? I can't hide in Alexandria forever."

Philo gazed downward as he stroked his beard in silence. His eyebrows arched as he raised his eyes to look at us with a question. "Tell me, what do you know about Gaul?"

Thomas looked surprised at the sudden change of topic. "Gaul? Isn't that the land northwest of Rome? If I remember correctly, it's full of savage men who sacrifice babies and virgins to pagan gods."

"That's what the Romans want you to believe," Philo said. "I have a friend with a ship who trades goods from Gaul, and he is due to set sail in a few days. I could ask him if he could take you as passengers."

Thomas seemed unable to put any thoughts into words. So I did.

"I'll tell Sarah that it is an adventure. If she thinks we are in trouble, she will complain the whole way. But if we tell her she is going to be the heroine who will save people in a new land, she will not whine about seasickness or about being taken away from her friends."

Thomas finally found his tongue. "Rabbi, we will miss you."

RACHEL

The funeral for Rabbi Gamaliel attracted people from all over the countryside around the city and beyond. Upon hearing the news of his death, James and all the rest of the members of the Sanhedrin tore the fabric of their robes to bare their hearts. Unlike the ceremonies for some of the more arrogant aristocrats in the city, we did not have to hire women to weep loudly at the Rabbi's burial. Hundreds of people were already wailing without any prompting. Even the new Roman governor, this man Felix who replaced Cumanus after the murders in Samaria, sent some of his lieutenants to show their respect. A lot of men I had not seen for many years came to Gamaliel's funeral.

And Saul came back to the city! When I saw him standin' there among the rest like he was royalty himself, I had to hold my mouth shut with both hands to keep myself from yellin' some things that ain't proper to say at funerals. He nodded his head this way and that to acknowledge men he knew back when he studied under our rabbi, but he wore a smug look on his face that told me all I needed to know. He hadn't changed a bit.

When James walked over to greet Saul, I sneaked along behind him close enough to listen.

"I am no longer known as Saul," I heard him sayin'. "My flock is mostly Gentile, so they call me by the Roman name of Paul."

One of James's friends laughed out loud. "So your name has gone from Saul, the namesake of Israel's first king, to Paul, which in the Romans' tongue means small."

Saul glowered in anger as several of the men nearby chuckled. "The Lord our God does not consider me small," he answered angrily. "In the years since I left here, he revealed to me his Son, Jesus the Eternal Christos, raised from the dead. And then he sent me to the holy mountain where Moses received the Commandments, and he told me personally that I was chosen to take the Good News to the world. And I have gone forth as he commanded me, and I have established churches throughout Greece."

James had perked up at the mention of the King's name. "You've seen my brother, Jesus? How is he? I have not heard from him for many months now."

Saul, or I guess I should say Paul, waved his question away as if he were an ignorant boy. "The man you knew as Jesus was revealed to me in a vision as the eternal Son of God. He was the Anointed One. Or as the Greeks call him, the Christos. And my followers call themselves Christians in his honor. The Lord our God selected me even before my birth to save the world through the Christos."

I had moved around to the side so I could see both of them now. James knitted his brows as he asked, "And what are you teaching these Gentiles about my brother?"

Paul puffed out his chest and reached out his arms to the sides as if he were givin' a speech to a big crowd. "I tell them that only by putting their faith in the Lord Jesus Christos can they come before the Father, that they are all evil and will be cast into Hell if they do not believe."

James held his head down for a moment so that his chin almost rested on his chest. Then he straightened up again and looked Paul in the eyes.

"I think you may have missed the point about what my brother preached. Yes, he led us all to know the Father, but he never claimed any glory for himself."

Paul rested his hands on his hips and leaned forward slightly as if he were still lecturing some boy. "No, it is you who never understood what the Christos was telling you, even though you knew him in the flesh. I never knew him as a man, but I know him as the eternal Christos, the savior of us all who has existed with the Father since before the beginning of time. He has revealed himself to me."

Like I said, I had to hold my mouth shut with both hands. I couldn't believe the arrogance of this man! Well, I could actually believe it really easily, remembering him as I did, but one still doesn't think her worst expectations to ever come true. I never knew anything about Paul's parents, but it was pretty plain to me that they never spanked him as a boy when he misbehaved or started thinkin' too highly of himself. Apparently that time we women sent him out of the country wasn't enough to correct the years of spoilin' he got as a child.

I noticed a woman standing behind Paul, her arms draped over the shoulders of a boy standing in front of her. She looked Judean but her clothes were Greek. And her clothes practically shouted out money. She had a long white dress that hung from her shoulders to her ankles, and a huge blue silk scarf covered the top of her head and wound around the dress almost like a toga. This lady looked rich. No, rich wasn't the word for it. This woman looked like she owned a country. Her son — I assumed he was her son — looked like he might be twelve or thirteen, and the cloth of his tunic would rival that of the High Priest.

I'd been lost in thought for a minute but snapped to when I heard James say, "We shall have to discuss this further later. Meanwhile, let us give honor to our Rabbi."

The funeral went on normal like. Important people made what I suppose were important speeches with what sounded like important words, though I couldn't be sure because I'd never heard half o' them words before in all my life. All the fancy folks went "ooh" and "aah" when they heard the important words, but I don't know if they understood 'em any better than I did. I've seen time and again, when somebody don't understand somethin' but they don't want to be seen as stupid, they'll pretend and go along with everyone else about how grand it was.

The Rabbi Gamaliel's son, Simon, had come home to honor his father. Young Simon, himself a rabbi, had been off studying these many years in Alexandria down in Egypt. But the son and father almost never communicated with each other in all the years I knew them, not after Gamaliel's wife died. From what I heard, they didn't disagree about the Law and the Prophets, nor about how folks were supposed to honor the Father at the Temple. I guess they had some sort of argument and the son left in a huff a long time ago, and the old man never talked about it in all those years. Gamaliel had a daughter too, but she married some priest and moved away long ago.

Anyway, Simon did all the things a son is supposed to do when his father dies. He sang Kaddish and walked along as they took the body to a cave where they put it on a stone shelf and anointed it with myrrh. After a year, someone would come and collect the bones and put 'em in a stone box.

I expected to serve him dinner and make up a place for him to sleep, but Simon left Jerusalem almost as soon as the funeral was over. I never knew why.

So, when we had supper, it was just me and James at the table. Rabbi Gamaliel had left the house to James. My boy still taught dozens of students, and he led our big meals for the poor and made all the rich men give alms for widows and orphans. Rabbi Gamaliel had said when he got sick that he wanted the Righteous One to continue his work here, so he left the house and a lot of his money.

I was never one to hide what I was thinkin', so I jumped right to the point.

"What did that snake Saul have to say for himself? Oh wait — he's callin' himself Paul now, to make sure we all remember he's Roman."

James' eyes sparkled in the candlelight, and his teeth shone white when he grinned. "Our former student fancies himself a great leader," he said. "I don't think he ever met my brother, but he claims to know him better than any of us, even Simon Peter, who traveled and worked with Jesus for several years. Paul says he's the son of God. Sometimes he seems to say my brother was God himself. That's funny, because I remember wrestling and calling him a smart ass quite a few times when we were boys growing up. So if he's God, I'm in big trouble."

I noticed his bowl was getting low, so I ladled more stew into it. We never ate meat anymore — the Righteous One said he couldn't bring himself to do it — so the stew was just barley with some roots and vegetables. The wine tasted a bit sweeter than usual.

"Well, your friend Saul or Paul or whatever he calls himself seems to be dressing and eating well," I said, dishing the last few drops of stew into my own bowl because James's dish was full and wouldn't take any more. "So I know somebody's taking care of him. When he was your student, I don't think he could tie his own sandals without help, and I know for a fact that he couldn't cook a meal even if he was starving. I saw that rich woman hangin' on his every word, so I'm pretty sure she's handlin' things for him. I'll introduce myself if I see her again."

James drank the last of the wine in his cup.

"Rachel, I don't know if the Rabbi ever thanked you properly for everything you have done to support his ministry through the years. He told me many times how often you sowed a seed in his mind that would later grow to a great truth that he had never thought of before.

"And me too. Remember that time when Gamaliel told you to teach me about the Passover by taking me to your kitchen and making me bake two loaves of bread, one with leaven and one without? And then you made me realize that the slaves fleeing Egypt had to bake unleavened bread because they were desperate to leave as soon as possible and could not wait for the leavened dough to rise. That lesson you taught me has helped to make me what I am today. If I have learned anything about God's righteousness, I learned it from you. And even my brother Jesus, the King, when he left Jerusalem after the Romans killed him, he told all his disciples that you were the person in charge. None of the men should do anything without checking with you first."

I swatted the side of his head. "You've had too much wine. Off to bed with you now. But drink some water first so you don't wake up with a headache." I had to turn away from him as soon as I could. My eyes were tearin' up like a baby and I didn't want him to see me cry.

The morning after the Sabbath, James needed to get out early. I had some bread and fruit ready by sunup for him to break his fast. Today was The Blessing. He started The Blessing a few years ago, and now hundreds of the poor came for every one of them. Every Sunday, the day after the Sabbath, before people started their work week, James would stand to speak at the top of the grand staircase leading up to the Temple. And not just the poor would gather on the steps to hear him, a lot of the city's rich folks and about half the Temple folks would come too.

This day the crowd was even bigger because of the gathering for Rabbi Gamaliel. Even though they needed to get to work — drawing water for the day and carrying it back to their homes, some of them going out to the farms to bring back carts of vegetables to sell at the marketplace, others working all the different sorts of jobs that have to get done to keep the city moving — the poor gathered on the steps to hear the Righteous One. But as I looked out over the crowd, I saw a lot of the visitors who had come for the funeral.

And there they were. Among the crowd at the bottom of the staircase, I could see Paul and the rich woman and a man who looked like he might be her husband. And there was the boy she had with her before. I suppose I shouldn't be proud o' what I was thinkin' at that moment, but I was secretly glad that the crowd on the staircase was so thick that Paul couldn't climb even onto the first step.

"People of Jerusalem!" James was at the top of the staircase, his arms held up and stretched out from his sides to include everyone. His voice was loud and clear, and the crowd hushed in an instant.

"You have heard that it was written that you should do for your neighbor as you would like your neighbor to do for you. Let me tell you a story I learned from my brother, Jesus. I think this really happened to him as he was traveling the countryside. A fine gentleman was traveling on the road. Thieves attacked him and robbed him of all his riches, leaving him for dead lying on the side of the road. A respected man of the Temple passed by but would not touch the man, fearful that to do so would make him impure. And later a respected merchant passed by, but he would not help the man because he could see he'd been robbed of all his money. But then the worst person you can imagine — a Samaritan! A man from Samaria saw the man at the side of the road. He gave him water to drink and then lifted him up and put him on his donkey. The Samaritan walked while the man rode. He took him to his home and gave him food and washed his wounds. He cared for him until the man was well enough to travel on his own.

"Now," James shouted, "which of these behaved like a neighbor? Was it the man from the Temple?" Dozens of voices shouted no. "Was it the merchant?" Even more shouted no. "Was it that terrible man, the Samaritan?" And now the whole crowd shouted yes.

James paused while the people laughed. Imagine a Samaritan behaving better than a fellow Judean!

James waved his hands for silence. "I think Simon Peter and John may have traveled with Jesus on that particular trip, so you can ask them later if I got all the details right," he joked, pointing toward the Galilean and the Jericho brother. "But I think we can all agree that the Father can reach out to touch you in ways you don't expect, using people you would not expect. So you must keep your eyes and ears open to see and hear."

He turned toward where I stood on one side of the stairs. I'm almost sure he was looking directly at me when he said, "Let me tell you another story. The Father's kingdom of heaven is like this: A woman had three measures of dough. And she took a small bit of leaven and hid it within the dough and left it alone. And when she baked the loaf, the leaven had spread through the dough and made it grow so big that you would think there was no room for it in in the oven. The word of God is like that — a little bit can grow in your head and make your life much bigger than you would ever have thought possible."

He held his arms out to his sides with the palms turned upward and turned right and left to include all his listeners. "Go forth now and do your work. Do your work for yourselves, for your families, and for the Father. Amen!"

"Amen," shouted a chorus of voices. Then the people turned and went their way.

PRISCILLA

Aquila did not seem to grasp the significance of the debate. Sadly, my husband often did not see the larger picture and needed a push from me to do the right thing. On this trip with Paul, I'd had to push more often than usual.

"Who cares what these fools in Jerusalem think?" he said as he lay back against a cushion. "We have established more churches and have more followers than these people will ever have."

Paul apparently wanted to compete with Aquila to see who could be the most obtuse. "I agree. These so-called Pillars of the faith — James and Peter and the dimwit John — they mean nothing to me. They remember Jesus as a man. But I met him as the Christos! He appeared to me in a vision and spoke to me, when the brigands of Jerusalem kidnapped me and carried me north. I think they meant to take me to Damascus but tired of their task by the time we reached Galilee. So they beat me and left me for dead, and that is when the resurrected Jesus, the Lord Christos appeared to me."

I never tired of hearing this story. I felt that I stood in the presence of God's Chosen One every time he told it. I wanted to move on to my next subject, but I let Paul continue. It was better to let him repeat the story again.

"The people who took me in and nurtured me back to health seemed to know all about Jesus. And they seemed to know that he had been raised from the dead, but they either tried to avoid discussing it or else they were woefully ignorant of the implications of his resurrection.

"When I had regained my strength, I traveled south to Mt. Horeb in Arabia, where Moses and Elijah spoke directly to God. I spent countless days fasting and praying, growing delirious in my hunger and fervor. And I believe God spoke to me through my own intellect. I came to understand the mystery."

Paul leaned back on his cushion, his eyes staring into the distance, a smile frozen on his face from whatever it was he thought he saw. I gave him a few more minutes to bask in his own glow, and then I spoke up.

"Paul, Aquila, I do not doubt anything you say. But listen to me. I am the one who has made this family rich. We employ many leather smiths who make wonderful products, but I am the one who makes wealthy merchants and their wives want to buy them. I am the one who convinces rulers like Felix and Cumanus before him to wear our leather jackets and sandals and harnesses at sporting events and feasts, so that all the other people see them and desire to buy our products as well.

"So, when I tell you," I continued, "that we need James to give his blessing on our work, trust me. It is true that the people of our churches in cities from Antioch to Athens all believe in Paul's Gospel. But they also have heard of James, the Righteous One who was the brother of our Lord when he walked the earth in the flesh. If James gives his blessing, the people of your churches will grow stronger in their faith that God has chosen you, and you alone, to bring salvation to the world."

Aquila shifted his weight on his cushion, but I ignored him. I kept my focus on Paul. If he would drop his pride and submit to James, Aquila would follow. I respected my husband, but I knew he would not dare oppose me if Paul came to reason.

Paul for his part, had stopped staring into space and gave me his full attention. As he let my words sink in, he seemed to squirm in his seat for several moments. He opened his mouth to speak but, catching himself, stopped and reconsidered before resuming.

"I see your point. As much as I consider him a pompous ass — and I have considered him so since we were young men studying together under Rabbi Gamaliel — I will allow him to have his say. But he does not know Gentiles, and I will not allow him to force Greeks and Romans to undergo circumcision. It's hard enough to get them to forget about their household gods. I won't make them cut themselves too."

I let him have that victory, but still gave a note of caution. "Absolutely. But you don't need to make that argument until after you've left Jerusalem. Get his blessing, and then we can deal with the circumcision issue later."

RACHEL

I'd never have been able to even approach her on my own, but I knew she'd bring her family and Saul — I mean Paul — to see the Righteous One. They wouldn't have come here unless they wanted something. And she looked to be the brains behind whatever their scheme might be, so I focused on getting to her.

Sure enough, when I was serving James some grains and milk in the morning, he said Paul was coming to see him that day at the school. James's students weren't all boys anymore. Some of them were men who had already become rabbis in their home towns and came to the city to get more respect. You could become pretty famous with the folks back home if you could tell them you had studied with the Righteous One, I guess, because in the last few years they had traveled from all over Judea and Galilee to join his class for at least a few sessions. Some, the ones with enough money, would stay for a month or more.

"Can I come to your class today, Rabbi? If you're havin' visitors, it might be nice if I could bring some little cakes and water for the folks to snack on."

James looked genuinely pleased at my suggestion. "Why, that would be wonderful," he said. "And it would teach Paul that he is too slow to forgive and too quick to judge. He confided yesterday that he is still afraid of you and thinks you only mean to do him harm."

I crossed my arms as if I were really perplexed. "Now, what on earth would give him that sort of idea?"

I cooked some cakes and drew some extra water that morning and loaded them into a basket for the short walk to the building where the class was held. Like I said, it was a mix now of smart boys from rich families and full-grown men. I made sure everybody got equal portions. The boys' parents could afford to keep them well fed. And the men — a lot of them were here because the people in their home villages pooled their pennies together to pay their way. So while I didn't want to deprive the youngsters, the men probably needed the food more and I wanted to make sure they got their share.

Paul, it turned out, didn't want any of the food I offered. He said he was still full after breaking his fast that morning. But I have to wonder if he was afraid that I'd try to poison him. He had certainly eaten plenty of my cookin' back when he was a student. But then, a lot had changed between us since those days. I was sure he probably remembered that my face was the last one he saw before the other women captured and beat him and had him spirited out of the city.

The rich woman was standing at the back of the room, watching as her husband and son sat with the other students listening to James talk about some passage in one of the Prophets. Like before, she had dressed like royalty that morning and looked like she could walk right into a meetin' with Governor Felix without so much as a curtsey.

I sidled up next to her. "Your boy looks like the smartest one in the bunch," I whispered. "You must be so proud."

I'd said the magic words. You can compliment a woman on her looks, on her clothes, on her cookin' or on her singin'. But tell her that her cub stands head and shoulders above all the others, and you'll reduce her to a gigglin' girl.

"Yes, I have taught him myself," she bragged. "His name is Lucas. I've taught him to speak, read and write in Latin, Greek and Hebrew. He has also studied healing arts from our physicians in Corinth. I hope he will grow up to become a great man."

I played along. "Oh, he sounds brilliant! And in addition to gettin' such a grand education, he's travelin' and listenin' to Paul. That must give him quite a bit to think about. By the way, if you don't mind my askin', what is your name and how are you connected to all this," I whispered, wavin' my hand toward all the students listenin' to James in the front of the room.

Now, I stand at least a head shorter than a lot of the men who visit us, so I'd grown used to them lookin' down their nose at me. But this lady was the same height as me, and her eyes were directly across from my own. But even so, she put a chill into the air that made me feel she was lookin' down her nose just like all those tall men. I guess in her life everybody bowed and scraped before her, and she'd grown pretty accustomed to puttin' people in their place — which by her way of thinkin' meant below her. I'd met plenty like her in my years.

But I'd also spent the last forty winters takin' care of the Rabbi Gamaliel, and now the Righteous One. Princes and princesses came to see them here, and all the greatest priests from all parts of the world stopped to say hello. None of them impressed me much anymore. No matter how much gold they carried in their coin bags, they all asked for second helpings of the meals I set before 'em. And they each acted as silly as the next if they drank a third cup of wine.

"My name is Priscilla," the lady said. "My husband Aquila and my son Lucas and I have been traveling with Paul for some time now. Paul is the Christos's messenger. He alone, out of all men was chosen to bring the word to all people throughout the earth."

It took me a minute to catch on. "Christos — oh, you mean the King, Jesus," I said. "You know, the King is James's brother, and he ate and drank at my own table. Why, after his crucifixion, when he came to the house, I led him to the upper room myself, and he told the men — "

"You saw him after his resurrection?" She clutched my arm like I'd offered to give her a gold coin. Though, now that I stop to think of it, she probably already had a lot of gold coins of her own.

"Yes, of course I saw the King. All of us did. The Romans tried to kill him, but they couldn't. Like I was sayin', I took him upstairs to where the other men were mournin' his loss, and he told them — "

She interrupted again. "The Romans weren't responsible for his crucifixion, it was the Judeans who betrayed him."

"No, it was the Romans. They took him across the Kidron Valley and hung him on a cross, and he died that very day. But his brother Judas's wife Mary went to the tomb a few days later to anoint the body, and he was alive. After he rested for a few weeks, he came back here to talk to his followers. And he told them that I — "

We had been talkin' in whispers, but now she spoke loud enough to catch some stares from some of the men tryin' to listen to James. "You only knew him when he was a man in the flesh. Paul has brought him to us in Spirit, as the Son of God."

"Oh, did you bring him with you? That's wonderful," I was sayin'. "The last time he was here, I meant to give him some blankets and new sandals for his travels. And we just got a shipment of some of that wonderful wine he used to make up in Galilee. I bet he'd love to have some of that."

From the look on her face, you'd think I had just called the emperor an imbecile to his face or somethin'. She backed away from me like I had pus from leprosy just oozin' off my fingers and open wounds on my face.

"The Christos is no longer a man of the flesh," she said in a voice that sounded like she was readin' straight from the Law and Prophets. "The Father has resurrected him from the dead and has raised him to heaven, where he sits at the right hand of the Father."

I held my tongue. I knew darn well where the King went after he came back to life, but I wasn't going to blurt it out to this stranger. After all, she was a friend of Paul's, and Paul was never any friend of the Righteous One nor the King. For all I knew, she might be tryin' to find out Jesus's location. She wasn't gonna get it from me. But I didn't want to make her suspicious by arguin' the point, so I changed the subject.

"It's a shame the Rabbi Gamaliel passed away. I remember when Paul and so many young men came here to study. Most of 'em are spread out across the empire now, so I'm glad you folks were close enough to Jerusalem that you could come here for this visit." I left the point hangin' in the air.

She took the bait, as Simon Peter would say. He was a fisherman for so many years, so he used expressions like that. Anyway, she said, "Oh yes, we were already on our way to Jerusalem. Paul wanted to tell James, John and Simon Peter about his mission among the Gentiles in the empire, and to get their blessing on his work."

Aha! So that's what they were after! They wanted James to put his own name and reputation behind whatever Paul and this woman Priscilla were doin' out in the provinces. It must be worth a whole lot to them to be able to use James's name or else they wouldn't have traveled so far to ask for it. I would make sure James didn't give them what they wanted without makin' sure they gave him what he wanted in return.

Just then, I noticed some commotion in the front where the men were talkin'. I was accustomed to men with different ideas arguin' their points. That's pretty much what James always presided over, and Rabbi Gamaliel before him. Women made sure everybody got fed, clothed and sheltered, while men spent their time arguin' about whose ideas were smarter, and whose muscles and private parts were bigger. That's just the way it had always been. So at first I didn't think much of it that there was a disagreement goin' on. But it looked like Paul's face was turnin' red, so I hushed Priscilla so we could hear what was goin' on.

"We have always accommodated the God-fearers," John was sayin'. "Throughout the empire the God-fearers show some sympathy for our ways, and they even adopt some of them in trying to woo our women to become their wives.

"But they refuse to circumcise because the loss of their foreskins would embarrass them in front of the other men in their gymnasiums, and they refuse to give up their pork and other unclean foods. So we tolerate their presence among us, but we do not accept them fully into our community."

"You hypocrites," Paul ranted. "You say you accommodate the God-fearers, but you hold yourselves above them. But I tell you that through the Christos, the Father has made all foods holy and he does not require circumcision among the Gentiles."

John raised his voice to match Paul's. "Are you suggesting we abandon the laws that the Lord has given our people since the time of Moses?"

"No," shouted Paul immediately. "But don't require the Gentiles to follow the same laws. They have come to the Father through faith in his son, the Anointed, the Christos. That should be sufficient for you."

James stepped into the middle of all the men, holding his hands up for silence. With all the shouting, it took a minute for things to quiet down.

"My friends," he said, "this is too important an issue for us to try to decide in one day. Let us each go home and sleep on what we have heard today and be prepared to return in two days to discuss it more." He paused a moment to look meaningfully at Paul and John. "And I suggest you take a moment to contemplate that the Lord our God gave you two ears but only one mouth. I believe that ratio tells us how much the Father wants you to speak, and how much more he wants you to listen."

Paul started to say something, but James turned on him in an instant and pointed a finger. "Don't."

All the men started workin' their way to the door to leave. Priscilla held her hands out for Lucas to come to her. Now that I got a good look at him, he looked like he had probably reached his twelfth birthday by now. His mother wrapped her arm over him protectively like he was still a toddler, and she waited for Aquila to get to them.

"It was so good for me to meet you, Priscilla," I called out over the noise the men were creatin'. "I hope we get a chance to talk more soon."

She turned and acknowledged me with half a smile, and then she walked out with her family.

MARY

Sarah was loving her adventure, but her parents felt they were suffering for the sins of all humankind. Thomas had grown very familiar with the sight of the sea water below us, because he spent so much time clutching the ship's rails and vomiting over the side. He had difficulty keeping any food down, and his face seemed to be taking on a greenish tint. If this voyage lasted much longer, I was afraid he would not. Last much longer, that is.

Myself, something in the food or drink had taken a terrible toll inside me. Unlike my husband, I could keep food down but then it seemed to pass right through me. I spent most of my time below deck, never more than a few steps away from my chamber pot.

But Sarah! She suddenly had her whole days to explore, because Mommy was too sick to make her study. She ran from the stern of the ship to the prow and questioned every crew member in between about his responsibilities and how he raised the sails and lowered the sails and did he ever have to row the boat when there was no wind and how did he drop and raise the anchor and how did the captain steer the ship and did they really use the stars in the sky to guide them at night and did they have wives and children at home and what time is supper going to be this afternoon and do we really have to eat that same gruel we had yesterday?

I was afraid the captain would grow so irritated with her that he'd throw her overboard, and Thomas and me along with her too. We had taught Sarah how to swim almost from the time she could walk. But I doubted she could manage to keep Thomas and me afloat, and we were probably too weak to save ourselves. The girl might get us killed.

The captain, however, apparently never had an inquisitive little girl as a passenger on his ship before, and he did not know how to handle it. The crewmembers started giving her little jobs to do — carrying small buckets from the galley to dump refuse overboard, or helping to lower a weighted line into the water to measure its depth, or relaying messages. They even gave her a title, Second Mate, no less! At night while I was laying on my blanket, praying for the illness to leave me, she would come and tell Thomas and me all the important tasks that she had performed that day and would solemnly inform us of the meanings of nautical terms she had learned. "And Daddy, if you stay so sick that you die, I've learned how to bury you at sea. There's a certain way to do it so that not too many fish will try to eat you. It will be a very formal affair, and people will talk about it for years to come." I'm sure this gave my husband great motivation to get healthy soon. I know it certainly motivated me.

When Thomas and I were finally able to join the others for supper on the third day, the cook and Sarah personally carried our bowls of stew to us and brought us cups of wine. "It's better to drink wine, Mommy, because sometimes the water's got germs that can make you sick. I've been drinking wine every day, and I feel great!'

Oh wonderful, so my little eight-year-old girl was going to be a drunk! But I was still too weak to complain. And I had to admit that the food and drink she served seemed to restore a bit of my strength. I complimented her and the cook. She had obviously prepared him for this moment: He bowed and she curtsied simultaneously, and then they turned together and returned to the kitchen.

Judas Thomas and I gingerly picked through the food, fearing the worst. But it stayed down for him and stayed up for me. After the meal, we both felt drowsy, probably due to a combination of our full stomachs and two cups of wine. The wind had dropped to a steady but reasonable speed, and the seas remained calm. I leaned my head against his shoulder and for the first time in days, we dozed comfortably.

SUSANNA

Abban spoke excitedly. He had been standing at the prow of the ship with the captain, peering and pointing into the distance. He clutched my hand but looked into his father's eyes as he spoke.

"We have come within sight of Malabar. You will see your homeland soon, Father."

Amrit's eyes sparkled and his lips quivered as he nodded simply. He did not attempt to speak.

We had mostly kept to ourselves on this sailing. For one thing, fewer people here spoke Greek, and almost none knew Aramaic or Hebrew. But Jesus Thomas and I were startled as we walked back from the galley to hear a familiar accent from a pair of passengers who likewise had kept incommunicado. Always outgoing — to a fault — my brother stopped to say, Shalom.

It turned out that the men were traders who usually sailed from northwestern Arabia down the sea and around the tip of land toward Malabar, where the spice trade thrived. "You will find many Judeans there," one of them said. "Our people hold important positions in most ports, and they trade in only the finest quality material."

I was ready to return to Abban's side but stopped when the man asked, "Have you visited Jerusalem lately and heard about the King?"

Jesus Thomas also stiffened, but quickly massaged his shoulder as if to ease a sudden kink. "I have not been there for some time. The King — do you mean Herod Antipas? I thought the Romans only gave him one-fourth of the old kingdom."

The trader gestured wildly. "No, not the tetrarch. A man named Jesus was proclaimed the King by the country people. The Romans executed him, but they say he was resurrected by God. They called him the Anointed One. The Greeks call him the Christos, which means the same thing."

My brother squeezed my wrist to warn me to silence. "I had heard stories that a Righteous One had arisen in Jerusalem. Is that whom you are speaking of?"

"No, no," he shook his head. "Jesus the Christos is the brother of James in Jerusalem. In fact, James leads many of the poor to worship in the Temple, and the people say he may become the High Priest one day. And their other brother, Judas — we heard that he was so saddened by the execution of the Christos that he killed himself. Everyone has been speaking of almost nothing else for these years since then. I am surprised you had not heard the story."

Jesus Thomas was playing dumb, giving the trader a chance to say more. "This Jesus the Christos was resurrected from the dead, you say?"

"Yes," the man said animatedly. "They say he rose after three days and appeared to his followers. And all Judeans now say that Rome is unable to kill their King, that God the Father and his son the Christos is mightier than Caesar."

"Your story gives me a great deal to think about," my brother muttered as he stroked his beard. "I will have to ponder this news."

We returned to where Abban and his father rested. My brother held a finger to his lips and spoke softly. "From now on, call me Thomas. No more Jesus Thomas. Thomas only."

A few hours later, we tied up the boat at a small wooden pier. The crew started unloading small crates and stacking them on shore, while the captain spoke to a local trader who had been alerted to the shipment's arrival and hastened to the harbor. Abban and I helped Amrit to his feet and put his arms over our shoulders as we walked him down the pier onto solid ground. He solemnly folded his hands in front of his chin and bowed his head slightly, then lowered himself gingerly to his knees. Even though we were on sandy ground at the seashore, he bent down and kissed the ground.

"How long have your travels taken you away from your homeland?" I asked.

Amrit stood erect and brushed the sand off his lips and beard. He looked stronger now that he was on solid ground. "I have been away many years. Even when I was trading spices, I only came as far south as the land near ancient Babylon and met with ships that had sailed north from here. Then I would transport the spices north to deal with the men passing in both directions on the great road that goes from the Middle Kingdom in the east to the great sea in the west. That is how I met your father and your brother all those years ago."

Abban grinned. "And that is where I acquired my affinity for silk. I have not worn any on this journey because it would draw unwanted attention to us. But in those days I spent most of my time out of sight studying mathematics anyway, so I felt free to wear colorful clothing."

True, I thought to myself. My husband still preferred colorful silks to the linens the rest of my family wore. In fact, now that I thought of it, all of Amrit's men wore linens too. What must they have thought of my Abban when he was growing up? Why, I was the only female in this traveling group, yet I appeared drab compared to my husband when he wore his usual garb.

A group approached us on the beach near the pier. Amrit's men fanned out in a protective wedge to either side of me. Although they maintained relaxed stances, I could see that each of them was coiled and ready to spring into combat if anything went amiss. Thomas, also noticing the men's shift in position, sidled up next to me and spoke softly into my ear. "In all the time I have known these men, and in all our travels together, they focused their defenses around Amrit and Abban. Now the defense centers around you. They truly have found their Rani, and they would give their lives to protect you."

His words surprised me. Yes, I had taken charge when situations called for it. And I had used all the wiles that Mom had taught me. The Stare, first and foremost, but also praising and punishing when it became necessary to encourage or discourage certain types of behavior. If the men started to become disrespectful, I could "slap" them with a few well-chosen words. And as Mom had said, when a man has developed a good habit, a few smiling compliments from a woman will burn the memory into his soul, and he will make that example of good behavior into an everyday staple of his character.

So yes, I had taught the men to respect me and molded their routines to reflect the attitudes I wanted from them. But I had not thought I had exerted so much control that they should bow to me as their princess or fight to the death to ward off any enemies. Thomas's words surprised me and gave me pause to consider how I must mold my own actions to remain worthy of their reverence. I must set a good example.

The central person of the group that approached us wore a trimmed beard and moustache over the dark complexion of his face. The men of Israel did not cut their beards — we had a custom dating back hundreds of years that they must not do so. But after just a few moments to adjust my thinking, I grew to appreciate the man's whiskers. He appeared about thirty years old, a few years older than me. His entourage did not take defensive postures like my group did, but perhaps they did not feel the need. After all, this was their home and they might have reinforcements nearby hidden from our eyes.

"Madam," the man said to me, touching first his forehead, then his chest and then swirling his hand toward the ground as he took a deep bow. "You have traveled many leagues to arrive here. Let us move to yonder pavilion where you may sit in shade and refresh yourself with a beverage. Would you prefer water or wine after your long journey?"

I glanced at Amrit to get a sense from him which response I should give. I had really grown accustomed to drinking wine because the water at some of the villages we visited often needed boiling before I felt safe drinking it. But perhaps I should avoid wine and keep my head clear.

But Amrit gave a slight tilt of his head and a sort of shrug with his eyebrows, if such a thing is possible. He indicated that it was probably safe either way.

"I would love to have a cup of your wine," I told the man. "Our fruit of the vine on this journey has begun to sour, and Amrit here has been telling me for weeks how wonderful your grapes here are and how sweet their fermented juice."

"Splendid," he replied, leading us toward the building.

PRISCILLA

I stood up from my seat at the front of the room, turning my gaze slowly from left to right over the roomful of women. Their chatter quickly ceased as they waited to hear what I would say. Aquila and Paul did not come to this meeting because I told them I needed to speak to the women alone. They had gone off to some open square in the middle of town to try to start up a conversation with anyone who had time to talk. Usually, after Paul had spoken for only a minute or two, most of the townspeople came to the realization that they did not, in fact, have time to talk. Others would stay to listen and would either rise up to shout Amen together or to try to seize Paul and have him thrashed.

That's why I addressed the women alone. Sure, Paul could excite the crowds to passion and sometimes even violence, often against himself. Perhaps he enjoyed making a martyr of himself. But I had a more practical mission. If we were to create a community to worship the Christos, we needed a strong organization governed by people with good common sense. We needed more than fancy talk. We needed people who could actually get things done.

I needed the women.

"You are all so beautiful," I began, "but I see strength and wisdom in your eyes as well. Your husbands are all lucky to have captured you."

They twittered in response. These ladies all had cups of wine sitting in front of them as they lounged together. Women of means, they could afford to drink wine in the afternoon. Their servants would never dream of imbibing so early, lest they fail to finish their daily tasks. But my audience in this room, which had been loaned to me by the wife of a wealthy merchant with whom I dealt often, all drank freely and more than a few of them were already slurring their speech.

"So tell me, you beautiful ladies of Antioch, before your husbands won you in marriage, did wealthy Romans and Greeks compete for your attention? And forgive me if this causes worry, but are their young sons now hoping to court your daughters?"

One woman stood up in a flowing white dress that draped from her shoulders and dipped to a valley that emphasized the ample swell of her breasts. In fact, now that I took notice of her, I would have thought invisible hands were holding those breasts up in defiance of the downward pull to which the rest of us succumbed. At her age I was certain she had nursed her babies, but her nipples pointed upward through the fabric like a thirteen-year-old virgin's.

"A Roman nobleman has asked for my daughter in marriage. He wants her not for his son but for himself. The old fool has hair whiter than my husband's, and I doubt he could even plant the seeds necessary to give me a grandchild!" Several women giggled behind their dainty handkerchiefs at this utterance; I suspected that they were quite familiar with men's overconfidence in their ability to perform. "My husband favors the match because he thinks our family will grow more rich and powerful, but I shudder to think of my poor daughter underneath that fat old man."

"Then teach your daughter never to get beneath any man," I said immediately, causing delighted gasps from around the room. "If she is forced into this marriage, she should stay on top. For one thing, she is more likely to gain pleasure if she is on top and in control of the motion." This drew more gasps, though I think some were in shock not because the concept was new to them but that I would speak so openly of sexual matters.

"But more important," I continued fervently, "all of us, and our daughters too, must retain our power. Our men can harvest food, fight wars, make speeches and write the history books bragging about their own achievements. But it is up to us women to make those achievements possible."

I moved across the front of the room, my hands stretched out in welcome. "Now, I did not ask you here today to talk about the best positions to take when having sex, though that topic can certainly perk up our ears in whatever setting." More twitters.

"No, I am here to talk about the Christos. You have heard Paul speak about him, and he is winning over a few men. But I am here to tell you that we women will reap great rewards if we turn our men away from the Greek and Roman household gods to worship the Christos and his Father, the one true God."

A woman seated in the middle of the group held up her half-empty cup and cried, "I want to hear about how to get more pleasure by staying on top." Apparently, she held status high enough for the rest of the women to see her remark as permission to laugh openly. It took a full minute before the gales of their merriment quietened down.

"And besides, wasn't this Christos just another man? I know a Judean woman who says the Romans killed him," called out another.

I held up my hands to silence the chorus of chatter. "Yes, if you ask the Hebrews, they might say he was only a man because that is how they knew him. And now they must hide their shame, because they did not recognize him as divine. Yes, through their treachery he was executed, but he rose from the dead! Paul saw him! And the Father has told Paul that the Christos is a part of God, that he is the Father's equal. Your household gods do not measure up to the grandeur of the Christos.

"So when the Romans and Greeks come courting you or your daughters, first you must stay on top — both figuratively and, I would suggest," I smiled at the woman who had asked for more information, "physically. Then when they come to understand that you are in control, you can make it known to them that if they wish to marry you, they must first come to know the Christos. The men will not force you to accept their gods. You will force them to accept yours — the one true God."

A rousing swirl of cheers rose from among them. Whether from the wine or a new sense of empowerment, I could not tell. But their smiles seemed to take on a new light of confidence.

RACHEL

Though I didn't much care for the woman and hoped I'd never have to stand in the same room with her again in this lifetime — and maybe not the next one either — I had to admit that Priscilla came through on her promise.

One merchant after another arrived at the city with cartloads full of food to be delivered to James. Followin' after what his brother, the King, had taught him, the Righteous One had been giving weekly "love feasts" where the rich and the poor were all invited to sit at the table together. I don't want to give the impression that very many of the rich took him up on the invitation, but some of 'em would come so they could appear holier than their other rich friends. Now, James called these get-togethers love feasts, but we served 'em more than just hugs and kisses, though they got plenty of those too. We gave out real food, and clean water and wine. It had started out small, but now so many people came that we had to hold it on the grand staircase leadin' up to the Temple. Most of the folks could at least bring their own bowl and cup, and we'd dish out a serving of stew and pour them each a cup to drink. Then they'd climb to a spot in the central part of the staircase to sit down and eat. We'd always keep a lane clear on either side of the staircase so people could go in or out of the Temple grounds up above, but the middle part was pretty full of people the first morning of the week, every week.

But don't you even get it into your head that James was bringin' more people to the Temple on Sunday mornings than he did on the Sabbath on Saturday. On Saturdays he'd stand at the top of the staircase and preach to the poor about the Law and the Prophets, and he'd give them blessings like some of 'em had never heard before in their lifetimes. And then at the feasts on Sundays he'd walk among the people and share stories about the King and some of the things he used to say before the Romans tried to kill him.

My boy James was gettin' real well known throughout the country for his love feasts. Some of the newer people even called him the priest of the poor, but most folks who had known of him for years still called him the Righteous One.

Anyway, when Priscilla, that rich friend of Saul's, I mean Paul's — when she made it known she was desperate for James to give his blessing to Paul's ministry to the Gentiles, well I made sure she knew that we had some needs of our own here in the city. If she wanted our help, I told her, then we could use her help too. I said we're feeding a couple hundred people every week and could sure make use of some extra food. We shook hands on the deal, her and me. She told Paul what to do, and I told James.

So now she was sending so much food to us, we had to find someplace to store it. Peter and his helper, John, found somebody who had a barn here in David's City below the Temple Mount, and they built a bunch of new shelves inside to stack up all the food. And though we women didn't try to do any of the cooking on the Sabbath, because James would never allow us to do any work that day, the cooking fires started burning well before sunup on Sunday. I had all the younger women doing most of the hard work, seein' as how I was startin' to get gray not only in the hair but even in my face, or so they told me. Besides, I had plenty to keep me busy, directin' all the cookin' and sendin' people to carry messages to James at the Temple and makin' sure we gave a bit of food to the Romans too so they'd look kindly on us. The soldiers didn't speak our language, so they would never bother tryin' to stay and visit with us — thanks be to the Father! But even if we didn't understand each other, a smile and a bit of food sends a nice message in any language.

James, bless his heart, took time off from the Temple to go with me to the barn one day after we'd got it set up and organized proper. He'd heard we had quite an operation goin', but this was the first time he'd seen it.

"Rachel, I can't believe you've been able to do all this!" He stood in front of a block of shelves that held about forty or fifty sacks of grain. In the darker corner of the barn, where it was a bit cooler, we stored a bunch of wheels of cheese. Next to it were figs and other fruits. If no more supplies came in at all, we could probably scrounge enough food for the next four weeks' feasts from what we had in the barn at the moment.

"Well, I couldn't do it if we didn't have so many young volunteers. I'm gettin' too old to do this sort of stuff on my own." I brushed a strand of hair back from my face to hang it behind my ear. "And we wouldn't get so many volunteers if it weren't for the good words you preach on Saturday, and you visitin' with everybody on Sunday at the meals. So you can take some credit your own self, you hear?"

James wrapped an arm around my shoulder and hugged me. He even kissed me on the cheek. Now that I think back on all the years, I don't think he ever did that before.

MARY

I hate standing in the middle of several talking men and not understanding a word they say. We had landed at a place on the southern coast of Gaul, and some men met the captain of our ship when he brought us ashore. Now, I grew up speaking Aramaic and Greek, and I knew enough of the ancient Hebrew to hold my own in a conversation. Outside of Jerusalem, not much conversation required Hebrew, so I never bothered to learn more of it. But here in Gaul, they spoke a language that seemed closely related to the Latin that the ruling class among the Romans used among themselves. I could understand a little bit of Latin in writing but could not speak it, and this version the Gauls spoke lost me completely. So Judas Thomas could follow along and translate some of it to me. But I didn't like depending on someone else to listen and talk for me.

"They say there is a village with several Judean families near here," Thomas told me. "I think we should try visiting there first."

We had landed at an area of beach that stretched in a fairly straight line from east to west. But the land rose into hills almost immediately on the west and north. In order to reach the village the men told us about, apparently, we would need to follow a trail eastward toward a tongue of land that poked southward back into the sea. Thomas gave some men a few Roman coins to help carry our possessions. Sarah walked the trail a bit ahead of us but worried me incessantly, running off the path every time she saw something new. "Mommy, look at these flowers," she yelled at one point. A few minutes later, "Mommy, look at that funny animal." Finally, I made her walk at my side and I held her hand. She yanked on my arm and pleaded whenever she saw unusual sights that she wanted to explore, but I would not let go. She would have time to explore after we got settled in this strange land.

We saw a few fields of crops, but they didn't appear to be enough to support many people. Thomas exchanged a few words with our guides and then explained to me that most farms and famers would be found north over the hills. The village we approached facilitated trade with ships sailing on the sea.

As we approached some small buildings not far from the water, I saw a man working a potter's wheel outside one of them. He did not wear a prayer shawl or any other identifiable clothing, but he did not need to. His beard, untrimmed on the edges and stretching down onto his chest, clearly told me his people had roots in Judea.

After the men had exchanged greetings through translations of their languages, the potter exclaimed loudly and said some words to Thomas in a heavily accented Aramaic. My husband waved Sarah and me over to join the conversation.

"My family has lived in this land for three generations," said the man, who introduced himself as Mateo. "But my grandparents and parents insisted that I teach my children the language of our ancestors and hold true to the old ways. Please, come sit down while I get wine for you to drink and water to wash your feet."

I thought I felt a tug of excitement on my hand when Sarah heard him mention wine, but I prayed it was just my imagination. Really, I told myself, you must force yourself to stop worrying. All of us drank wine as children, and most of us turned out all right.

Thomas and Mateo chatted about the local Judean community. Though small, it thrived, according to Mateo. Several other men excelled as craftsman, like himself, while others farmed the land producing grain and grapes. Gaul had good weather and soil for making wine, he said. In the back of my mind I wondered if they would have anything to match the wine Jesus had helped the Galilean vineyard produce, the so-called Nectar of Nazareth.

As we talked, a girl about Sarah's age came around the corner of the house and stopped suddenly when she saw the strangers sitting there. "Annie," Mateo called, "come meet our visitors. They have just sailed from Egypt, and before that they lived in our people's homeland, Judea. This is their daughter, Sarah."

The two girls gazed at each other in silence for a moment. Then Annie asked, in halting Aramaic, "Why is your skin so dark?'

"I don't know," Sarah responded. "Why is yours so light?"

Mateo looked embarrassed and was about to say something, but Thomas laughed loud and long. "Annie, that question followed my brother and me all through our lives. It's a long story and someday, if we have the time, I will tell you."

RACHEL

Rebecca always followed orders, so I had learned to depend on her. I told her yesterday afternoon that I needed her to fetch Mary's brother from his family home in Bethany. Sure enough, this morning not more than three hours past sunup, here she was knockin' at the door with Lazarus in tow. But I don't mean to make it sound like he was following her like a lost boy. James had lived with Mary and Lazarus all through his early years while he was studyin' with Rabbi Gamaliel, so I knew Lazarus well. As a boy he always struck everybody as an odd one, a kid who spent more time listenin' to the voices inside his own head than payin' attention to goings-on in the real world all around him. But James told me that his brother the King taught somethin' to Lazarus, and he became sharp as the edge of a Roman's sword. Not that he'd ever cause you harm, but he could cut through lies and nonsense with just a few words.

So I invited Rebecca and Lazarus upstairs to rest after their long walk into the city, and I carried water and towels up for them to wash their feet. I gave them each a cup of wine too, even though the sun hadn't reached midday yet.

"Thank you," he said. Ever since his father, Benjamin, had died years earlier, young Lazarus had taken on a more regal air. Well, I called him young, but he must be almost thirty-five by now.

I got right to it without wastin' time. "I asked Becca to bring you here because James heard some scary news. The governor says he's gotten new orders from Rome to start seizin' property for the empire. Seems they ain't stealin' enough from us in taxes, so now they're gonna start stealin' land too."

Lazarus rested his chin on his right hand, his fingers absent-mindedly writhin' through his beard. "I see. And you're telling me this because James thinks the Romans will come after my family estate?"

"Yup, it's almost certain. That's why he asked me to give you the news here instead of tellin' you himself up at the Temple. If the Roman guards up there see him talkin' to you, they'll figure he's warnin' you and will attack your home sooner than you can get prepared."

Becca leaned forward, her face frightened. "Are they gonna hurt anybody? My husband's cousin works out there on the farm. I should go warn him right away."

I reached out and put my hand on her arm. "Hush, we're not gonna give ourselves away to the Romans. They're watchin' everybody, so don't you do nothin' that will tip 'em off that anything unusual is goin' on."

Lazarus stood up and walked over to the window, looking out at the narrow lane below. He stood there with his back to us for a minute before he finally said something.

"I have always paid my taxes in full, and I have refrained from making any public statements that could be interpreted as a threat to the governor or the empire. If they are going to move on me, they will probably have trumped up some false charges to justify arresting me and seizing my land, which means they plan to either imprison me, sell me into slavery, or kill me." He turned back toward me. "I have more than twenty men and their families working for me. Did James say whether the Romans intend to arrest my workers too?"

"He doesn't think they will." I squeezed Becca's arm when I said this, to let her know I thought the cousin would be safe. "The Romans still need people to farm the land. They want the estate for the food you grow and as a resting place for soldiers between here and Jericho. He didn't hear them say anything about building a fort or anything like that. They probably just want a comfortable house for the commander and plenty of room for tents for the soldiers. So they'll probably leave your workers alone, except they'll appoint a Roman to oversee them and give orders."

Becca's kinfolk don't have much money. Fact is, they got a bunch of friends who all call themselves The Poor. It started out as a joke among a small group but kept growin', and by now The Poor included several hundred people in the city and surroundin' countryside.

Lazarus started pacing back and forth, not saying anything. In that moment he sort of reminded me of his days as a boy, wrapped up in some idea in his head, and not necessarily aware of his surroundings, so I spoke up before he got lost.

"And there's one more thing. James got a letter from his brother Judas Thomas and your sister Mary."

Lazarus stopped suddenly and turned toward me, and his face got focused real quick like. "Mary? Is she well?"

I nodded. "She's just fine. They left Egypt because they heard the Romans had people out lookin' for Judas. They've gone to Gaul, which I guess is someplace t'other side of Rome. They've met a few other Judean families there, and they're settlin' on a piece of land they say is good for growin' grain and grapes."

He went quiet again, thinkin' it through. Meanwhile, Rebecca and I started to straighten up the furniture in the room, and we picked up the cups and the towel and water bowl that I'd brought up. She helped me carry the stuff downstairs to the kitchen. "Do you really think our cousin will be safe?" she asked while we stacked the things on a table.

"Don't worry," I squeezed her arm again. "Those soldiers don't know the first thing about growin' crops. They certainly aren't going to reap the crops themselves at harvest time, and most of 'em probably don't know how to cook the food after it's been harvested. Your cousin and the rest of The Poor will be safe. But you can't warn him or else the soldiers will launch their attack before we can get ready."

She bobbed her head up and down to show she understood. We went back up the stairs to see Lazarus. He looked like he'd made up his mind.

"I can leave enough money for the workers and their families to support themselves, and I can take enough to pay my way to Gaul. One of James's kinsmen is a trader of tin. His name is Joseph, and he hails from Arimathea. He often ships much of his ore to Rome and other ports west in the great sea, so I will ask his help to go to Gaul. I'll join Judas Thomas and Mary there," he said. "Before I get ready to leave, I'll need to speak to James about the particulars. Where did they settle in Gaul? How much can I bring with me? I never thought it was an advantage that I do not have a wife and children. But if I have to flee the country right away, then I am fortunate I don't have to spend a lot of time getting a family ready to go."

I made him sit down. He looked all worked up.

"We'll work all that stuff out. You just stay here 'til this afternoon when James comes home, and we'll set it up for you."

MIRIAM

I had Simon keep the logs for me. My eyes did not see as well as they used to, and writing the small figures on the parchment sometimes made my fingers and wrist ache. Even though girls in my day mostly never learned to read, my mother, Anna, had made sure that I could communicate in writing and I, in turn, passed that knowledge on to my daughters, Joanna and Susanna. They would teach their children as well. And I had made it known to Judas before he left that if he did not make sure my granddaughter learned to read and write, I'd hunt him down no matter where he hid in this world to show him how much pain he could cause to himself through disobedience to his mother.

So it wasn't that I could not keep the logs of trades myself or keep track of the pricing necessary in our bartering to keep it profitable. No, I just had to admit that I was getting old. Besides, Simon needed to learn to manage things. When he was a young boy, Simon was the slowest of my sons when it came to learning to read. That's the main reason Joseph taught him to lead other boys as scouts and guards for travelers. Later they became armed escorts, protecting merchants from robbers as they moved their merchandise through Galilee to markets or to the ports of the great sea to the west of us. Eventually, Simon was leading a small army that operated right under the very noses of the Romans.

But Simon needed to learn how to manage the business too. So I would force him to complete the logs. I blew out the candle on the table and stood up to stretch my arms, and then I walked outside.

Simon and two of his fellows were speaking to a man standing beside a wagon full of sacks. A woman and boy sat on the buckboard. I guessed they were the man's family and they were traveling — not the regular sort of traders who usually stopped here.

"Ma'am, why don't you and your boy come inside and have a drink of water and wash your feet. Have you eaten today?" I asked, shielding my eyes from the sun as I looked up at them.

"Why, thank you. That's very neighborly of you," the woman said as she and the boy climbed down.

I called out to one of Simon's men. "Jacob, get these oxen some water and hay. And Salome," I called to one of the women who worked in the house, "see if you can get some water and cakes for our guests."

When we had moved inside, the man bowed deeply. "In the name of the Christos, we thank you for your hospitality. My name is Matthias, and this is my wife Leah and son Jonathan."

I tilted my head as I replied, "You are welcome. But who is this Christos of whom you speak?"

His eyes lit up like a merchant who had been given the opportunity to sell all his wares at double price. "Have you not heard of the events in Jerusalem? The Christos, the Son of God, has been raised from the dead and is seated at the right hand of the Father. He has come to save us all!"

"Praise God," I replied with caution. James had told me many times over the years to act carefully with wild-eyed converts. "And this Son of God. Does he have a name?"

Just at that moment, Simon walked into the room. I tried to motion him to remain silent, but he was not looking in my direction and missed the signal.

"Yes, it is Jesus of Nazareth," Matthias proclaimed loudly.

"Oh — Jesus? Have you seen him?" asked Simon. "I wanted to tell him there is such a high demand for the Nazareth wine that Nathan has increased the price."

I finally caught Simon's eye and shook my head subtly, giving him a sign to keep quiet.

Matthias momentarily looked confused at Simon's remarks but then shook it off. "No, I have not seen him, but I have felt his mighty arm at work in my life and in the world around us. No, I learned of him from Paul when he visited Antioch. Paul said Jesus welcomes us Gentiles into his church, that the Father does not require circumcision for us to become one with the followers of the Christos."

Simon opened his mouth as if he were about to speak, but I stepped on his foot.

"I see. This Paul that you speak of — I think I may have heard of him before. Wasn't he in Jerusalem years ago?" I asked.

"Yes. His name was Saul of Tarsus, and he became famous as a persecutor of Jesus's followers. But he says he saw the risen Jesus, who was resurrected by God after his crucifixion by the evil Judeans in Jerusalem."

At that moment Salome entered carrying a tray with three bowls of a vegetable stew. She set the tray down and handed a bowl to each of our guests. The boy, Jonathan, started to lift the bowl to his lips immediately, but Matthias pushed it back to the table. "We thank you, Lord, for this food, in the name of the Father, the Son and the Holy Spirit." Then all three of them began eating.

I pressed him a bit. "The Judeans did not crucify him. Only the Romans have the authority to execute a man."

Matthias looked up from his bowl. "Paul says the Judeans worked in secret to turn Jesus over to the Romans because they were jealous of him. But now the risen Christos is victorious. Why, Paul just won a victory over the most evil of them all, James in Jerusalem. James wanted Gentiles to submit to circumcision. But Paul proved that Jesus the Christos does not require circumcision."

Before I could say anything, Simon grunted angrily. "I'm sorry, Mom, but I can't listen to this anymore. Matthias," he said, focusing his glare on the man, "I was there in the courtyard at the Temple when the Romans seized Jesus. No Judeans turned him in. A riot was erupting at the Temple, and he sacrificed himself to get the rest of us out before the Roman soldiers attacked us. And don't you dare say a word against James. He is Jesus's brother, and all Israel reveres him as the Righteous One."

I put my hand against my son's shoulder. "Simon, our first responsibility is to provide hospitality to our guests."

"Yes, Mom, but I also have a responsibility to declare the truth. If this Paul is spreading lies about Jesus and James, I have to speak out."

Matthias bowed his head. "I am sorry if I have caused offense. Perhaps we should leave after Jonathan finishes his bowl."

"Where are you going from here?"

"We are making our way back to Antioch."

"Then you shall stay here tonight," I responded immediately. "The next place on the road where you can find safe shelter is almost a full day's walk from here. I won't stand for you endangering your wife and boy out on the road.

"And tomorrow," I added, turning a stern eye on Simon, "my son and some of his men will escort you on the road until you reach safety."

MARY

Sarah stood in the middle of a circle of girls, who each were peering at portions of a scroll and trying to decipher the characters. Though all the girls had pale complexions, they had quickly accepted my dark-skinned daughter as one of their own after Annie introduced her to the group. And she could teach them to read and write, and she seemed to have such profound things to say about everything in life. I probably held a biased view, but I thought my girl was the star of the group.

I turned to go back into our small house. This seemed almost like a tiny shack in comparison to the estate my family had run in Bethany, outside Jerusalem. And it could never compare in size or quality of construction to Judas Thomas's family compound at Sepphoris. But we earned this house and the surrounding land all on our own. Thomas had quickly caught on to the local flow of goods and started facilitating trades that helped our neighbors. Mateo had spoken truly — the grapes grew well here and produced an outstanding wine. The farmers mostly grew all they needed to eat, but they lacked the sorts of spices we had come to take for granted in Judea and Egypt. A ship from across the sea in Africa had stopped by the harbor during a mild storm, and Thomas struck up a deal with the captain to trade several barrels of the local wine for a number of crates of exotic peppers, roots and dried flowers that made even the dullest gruel practically dance on one's tongue. Afterward, Thomas began importing large quantities of the spices. After we became a source on this side of the sea for those spices in addition to our wine, other ships came to trade for those commodities and brought products from their own homelands. We were now also trading in gemstones, precious metals, and cloth of various weaves.

I heard the door to the house opening, but I already knew it would be my husband returning from the harbor after meeting a ship there. An inventory of goods on the table before me was demanding all my attention.

"Mary, I'm home," rang out Thomas's voice.

"I'm in here," I replied, continuing to study the inventory.

"I met some interesting men at the harbor and brought them home for dinner. I hope you don't mind."

I thought to myself, if you already brought them home, then it's too late to ask me if I mind. We Judeans offer hospitality to strangers quite cheerfully — it has been taught to us by our parents for countless generations and is even written into our scriptures. But our husbands have always assumed the "cheerful" part for themselves and assigned to us wives the "hospitality" responsibilities. I would lecture Thomas later, after we fed the strangers and sent them on their way. Meanwhile, I would force myself to wear a gracious smile for our guests.

Thomas entered the room with the men behind him, obscured from my line of sight. I started to get up. At that moment Thomas stood aside and I saw a face I recognized from all the days of my youth.

"Lazarus!" I ran to my brother and threw myself at his chest, wrapping my arms around him. He staggered backward at the force of my trajectory but regained his balance and hugged me tightly. I showered him with kisses, tears suddenly springing from my eyes and rolling down my cheeks.

"Why are you here? Has Jerusalem fallen? Is James all right?"

Lazarus smiled grimly. "Jerusalem still stands. It was James who warned me that the Romans planned to arrest me." Seeing the sudden shock on my face, he added, "No, I did not do anything wrong. They were only looking for a pretext to steal our estate to house some of their officers and feed their soldiers. I was assured they would let our farmworkers continue to till the land, but the army would seize the crops without paying the middleman. Me."

He nodded to the other man next to him. "Mary, I think you remember Judas Thomas's kinsman, Joseph. When the Romans executed Jesus, we moved his body to Joseph's family tomb in the Kidron Valley. Of course, as it turned out, we only needed his generosity for three days."

I clutched Joseph's forearms in greeting just as a man would. "Yes, of course I remember. I am so happy to see you."

Joseph beamed. "I have brought a shipment of tin. Perhaps I can find merchants in this area who would trade for my wares.

Thomas laid his hand on Lazarus's shoulder. "You say my brother got word to you? How is he?"

"James is fine. In fact, I suspect he learned about the plot because the Roman governor is considering making James the High Priest for at least one term. James has been called into many discussions with various Roman dignitaries about how they can maintain the peace even while they continue exacting as much money and goods in taxes as possible from Judea."

Thomas looked confused. "High Priest? But what of Annas's family?" I wondered too — Annas and his sons had held the high priesthood during almost every term since we were young children.

Lazarus walked several paces across the room before turning back to face us both. "I suspect that many people are plotting behind the scenes. Annas's family knows that James is recognized throughout the country as the Righteous One, and the people will listen to his every command. And the Romans' know that James's followers still acknowledge Jesus as the King, and they believe that he is still alive. I think Annas's sons expect Rome to squash James because they cannot accept the notion of any king higher than Caesar. But James's faction says loudly and repeatedly that Jesus's kingdom is not of this world, so they are no threat to the emperor. Meanwhile, the Romans want to encourage James's pacifism to counter the Zealots' calls for revolution.

"So — each for their own reasons — all three groups see James's elevation to High Priest as a victory. It will take the responsibility off Annas's family if something goes wrong, it will relieve the Romans of the threat of an armed uprising, and it will convince the common people that God's kingdom is coming here on earth."

Thomas folded his arms across his chest. He did not have to say, Harrumph. Anyone could see it in his face.

"So while these competing political interests are setting up my brother to become a martyr, the Romans seized your property with the threat to execute you for treason?"

Lazarus grinned. "The Lord works in mysterious ways. At least we may have James entering the Holy of Holies soon to pray for us all."

PRISCILLA

Paul and Aquila spoke excitedly among themselves as they sat in Aquila's workshop, stitching hides together. I couldn't tell if they were making a tent or just a pair of jackets, and I doubt if they had stopped to figure it out themselves. If I'd had some definite orders for goods that had to be filled at the moment, I would have stepped in and directed them to focus on a size and shape to fit the order. As it was, however, we had no requests pending and I could allow them to work merrily as they chatted, thinking to themselves that they were doing something productive. Paul had traveled from his home in Antioch to visit us here in Corinth. Whenever he stayed with us, he liked to tell others that he paid his own way with his tent-making. Actually, I paid all his travel and living expenses, but I thought it important to let him believe in his own self-sufficiency.

Paul and my husband were alike in that way. Both of them held Roman citizenship. Aquila and I had actually lived in Rome until Emperor Claudius expelled Judeans from the city a few years earlier. Fortunately, I was able to convert my personal wealth to jewels and precious metals that we could easily transport under heavy cover, and my family had built up a wide network of business partners in the eastern empire who could offer us refuge as we sought to establish a new home. As we traveled, Aquila would stitch together tents out of hides that we acquired from traders on the road, which I in turn would use to barter with other traders. The tents didn't really generate a large profit, but they kept Aquila busy, and now Paul too.

What I really wanted was to make a triumphant return to Rome, and Paul afforded me that opportunity. We could never force our way back militarily, but we could return if we represented an idea for which the emperor's people hungered. Their household gods performed many wondrous feats in the myths they passed down from generation to generation. Gods and sons of gods could hurl thunderbolts, raise the seas or demolish mountains. I wanted Paul's new god, the Christos, to stand taller and mightier than the Roman and Greek gods. I wanted everyone to beg us to come tell them about Paul's god. I wanted them to beg *me*.

"Boys, come here a minute," I called to them. "I want us to talk about creating some basic rules of behavior for the churches. Lucas," I called to my son in the other room, "you come also. I want you to listen in on the discussion so you can record it later."

SUSANNA

The trader from Antioch had brought a large load of saffron, which was rare here. Jesus Thomas nonchalantly nodded to signal interest, but just barely. He did not want the other man to raise his price. For that matter, the trader had not indicated yet what he might want from us in exchange. Abban and I pretended to be preoccupied with reading a translation of one of the Vedas. After our first few months of living here, we decided that studying the Vedas would be the best way for Thomas and me to learn to understand our neighbors. I thought the words of these ancient texts contained many references to places and people of which we knew nothing, and some of the phrases repeated often made no sense without some cultural explanation. Amrit especially enjoyed teaching us about the customs contained in the Vedas. The old man seemed to come alive explaining histories he had learned in his youth. And as we learned more of the people's history and legends, we found it easier to learn their language too. Thomas could speak it better than I, but he spent much more time talking with people in the town around us and bartering for food.

As the trader from Antioch inquired about the wares that we had available, Thomas took the opportunity to ask for news from home. We seldom got the chance to speak to anyone in Aramaic anymore, so that was a treat in itself. But the news was even better.

"Yes, the Righteous One has become one of the most popular men in Jerusalem," the man was saying. "The people revere him for his holiness but also because he can tell them about the Christos, who was his brother. Even we in Antioch have learned of the Christos, and many people worship him."

"The Anointed?" Thomas asked, using a more familiar term than the Greek word. "Who is this Anointed? You say he was James's brother?"

"Yes, yes," the man replied excitedly. "When he was in the flesh, his name was Jesus. But God the Father raised him from the dead on the third day. And he is seated at the right hand of the Father."

"Hmm, I had not heard that story," Thomas's brows knitted together as he spoke. "And you say The Righteous One is telling this story in Jerusalem?"

"No, Paul is telling us in Antioch. He has seen and spoken to the risen Christos himself, and he has received a vision from the Father."

Thomas held the tips of his fingers together almost in a posture of prayer. "This Paul says the risen Jesus appeared to him personally. Tell me more about this man Paul. By the way, what is your name?"

"Isaiah. My parents named me for the ancient prophet. This man Paul was formerly known as Saul. He used to persecute the followers of Christos. But after the risen lord appeared to him in a vision, he changed his life and he changed his name to reflect that new life."

My entire body felt like it was vibrating violently with the urge to shout, but my brother nudged me ever so subtly to hold my tongue.

"Saul. Hmm, yes, I think I have heard of this Saul before. He opposed the Righteous One, and I heard rumors that he participated in martyring one of the faithful. But now you say he has adopted a new life, and even a new name. Tell me more," Thomas said.

Isaiah's face lit up, clearly happy to have found a willing audience. "He says there are three aspects of God. There is the Father, who is the creator. There is the Son, who is the incarnation of the Father in this world. And there is the Holy Spirit, which is invisible but is present everywhere to hear our prayers."

Isaiah reached out and clutched Thomas's hands. "You seem open to Paul's teachings. Would you like to be baptized? We can do it right now if there is clear water nearby."

Now Thomas openly grinned, shaking his head slightly from side to side. "John baptized me many years ago in the Jordan."

"But John's baptism will not save you. You must be baptized in the name of the Christos. Paul said so."

Now Thomas reached out and put his hand on Isaiah's shoulder. "Did this Paul somehow make you think that the Father will not speak or listen to you unless you say just the right words, or make just the right motions at the altar? You greatly underestimate the Lord our God."

Isaiah looked into Thomas's eyes as if he were about to say something. But apparently what he saw there struck him dumb. His mouth fell open but no sound came out. He seemed to quiver for a moment, and then he slowly sank down to one knee, his gaze never leaving Thomas's face. I felt the presence of the Father in the room too.

"The Father is within each of us," Thomas said. "The Spirit is within each of us. We are all his sons and daughters, with whom he is well pleased."

Isaiah bowed his head for a moment and then looked up again. "Tell me what I must do."

JOANNA

I had tried to tell Mom that she was too old to travel, but it would have been easier to tell the wind to stop blowing or the sun to stop shining.

"It was for this that your father and I were born," she had scolded me. If she were stronger and faster, I believe she would have caught me and turned me over her knee for a swift swat on my hind side. Fortunately for me, I recognized the glare in her eye and jumped backward out of her reach before she could grab my arm. I knew she only intended it in good fun, but I had learned only too well in my forty winters not to give her an advantage if I could avoid it.

So here we found ourselves traveling the long, hot road to Jerusalem. The path along the east side of the Jordan had passed uneventfully. But now, after fording the river to the west bank before it reached the dead lake, we climbed up the hill past Jericho on the road to Jerusalem, and the crowds of people ahead of us making the pilgrimage to the holy city made our climb go very slowly. Some of our fellow travelers joyfully sang psalms, and their children danced as we made our way. Everyone seemed to be talking about the great news. Not only would the Temple ordain a new High Priest, but for the first time in most people's memory, he did not come from the clan of Annas.

And what man would the Temple welcome as its new High Priest?

None other than my eldest brother, James. Better known as the Righteous One of Israel, the greatest hope of our nation. I knew quite well there was no way on earth that I could have kept Mom from coming to witness this event.

Despite her determination, I still made Mom ride on a wagon pulled by oxen for the whole distance. We were bringing offerings from many of our neighbors near Bethsaida. Simon and Judith had collected some offerings for the Temple from some members of the community in Sepphoris, and also packed supplies for James on the cart. Their son Judas, now five years old, argued that he was big enough to walk with the adults alongside the wagon, but Mom convinced him to sit on the buckboard with her by saying she needed someone to protect her if bandits attacked. So he sat next to her like a proud and fierce little warrior, scanning the areas on either side of the road where robbers might be hiding. He wore a stern expression on his face, as if he would thrash and throw down any attackers who dared to approach. Mom intertwined her arm with her grandson's as if the boy really were her protector.

As we passed a side path on the left that led to Bethany, Simon caught up with me to walk at my side.

"It burns my soul every time I think of how the Romans seized Uncle Benjamin's estate," he hissed angrily. "If I and my men had been here, Lazarus would not have had to flee to the west."

"Patience, brother," I said. "Going to war with the oppressors will not restore our nation. It will only give a momentary satisfaction of the lust for revenge. And then the Romans would kill us or sell us into slavery, and the world would forget us anyway. No, do not blame yourself for the sins of the Roman oppressors."

But Lazarus's evacuation from his estate presented a more immediate concern: Where would we stay? Ever since I was a little girl, every time we had made this pilgrimage to the holy city, we would stay in Bethany and then make the short trip into Jerusalem each morning and return to the estate in the evening. With all these pilgrims coming to the city, there would probably be no room at the inn. The house where James lived, which he had taken over from the old Rabbi Gamaliel after he died, did not have enough space for all of us.

Simon said not to worry. "After the Romans executed Jesus, Rachel, the woman who cares for James's household, found places for me and all my men to stay. I think Rachel will find somewhere for all of us to stay on this important occasion."

I nodded. "I have heard good things about this Rachel."

"Jesus said it best," Simon told me. "James's home is now the central headquarters for all the sons and all the daughters of the Father, and Rachel is the boss."

MARY

Some things never changed. When I first started holding prayer meetings, the women of the community came but their husbands stayed home. I heard some of them just dismissed the meetings as a "women's club" of sorts. Others objected to the fact that Sarah, my daughter, was teaching their girls to read, which the fathers thought was a waste of time. Later, when it became clear that their wives were experiencing the Father in a way they never had before, a few of the men joined us. And of course, after they experienced it themselves, the men spread the news far and wide, speaking as if they personally had discovered the path to God, telling other men to follow them to the sacred meeting place. They would never admit that their wives had dragged them here against their will and forced them to listen to me.

And now, as the crowd filed into the room and took their seats, the old ways persisted. The men took the seats in front and sent the women to cluster on benches in the dark recesses at the back. The wealthier merchants elbowed their way past the farmers to the best seats, but even the farmers shouted to their wives at the back of the room as if calling orders to servants. And now they all sat expectantly, waiting for me to put them in direct communion with the Father.

Today would be different.

"Let me tell you a story that the King often told the people in Jerusalem." Today as I spoke, rather than standing still at the front as I normally would, I drifted among the seats. Each man would sit up straight as I approached his seat and look up expectantly at me as if he thought I might single him out for honor. I would make eye contact with each of them before moving on to the next.

"My brother, the King," I emphasized his title and paused for a moment, to make sure they remembered who had told this story, and my relationship to him. Jesus probably would have laughed at me for playing such an obvious trick, but he would understand. Sometimes, to open a man's mind to new ideas or information, it was necessary to whack him first with a large blunt object. Not an actual physical object, but a none-too-subtle verbal admonition.

"The King told the story of a great wedding feast. Everyone in the village had been invited. The villagers who considered themselves the most important jostled for the seats closest to the father of the new husband, because he was the wealthiest man in all the village and the surrounding countryside. Each of the guests wanted to be close enough to the head table that the host would see them. They thought that if he saw them sharing in his joy, he would remember them when it came time for him to buy food for his household, tools for his farm, and jewelry for his wife."

I continued to stroll from seat to seat, working my way through the crowd. The men I had already passed at the front of the room now had to turn in their seats and crane their necks to watch me as I spoke.

"What they did not know was that the host's brother and his family had traveled from afar to attend the wedding, and they had arrived too late to clean up after their journey. Wearing their dirty travel clothes, they did not want to shame the host, and so they had taken seats in the back."

By now I had reached the back row of the men. I moved behind them toward the women, so that all the men had to turn completely around.

"Seeing his kinsmen, the host brought them forward to the seats of honor at the front. He approached the men already seated there and apologized to them but said he must ask them to leave those seats. The brother and his family, though embarrassed that they had not had time to put on their finery, took the seats of honor. The host told the wealthy guests to go find seats at the back."

I paused to let it sink in. "The King said not to exalt yourself. It is better to take a humble place and be called forward to the seat of honor, than to take the treasured spot for yourself but be told to leave."

I stood among the women and stopped moving. I reached out and clasped the hands of two farmgirls on either side of me and told everyone in the synagogue to hold hands with their neighbors. All the people in the room had attended before and recognized this as the beginning of the service. The men were forced to turn their chairs around to face the back before they could reach out to join hands. So now, in effect, their seats were in the back. They all fell silent, and we all closed our eyes as we felt the presence of the Father's spirit among us.

JUDITH

I swatted Simon on the side of the head. Hard. And I cocked my arm with my hand up, ready to hit him again if I didn't get the right answer from him.

"Hey — what was that for?" Simon whined, ducking his head away from any future blows.

I put my hands on my hips and fixed my eyes on his. He already knew where this was going if he didn't knuckle under, so I didn't use the Stare yet. But I didn't release him yet either.

"You can see very well that Rachel's back is starting to hunch and her hair has turned whiter than a priest's robe. But you're leaving her to climb the stairs by herself? And after she fed you that wonderful dinner last night?"

"But Mom needs help too."

"Yes she does, and it's about time that you noticed," I threw back at him. "So why are you and your men sauntering along like boys who have finished their chores? Get busy and help the women who need it, or else I'll put you in a world of hurt."

He tried to grin as if I was joking with him. But when I raised my hand to whack him in the head again, he quickened his pace and touched the shoulder of three of his guards. Together, they went to escort Rachel and Miriam, lifting the women by both elbows up each step of the grand staircase to the Temple.

When we entered through the porticoes at the top of the stairs and entered the outer courtyard, we found ourselves in a crowd so thick that our elbows rubbed against complete strangers on either side. I prayed that all these people had taken thought to relieve themselves before coming here. It wouldn't do for someone to start makin' water in the middle of this crowd, especially during such a sacred occasion. The public latrines were too far away to get to in a hurry, and the crowd was too thick.

Simon and the others had practically carried Mother Miriam and Rachel up the stairs, but now the old women stood on their tippy toes craning their necks to see. They both stood tall and proud, Miriam because she had given birth to the Righteous One of Israel, and Rachel because she had cared for him like an aunt ever since he was a teenager. The two of them held hands with each other like sisters.

A hush fell over the crowd as several priests came out onto a raised platform facing the crowd.

"We have a break in tradition," one of them announced in a shouting voice. "Though it is not the Day of Atonement, and he has not formally been appointed High Priest yet, Jacob bar-Joseph, or James as you all call him, has already entered the Holy of Holies."

A collective gasp swept across the crowd. None had ever heard of such a thing. Would God rain down fire and brimstone in response to someone other than a duly crowned High Priest entering the most sacred inner vault?

But before a minute had passed, James appeared and climbed up the stairs to the platform.

Miriam suddenly straightened like a wasp had stung her backside. A mother's anger flashed on her face. "Couldn't you at least have worn a clean robe?" she barked loud enough for all of us to hear.

Laughter began to break out as others in the crowd saw what had upset Miriam. Dark smudges of dirt started in front of James's knees on his robe and continued in parallel lines down the front of the white linen toward his toes. As more people pointed at him and laughed, James looked down at the front of his robe. When he saw the source of the merriment, he shrugged, smiled broadly and held his palms out for silence.

"My fellow Judeans," he called out in a clear voice, "forgive my appearance. I have spent this entire day on my knees, beseeching the Lord our God to look with favor upon his chosen people. And as you can see," he added, pointing at the lines of dirt on his lower robe, "when I moved about in the Sanctuary, I did so crawling on my knees and shins."

James made a show of reaching down to massage his lower legs. "In fact, it feels like I am developing some hard callouses on my legs. Pray for me, that I will be able to walk."

I heard a man cry out, "The Righteous One will have knobby knees!"

"Knobby knees!" cried another on the other side of the crowd.

I thought things were getting silly when about a dozen men began loudly chanting, "Knobby knees, knobby knees." What should have been a sacred event was turning into a comedy like the Greeks enact on their stages. I had never heard laughter become part of our holy worship at the Temple, so I found myself too shocked to form a coherent opinion in the instant.

But then the laughter fell suddenly to a hush as James held his hands up for silence.

"My brethren," he called out in a strong voice that carried to every corner of the courtyard, "let the entire world see us as a holy nation. Let us all get knobby knees together."

With that, James fell to his knees in prayer. And, astonishingly, the hundreds of people in the outer courtyard of the Temple all fell to their knees in silence as James chanted a prayer loudly. I learned later that the people outside the porticoes on the grand staircase below, and even those in the streets beyond the staircase, saw what was happening and also knelt in silence.

A holy nation indeed.

SUSANNA

Fortunately, the Judeans at Musuris spoke the local language fluently and could translate. Their tiny synagogue would not handle the crowds that Jesus Thomas was attracting, so he had given very specific instructions on the dimensions and building materials he wanted them to use for construction of a new, larger facility. It was rising near the banks of the River Periyar.

"Thomas, the man says it would be much easier if we built it with wood. Trees we have aplenty, but the type of stone you are requesting is quarried far from here and must travel overland," explained Aaron, one of the longtime residents here.

Thomas kept a patient expression on his face. "First, remember that stone's purity is eternal. But more importantly, it will not rot or burn. We want this synagogue to stand the test of time.

"And the stone is not just for this structure," he added. "I have visited with some of your so-called Brahmins, and we will build a second house of worship on the Hill of the Judeans, or Judanknnu in the native tongue. We will welcome the lower castes here at Musuris, but the Brahmins insisted on having a separate structure."

Aaron turned to me with pleading in his eyes. "Rani, your brother will not only make us transport the stone at great cost and labor, but now he will also force us also to carry it uphill."

The man seemed to think that I had the authority to overrule Thomas, that I was the merciful princess who could order my brother not to demand too much of his workers. Little did he know that, back home, the country revered Thomas as the King. I stifled the urge to giggle at the perception here that it was I who wore the crown.

I put a sympathetic but firm tone into my voice. "We all must work hard for the Lord our God. But do not fear. The Father smiles when he sees your devotion. He will bless you and your family."

Aaron's face hardened for a moment, but Thomas reached out and placed his hand on the man's arm. Their eyes locked for just a brief moment, and Aaron's tension eased. "I will tell the others," he said.

Aaron did not exactly have a spring in his step as he walked away, but neither did he look as surly as he did a few minutes earlier. I made a mental note to reward him with some words of praise for his work in front of his friends in the near future. His soul needed a boost.

"Thomas," I turned to my brother, "we have to be careful not to drive them too hard. Don't forget that we are guests in their land, and we have only been here a short time."

His grin spread from one side of his face to the other. "Ah, but they are the ones who need more space. The Father has touched them, and now they are clamoring for synagogues large enough to accommodate them and their many friends."

He winked at me mischievously. "Don't tell anyone yet, but I have received requests from five other towns too. Our builders will have plenty of work to keep themselves busy for quite some time to come."

Five more towns? That could turn into an administrative nightmare. Not only would I have to maintain order among the builders and their laborers but would also have to manage good relations with the citizens of each town. I had seen too many do-gooders with high intentions fail because they inadvertently caused offense to their new neighbors. The non-Judean people here had their own faith — or I should say collection of faiths woven together — and we did not yet know how well our relationship with the Father would coexist with theirs. An innocent but ill-chosen word or act could easily ignite a war. The history of my people, with a few brief interludes of independence and self-governance, traced through a long succession of dominance by pagan empires and cruel invaders. We survived by maintaining our identity without offending the surrounding majority. I worried that this rapid growth could have fatal repercussions.

Thomas looked me in the eye. I wanted to tell him my fears, but in that moment they seemed to fade in importance. I nodded in acquiescence. "Five more towns. Yes, we will have seven."

"Don't worry," he said. "In the other towns, we will not build extra synagogues for the Brahmins. I think they need to learn to tolerate the presence of the peasants around them. They can start by worshiping the Father together."

JOANNA

Mom died with a smile on her face. She had seen her first-born son grow to become revered as the Righteous One of Israel and rise to the office of High Priest in the Temple at Jerusalem. She had seen her second-born son become revered as the King and lead many thousands of our people into communion with the Father. She had seen her third-born son lead a tax revolt to halt an unjust war, and father her first grandchild. She had seen her youngest son lead a small army to protect the people of Galilee in their travels, and father her second grandchild.

So, judging just by her sons, Mom could go to the Father with her head held high. But she died proud of her daughters too! I had married Herod Antipas's personal steward, and Susanna had wedded a veritable prince from the East. Mom's grandchildren, at least those born of her daughters, would live in royal surroundings.

One of Dad's kinsmen had become successful as a tin merchant. His name was also Joseph, and he hailed from Arimathea, a small town northwest of Jerusalem toward the Great Sea. But he owned a tomb for his family near the city here — the same tomb, in fact, where Jesus's body was laid after the Romans tried to kill him. After an elaborate and well-attended funeral — she was, after all, the mother of the new High Priest — we placed Mom's body on one of the stone shelves in Joseph's family tomb. Joseph had sailed to the west with Lazarus and could not attend, but his kinfolk assured us he would approve. Judith and I had washed the body and anointed it with myrrh. We had no expectation that she would rise after three days, like the last time a member of our family was placed in this same cave. But we held no resentment — Mom had a wonderful life, and her time had come.

MARY

Fortunately, Lazarus had learned to speak Latin when we were growing up in Bethany. Although he was a quiet, withdrawn boy who often seemed to get lost in the wilderness of his own mind, Father wanted him to be able to speak to the Romans when he came of age. And not all Romans spoke Greek, so he would need Latin also. The language that the Gauls here on the southern coast spoke seemed related to the language of the Romans, so my brother caught on quickly.

The three of us — Thomas, Lazarus and myself — had fallen into distinct but interdependent roles. I led the spiritual gatherings of the former Judeans living here, plus an increasing number of Gentiles.

Thomas, in addition to handling much of the trading with the ships that stopped at the port here, spoke to people of Jesus's actual sayings. As had been the case in Alexandria, a few scribes attempted to copy down the sayings and collect them together. These scribes made copies of these sayings that could be carried to synagogues in villages too far away for us to visit each week.

And Lazarus would train selected people to lead the spiritual meetings in those villages. He surprised me, demonstrating that he had a gift for administration. He kept a chart of the three levels of training that Thomas and I would give and created lists of the people who had completed each level. Separately, he wrote out descriptions of what duties could be performed at each level.

Lazarus told us that, in the years since we had fled Jerusalem, James had established a popular ritual. Before his execution Jesus had started a tradition of having open meals with all who wished to come — the rich, the poor, the merchants, the farmworkers. No one was considered unclean, and no one would be turned away. These communal meals went against tradition; one is not supposed to sit at table with anyone who is not considered ritually worthy. But they all came to Jesus's meals, and James had continued the practice in Jerusalem. Now, for the past number of years, hundreds came to James's meals each Sunday on the steps leading to the Temple's porticoes.

In Gaul we did not have enough food to give everyone here a full meal. But at our gatherings, after praying and communing with the Father, we would distribute just a piece of bread and small cup of wine to each person. Members of the community considered it a great honor to be chosen to give the bread and wine to the worshippers.

So the three levels of responsibility for Lazarus's crews were these:

First, after basic instruction in Jesus's teachings, Lazarus would anoint them to spread the good news and urge their neighbors to attend a gathering.

Those who had completed the second level would be anointed in a public ceremony to become deacons, and they would be allowed to distribute food and wine at our symbolic communal meals. Even in Jerusalem, deacons had been authorized to go out as messengers from the Temple. Our deacons here in Gaul had the authority to go out and minister to people who could not attend the gatherings.

And third were the priests. Men and women who had studied the Law and the Prophets as well as the teachings of Jesus, and who could speak well enough to pass on their understanding in front of a gathering of people, would also receive anointment as priests at a public ceremony.

Lazarus would anoint those inducted at each of these levels with sacred oil on their brows.

Of course, there was a fourth type of anointing, but it was done without oil. When a new believer had attended a number of gatherings and expressed a desire to become a member of the community — whether Judean or Gentile — Lazarus or I would baptize that person in a flowing stream just as Jesus had baptized us in the Jordan all those years ago.

Some of the people in the villages took note of all the anointing going on within our growing community of faithful. A sailor in one of the trading ships heard them talk and mentioned the same thing was happening in other parts of the empire. The practice started with the Anointed One, he said, which I guess is what they called Jesus in those other parts. But the Greek term was the Christos.

The word caught on, and all our members started calling themselves Christos. I had to keep myself from giggling; they seemed to think the word was the plural of Christo. Anyway, we now had a wide network of hundreds of Christos throughout the region, and our numbers kept growing.

JOANNA

A courier from the palace had come to the gate in the evening with an urgent message for Joses. "Agrippa needs you to come immediately."

The request surprised my husband, because the king seldom visited Sepphoris. When he did come here from his palace in Caesarea on the coast of the great sea, he almost never asked for Joses to return to the palace after supper. But Joses would never allow a courier to sense his alarm at the unexpected summons. In a calm, seemingly bored voice, he asked, "Did he say what it is about?"

"He did not say, but a Roman officer was with him in the court when he gave me the order."

"Very well." Joses went so far as to yawn and stretch his arms out above his shoulders. I thought maybe this was going a bit too far to demonstrate his nonchalance, but I kept quiet. "Tell Agrippa I will be there as soon as I can. It shouldn't be more than a few minutes."

After the courier left, Joses seemed to wear a more worried expression. "I don't know what this is all about, but I don't like it. Plans that are hatched in the dark of night usually don't turn out well."

He tried not to show concern, but I could see it in his eyes. "Please come home as soon as you can. I will wait up for you."

"No need to do that," he said, trying to keep the casual tone in his voice. "I'm sure it's just some routine matter he wants attended to before he moves on to another city in the morning."

After he left, I sat in the dark room by myself. Agrippa, or more properly Agrippa the Second, did not seem as cruel as the others whom Rome had appointed to rule over Judea or Galilee or, in some cases, both regions. But like all the other Herods before him, he had risen to power by ruthlessly eliminating his rivals, even members of his own family.

I tried laying down but knew it was no use. Sleep would elude me until Joses came home safe. I could not think of any reason why Agrippa would harm him, but I learned years ago that a reason is not always needed. There was no reason for the Romans to seize my brother Jesus and hang him on a tree, other than that they wanted to make a public example of him to quell any further violence at the Temple. They claimed that they brought us Pax Romana, the so-called Peace of Rome. But they imposed peace with a sword.

Joses had survived a succession of several rulers. After Agrippa the First engineered the ouster of his uncle Antipas, he and other members of his clan engaged in devious and sometimes fatal intrigues to gain favor over each other. The elder Agrippa even harassed many of my brother James's friends in Jerusalem and executed James, the son of Zebediah. That Agrippa died when he blasphemed in public, allowing his followers to proclaim him a god. And now, after a rapid succession of rulers over the past number of years, we had his son, also called Agrippa, ruling the land.

They did not so much rule by the sword, as did Rome, but by the knife. And when they stabbed, it would be in the back.

That is why the summons this evening struck terror in my heart. Joses performed his duties properly and efficiently, not siding with one faction or another in any palace rivalries. So Agrippa the Second should have no reason to attack Joses. But that assurance provided no comfort to me as I sat alone in the darkened room.

Finally, I heard the front gate outside opening. Rushing out the door, I ran and wrapped my arms tightly around my husband. "You're safe!"

He returned my hug. My heart was beating so hard that surely, he must have felt it thumping against his chest.

"Agrippa wanted my advice. Do you recall Saul of Tarsus?" After searching my memory, I mumbled assent. "You remember that he came here after he was kidnapped from Jerusalem, and he briefly spoke to Jesus. Well, he has told people far and wide that Jesus was anointed by the Father and raised from the dead, and that this risen Anointed One spoke to him, Saul, and sent him into the world to save all the Gentiles. He has followers in several cities in Syria and Greece. He no longer goes by Saul but changed to his Roman name, Paul."

Entering the house, I struck a flint to a small stick of kindling and used the flame to light a lamp. "James told me about this Paul, that he claimed to know Jesus better than his own family and friends," I said.

"Yes, the same man," Joses said with a grin. "Well, he caused so much trouble on his last visit to Jerusalem that Agrippa had him arrested. The man is so disagreeable that Agrippa was tempted to sell him into slavery, but some woman who manages Paul's affairs made an appeal for mercy. She said Paul is a Roman citizen and asked that Paul be sent to Rome so he could make his appeal directly to the court of the emperor. She said that she and her husband would go along and would even pay for the prisoner's travel expenses. Agrippa thought this sounded very suspicious, so he asked me what I thought."

That didn't make sense to me. "Why would he ask for *your* advice?"

Joses grinned even more widely. "Joanna, we have kept many secrets over the past twenty-five years, and our neighbors have supported us. But Agrippa is quite aware that Jesus and Judas were your brothers. And he already knew that the former High Priest, James, is the eldest brother in your family."

Seeing alarm on my face, Joses quickly added, "Don't worry — he is not seeking your brothers. He just wants to know what to do with Paul."

I rested my chin on my knuckles, trying to think it through. "What would happen if he was sent to Rome? And what would happen if he stayed here?"

"That's what Agrippa wanted to know. Is there a community of supporters in Rome that would help him if he went there? On the other hand, do enough people in Judea and Galilee support Paul that he would prosper if Agrippa kept him here? He sensed that the woman Priscilla had ulterior motives for appealing to Rome."

"Priscilla?" My eyes went out of focus as I searched my memory. "I've heard that name before. I think Rachel mentioned her once in Jerusalem."

Now Joses guffawed with an explosion of breath. "I doubt if Rachel spoke of her as a friend. For one thing, I learned years later that it was Rachel who arranged for Saul's kidnapping and banishment from Jerusalem. And I'm told she and the women who worked with her on the plot cracked several broomsticks over Saul's head before they had him carried out of the city."

I snapped my fingers. "I remember the story now. They suspected him of arranging for the mob to stone young Stephen. The people still tell the story of his treachery. So maybe that's it — he wants to go to Rome because he fears for his life if Agrippa keeps him here."

Joses nodded. "That's one possibility. But Agrippa also suspects this Priscilla is looking for any excuse to get back into Rome. Claudius expelled the Judeans from the city several years ago because they would not assimilate with the pagans. Agrippa said she's an astute merchant and probably wants to get back to the wealthy customers she lost."

"But," I said, "what is that to Agrippa? If the woman just wants to sell some products to Romans, who cares?"

Joses pulled his tunic over his head to get ready for sleep. "I think he's worried that this Paul wants to preach in Rome. If the man somehow gains followers in the capital city, Agrippa doesn't want to take the blame."

RACHEL

Thanks be to the Father that James only served one year as High Priest. The constant meals for visitors from far off, with rabbis visitin' from villages out in the country, and the so-called dignitaries sent by the leaders of other kingdoms to try to make friends. Hmmph! Dignitaries, they called themselves? I thought the word would mean that they had some bit o' dignity or could at least pretend to act dignified. But I found every one of 'em to be a pompous ass whose mother probably never spanked him when she shoulda.

But like I said, it was over now. James served one year as High Priest, and folks all over the country got to braggin' 'bout how his legs got knobby with callouses from prayin' on his knees so much for the good of all Judeans. Truth be told, even though lots of people laughed about it, they were all right proud that their High Priest didn't seem to place much stock in the "High" part of his title.

Whatever political crisis Annas's family thought was about to hit when they allowed James to be appointed, never happened. The country ran itself like there wasn't a care in the world. Myself, I think it was because James prayed for us all so much. But the powerful folks — they figured it was because they were so clever themselves, somehow. So they asked the Roman leaders to appoint one of their own folks to High Priest when James's term was up, and they did. So now I didn't have to cook so many special dinners at home.

We still had the weekly love feasts for hundreds of people, but I'd long since gotten the younger women to handle those. I was way too old for all this stuff.

So it was just the two of us when James and I sat down for supper. He looked kinda thoughtful. I couldn't tell if he was happy or worried, so I asked.

"Oh, I guess everything goes well for me today," James said, returning his gaze to the bowl of stewed vegetables on the table in front of him. Suddenly grinning at me, he asked, "Do you remember your good friend Saul? The one who studied here so many years ago, and who now calls himself Paul?"

"Yes, no matter how hard I've tried to forget him, I remember him well. What sort o' trouble is he makin' now?"

"Well," James paused for a moment while he chewed his food, "you may have heard that he was arrested in Caesarea for causing a disturbance. His friends Priscilla and Aquila suggested to Agrippa that he should send Paul to Rome to plead his case before the emperor, and he has decided to do so. Several people close to the case tell me they doubt that Paul will ever return here after he gets to Rome, because Priscilla is so eager to reunite with her friends there."

I took a long sip of wine from my cup. I never drank much wine in my younger days because the work of running Rabbi Gamaliel's house kept me so busy at all hours of the day and night. But these days a good cup — or two, or sometimes three — went down well and gave me a chance to get all philosophical like James and his priestly friends did.

"So Israel is safe now." I never used to grin much either, but I had a big grin on my face now. "I wonder if Rome will be?"

Another thought occurred to me at that moment. "Your friend Simon Peter went to Rome a few years ago, didn't he? What do you hear from him?"

James arched his eyebrows as he looked up from his bowl at me. "I received a letter from him at the Temple, written by the young scribe who works with him. A large number of Judeans have returned to Rome. Many of them have joined our people here in calling my brother their King, though they only do so in secret because Caesar would not tolerate it. This Nero who holds the throne now — our people tell me he's volatile, so they are very careful not to offend him."

"Careful not to offend the emperor?" I barked, laughing. "That does it, then. Paul is doomed."

James didn't laugh, but he joined me with a grin of his own.

MARY

"Your Sarah has grown into quite the lady. A Madonna," said Ruth, one of our deacons.

Indeed, my little girl practically sparkled, or at least in my own eyes. Dressed in a white robe, and with her curly black hair tied back, she stood before row upon row of children sitting on the grass in the open yard in front of our meeting hall, teaching them from the Law and Prophets and interspersing readings from Thomas's collection of sayings uttered by Jesus. She stood out among the other children not only because of her dark complexion but also her leadership.

Everyone acknowledged Lazarus as our overseer, or *episcopus,* as the Greeks would say. He set the rules and established the practices for adult worship in our growing movement among the villages throughout this region of Gaul. But Lazarus had never become a husband or father, and he knew nothing about children. He never learned how to feed them, or how to teach them to feed themselves, how to speak, how to refrain from speaking when quiet was called for, how to do their chores, or how to discipline them when they failed or refused to do their chores.

That's where Sarah stepped forward.

Although the farmers hereabouts had resisted at first when my daughter started teaching their children to read and write, they now boasted that their offspring could read edicts from the emperor and sign agreements. The children could ask intelligent questions of the local magistrates and argue their parents' claims. Some parents went so far as to predict their children would one day become ambassadors, pleading the villagers' cases before the authorities in Rome. And now Sarah, just thirteen years old herself, was also teaching their children how to study the Scriptures, so that they would assume moral leadership of the community someday.

"Madonna. What does that mean?" I asked Ruth.

Ruth looked up from the grain she had been milling in a large bowl. "A Madonna is not just a lady, but a symbol of virtue. She is pure in the eyes of the Father."

I suppressed a laugh of derision. "So you say. But you don't have to pick up after her at home, or yell at her to do her household chores."

"You speak as a mother, too close to see what is plain to the rest of us," Ruth scolded. "Our children will create a better world than the one their parents gave them. And Sarah will teach them how to do so."

Ruth stood and looked me straight in the eye. "The Black Madonna. That's what we call her in the countryside."

PRISCILLA

Like many men, Paul seemed to believe that if he just spoke more loudly, that I would better understand his reasoning and come to accept his point of view. But he was arguing the same point for the fourth go-round, having raised his voice even louder each time I rejected his position, so now he was almost shouting. He had worn out even my vast patience with him. I could only imagine how much sooner anyone else would grow exasperated and possibly even resort to violence.

"No, I do not want Thecla to accompany us to Rome," I repeated firmly, referring to the young deacon of Antioch. "And stop shouting at me or else you will get no supper tonight."

"But you don't understand. Thecla is such a great symbol of virtue," Paul pleaded again. But his voice was softer, and some of the righteous conviction had gone out of his tone. He seemed to know he was losing, but just hoped to have the last word before the subject was closed.

"Thecla is a sign of chastity," I corrected him. "Yes, she speaks well before large crowds, and many revere her. But she tells women to remain virgins and tells men they should never touch women."

Paul didn't seem to understand my concern. "What is wrong with that? God might sweep us all up into heaven at any moment. We *should* remain pure."

"You don't know that," I shot back. "No one knows when the end will come — you told me so yourself. But meanwhile we are about to travel to Rome and try to convince people to give up worship of their household gods. Those gods encourage people to enjoy sex, they celebrate wine and good food, and then they say to have more sex. If you take Thecla into Rome, the crowds will shun you."

Paul looked crestfallen, like a boy who has been told he cannot go outside to play. "But shouldn't we be telling the people to live cleaner lives?"

I reached out and held both of his hands for a moment. "Trust me, I have made a great fortune selling people things that they didn't think they wanted to buy before they met me. Our mission involves the same sort of persuasion. First you tell them how wonderful the Father is. Then you tell them how much better their lives are going to be. Not until they have joined you and become fervent followers do you bring up these other things. But the first thing Thecla would say to them is that they must deny themselves pleasure. The first thing they would say back to Thecla is that if she doesn't get out of Rome immediately, they will turn her over to the emperor to be burned alive."

I lifted his chin so that he had to look me in the eye. "And they might drive you out of the city too, as so many in other cities have done. And that means you would not have the opportunity to tell your gospel there or spread it out from Rome throughout the empire."

As the implications sank into that obstinate mind of his, a look of comprehension finally dawned on Paul's face. He relented.

SUSANNA

"Rani, where would you like these benches placed?" The men had fashioned several long benches out of hardwood boards. During construction we had found that we could not use stone to build everything in our seven new synagogues. The walls, yes; the altars, yes. But the roofs, doors and benches, no. Thomas gave very general instructions about the buildings' construction, but he was useless when it came to details. For instance: Rabbi, do you want the people to stand or sit? Oh, I suppose it would be better to sit. Yes, sir, on individual seats or benches? Hmm, benches would probably be more efficient. Yes, sir, where would you like the benches? Um, somewhere inside the synagogue, I guess.

We did not have time for guessing. So I took charge. The men already acknowledged me as their princess, and somebody had to instill order on this bunch of reckless oafs or else we'd never finish our work.

"I want the benches on either side of a center aisle leading to the altar. But I want you to fan them out in a semicircle so that all the people can see the altar and they can see each other too. Like this," I said, holding my arms parallel to each other with my hands curved in front of me to indicate where the first bench should go, and then repeating the gesture for the second bench, and so forth.

The men carried the benches in one at a time and arranged them somewhat in the manner I had told them. When all of them had been brought in, I gave more specific instructions on each one, starting with those in front — move this one forward a couple fingers' width, scoot that one back the length of one hand, turn this one at more of an angle.

"But Rani," asked one of the men, "Thomas has said he wants us to allow all castes to enter here, and women too. Where will they sit?"

"They will sit on the same benches as everyone else," I snapped, perhaps more sternly than necessary. "Forgive me, I should not have shouted," I said quickly. These men supported us on our demand to give equal attention to all. They expressed shock that we would go against the norms, but they did not oppose the move, or at least not openly. If any of them secretly harbored resentment, he had not let on within my hearing.

When Thomas had led them in prayer and they each personally felt the presence of the Father, these men of Malabar all pledged their loyalty. Many of the people in this region followed the teachings of some ancient man they called the Enlightened One. Some also called him the Buddha. Hundreds of years earlier, he had taught a path to obtaining peace with God and the world around us. Thomas listened intently to many of the teachings that the people attributed to this Enlightened One, and he pointed out the similarities between that sage's sayings and our own.

Isaiah, the man who had come to us from Antioch, told us of the new customs that were developing there. For one thing, apparently, they had heard about the communal meals that Jesus Thomas used to lead in the countryside when we were still in Israel. But the Antioch people did not give a full meal; rather, they offered each person just a small bit of bread and just a sip of wine, all from the same loaf and cup. It did not provide enough sustenance for the day like our meals had done, but it gave the people a symbolic gesture of equality and unity. Thomas said it sounded like a good idea, so he incorporated it into our meetings at the synagogues. After an opening prayer, Thomas would invite someone to read a translated lesson from the Law and the Prophets, and then Thomas would speak about how the ancient scripture could give us a lesson for today's world. Finally, he would bless the bread and the wine and distribute it to the people.

When a member of one of the synagogues brought a newcomer to us who wanted to join the community, Thomas would baptize the newcomer in flowing water just as John had baptized him in the Jordan.

"But Thomas," Isaiah protested, as he had when he first met Thomas so many months ago, "Paul in Antioch says you must not baptize as John did but should do so in the name of the Christos."

Jesus Thomas usually smiled when anyone brought him a question, but he did not smile this time. "If Paul has a problem, that is between him and the Father. We will baptize as I have said."

MARY

"Uncle Lazarus, I think you, Mother and I should lay hands on Daddy for healing in a ceremony at the church," Sarah said to my brother, a confident look on her face. We had long gotten into the habit of calling our synagogues churches, because so many Gentiles had joined us.

The people recognized that my daughter had healing power, and I was proud that she was so confident she could help Judas Thomas. But inside, my heart seemed to rip my breath right out of me. Thomas had fallen down a rocky cliffside weeks ago, and villagers carried him home gingerly and laid him on a bed of straw. We hoped he would recover when his bones mended, but his feet had grown green with pus and he could not breathe without coughing fluid down the front of his beard. Lazarus and I privately exchanged worried looks. Even Thomas clutched my brother's hands one morning and told him how to manage the trading business after he died.

Yes, we believed in the Father's power to heal. But we felt the Father was preparing to call Thomas home.

"Sarah," Lazarus said softly, "I have spoken to your father, Judas Thomas. He is happy with the life he has lived, and he says the Father blessed him many times over when he married your mother. And he especially says you are the light in his life, and you are the Father's light for all the people in Gaul. It is time for Thomas to pass the torch to you, and he asked me to tell you to carry that torch proudly in the traditions he has taught you."

Tears sprang into Sarah's dark eyes. "But I think I can heal him," she pleaded.

I wrapped my arm around her shoulder. "Sarah," I whispered. "I have spoken to him too. Daddy says it is his time, and he asks that you let him go."

She looked searched Lazarus's eyes and then mine. As the realization hit her, she buried her face in my shoulder, rocking with sobs. The three of us cried together.

REBECCA

The good lady Rachel always trusted me to take care of things for her when her arms and legs got too stiff for her to do much on her own. And now that her eyes were growing dim, I had to pretty much move into the house to handle all of all the work all of the time. Rabbi James — our Righteous One — he told me to do anything and everything necessary to keep Rachel comfortable. He said I didn't need to worry about him, he could take care of himself.

Of course, Rachel told me the exact opposite. She said not to worry about an old woman like herself but to make sure James ate his meals on time and washed his hands and face afterward and wore a clean robe when he went out to the Temple. She sounded just like every other mama I'd ever heard getting after her little boy to keep his nose clean and pick up after himself. If I didn't know better, I'd swear she was his real mother. But I was there all those years ago when his mother Miriam told us all that Rachel was in charge and that we should help her protect James.

I didn't usually speak directly to Rabbi James much, him being so holy and all, but one evening at supper he asked me a question as I was bringing his vegetable stew to the table for him and Rachel.

"Rebecca, not as many people are coming anymore to the Agape, the love feasts. Rachel doesn't get around as much as she used to, but she said you might know why the numbers have fallen. Is it that they don't like what I preach to them?"

"Oh no, your worship!" When I realized what I had called him, I blushed and stammered. "I mean Rabbi. No, Rabbi, a lot of the Poor have moved to Pella, north of here and on the other side of the Jordan. They have their own feasts there, but I don't know if they're as big as the ones we have here in the city."

"The Poor?" He raised his eyebrows at me. "Do they all live in poverty?"

I caught myself, and realized I needed to slow down. "No, Rabbi. That's just what we call ourselves. Listening to you, we came to realize we're all poor in spirit. So we call ourselves The Poor, and we follow what you and your brother, the King, have taught us."

Rachel dipped her bread in the gravy of the stew but didn't say anything.

"Anyway," I continued, "the Poor have been worried lately that life here in Jerusalem is getting dangerous. The Zealots keep trying to raise an army to fight against the Romans, and some of their craziest members attack anyone who doesn't support them. Some of the rich folk in the city have even been stabbed. But even worse, there are some people who support the new High Priest who are really jealous of you and all the people that follow you. They make things pretty uncomfortable for us."

James stared off into space while he tugged at his beard with one hand absent-mindedly. It was Rachel who finally broke the silence. "Rabbi, I think you need to be careful or these demons will kill you."

His eyes came back into focus, and he smiled at her. "No, I am more worried about these people who felt they must leave the city. You say they call themselves the Poor? I will ask around — quietly! Don't worry, I won't draw attention to them. But I must look more deeply into this issue. Thank you for bringing it to my attention."

He didn't ask any more questions, so I didn't say anything more. He kept really quiet for the rest of that evening.

SUSANNA

My builders in Niranam, a village on the river, seemed determined to finish constructing their synagogue sooner than anyone else. Honestly, I never meant for this to become a competition. I told the men it was more important to do it right than to do it fast. I wanted their synagogue to stand not just for seventy generations, but seventy times seventy.

Word about our building activity apparently traveled fast and far. Just yesterday, Abban shared some startling news as he and I were sipping sura with Thomas at a small table in front of our house. I appreciated the rare chance to get a moment's rest in the open air.

"I have received a message from a realm far to the north," Abban said, his eyes sparkling. "An emissary from none less than King Gondaphorus himself has come to me. He says the king has heard great things about our construction projects here and has requested that you come design and build a new palace for him."

"Gondaphorus," I mused. "Tell me, where is his kingdom?"

My husband pointed north, as if I would be able to see it if I just turned my head in that direction. "This side of Babylon," he said. "We passed his country when we traveled here several years ago. I did not stop there because, for one thing, my father wanted to come home to Malabar. But the people in the north are not like us, and I did not have time to try to learn to trust them."

Jesus Thomas leaned forward. "Why would he want a new palace?"

Abban shrugged. "I have no idea. But from what the people here in the south tell me, he has a ravenous hunger for greatness. He wants to attach his name to the biggest and most beautiful things because he believes his name will become eternal in that way."

I watched my brother's eyes. Even though the corners of his mouth did not move, his eyes seemed to be grinning. I felt mirth in the air, though we were not laughing. Apparently, Abban felt it too, because after a moment he snorted and hit the tabletop with the palm of his hand.

After making eye contact with me and raising one eyebrow to make sure we agreed, Thomas sat up straight and turned to Abban.

"Tell the messenger this. The money the king set aside to build the new palace, he must take that money and spend it on the poor people of his land. Build schools so their children can learn to prosper. Buy them better animals and equipment to run their farms so they can feed themselves and their neighbors. Hire workers to build better roads so they can trade their goods and bring greater riches to all of the kingdom."

Thomas paused and let his chin sink onto his chest, and he closed his eyes. But a moment later he raised his head and opened his eyes wide.

"If he does those things, his name will live forever."

PRISCILLA

My villa near the Tiber River had long since been taken over by some partisans favored by the emperor. I would wait for a better day to try to reclaim my property. A former business associate offered rooms to Aquila and me. When I pleaded for an extra room for Paul, he hesitated at first but eventually relented. He had a storage shed near his stables in the back of his property. If Paul could clean out the shed and make himself a bed from the hay and other materials that he might find out there, he could stay.

"But how am I supposed to make living quarters for myself?" Paul asked when I informed him of my friend's offer. "I am no carpenter."

I tried to keep my impatience with him out of my tone as I answered. "Think of it like one of your work projects. Suppose that you are stitching pieces of hide together into a tent. But in this case you are bundling clumps of hay together into a bed for yourself. In fact, you may want to take some pieces of hide with you to stitch into a cover to go over the hay. It can get very itchy if you lay directly on it, you know."

A light came into his eyes as he realized this task might come within his area of skill. Picking up his kit of sewing needles and twine — I don't think it had really sunk into his thick skull yet that he could not stitch the hay together — Paul set off for the storage shed at the rear of the villa. I think I heard him actually humming a gay working tune to himself as he went.

With Paul out of my way, I could focus on our more immediate concerns. I must reestablish my business contacts in the city and use my credit to obtain raw material for Aquila and Paul to make their coats and tents. That would give us a small bit of income, which I would use to buy and sell more expensive items. Within a few months I hoped to have enough income that we could rent at least a small house in the city. When this Nero was driven from office — as all emperors were in one way or another, either by old age or younger rivals — when Nero was gone, I would reclaim my villa by the river.

But I also had to renew my acquaintance with a few well-placed officials in Nero's court. Paul had been released to my custody upon the promise that I would present him to the emperor for judgment. This required some finesse. I could not just walk him into the court and let them prosecute the charges against him. If I did that, Paul would begin speaking and the emperor, or more likely some lower-level judge, would just have the guards drag him off to prison to force him to be quiet. I needed to draw this process out longer so I would have more time to establish myself.

"Aquila, get yourself ready. We must go out," I called to my husband.

SARAH

One more piece of news, not good. Joseph, the tin merchant from Arimathea who had brought Uncle Lazarus here to Gaul from Judea last year, said he planned to leave. Mom, still mourning the passing of my father, Judas Thomas, implored him to stay a while longer, but he would not change his mind.

"The Romans established a foothold in Britannia under Claudius, but I hear that a queen named Boudicca is resisting the emperor's forces," Joseph said. "I hope to meet her and teach her what we have learned from your brother, the King. And though I do not care for war, perhaps I can help her and other Britons lay hold of enough metals to forge weapons to defend themselves and keep the Romans at bay."

"That sounds dangerous," Mom warned. "You will live much more safely if you stay here, and you can help spread the word of Jesus's ministry far and wide here in Gaul."

As luck would have it — or, looking back now, perhaps it was not luck but rather divine intervention — Lazarus walked in at just that moment with one of his deacons, a woman named Marta. He was speaking to her as he came in and continued to rattle off a list of chores for her and the other church leaders. "We have made contact with a small community of the faithful at the capital city, Arles. I want you or one of your sisters to travel there with a copy of Thomas's book, so the people can study Jesus's wisdom. Find out how many of them can read and write. Make certain that you identify the wisest person of their community and entrust the book only to that person. And you might suggest that the community assign some trusted scribes to make copies of the book so they can spread the good news even further."

Just then Lazarus stopped and looked up, seeming to notice Mom, Joseph and me for the first time. "Oh, hello. And what have you all been doing this morning?"

Joseph laughed long and hard. Clutching his stomach with his left hand as he regained his breath, he wagged the finger of his right hand at my mother. "I was just telling Mary that you do not need my help here to spread the good news in Gaul. You have organized your church well, and you are sending out apostles to share the word. I will serve a greater purpose in Britannia."

Marta, who had been carrying an armful of fruits, set them down on the table and excused herself. She told Lazarus she would consult with him later that afternoon, and she left the house.

My uncle, not realizing that he was inadvertently taking sides in what, moments earlier, had been an impassioned argument, turned to Joseph and replied, "Oh, quite right. I think we have everything here in southern Gaul under control. What will you be doing in Britannia?"

Joseph grinned at me. "Hopefully," he said, "the same thing that you, Mary and Sarah are accomplishing here."

JUDITH

"Judas, have you finished your reading of the Law and Prophets today?" called out Joses. He had just gotten home from his day's work at the palace in Sepphoris. He looked tired, but he would not rest until he had checked off his inventory of the chores that were supposed to have been done here at home.

"Almost," our son Judas called back. "I was taking some training in sword fighting this afternoon. I had to finish that first before I could start my reading exercises."

I stayed out of the argument that I saw coming. I had already worked out Judas's schedule with the boy and knew that he would take care of his reading exercises. But Joses felt that he had to prove himself, had to show that he exerted as much authority at home as he did at work, so I let him continue to question Judas. I busied myself mending a tunic that had a tear behind its shoulder.

"The reading is more important," Joses said. "You know, it was your uncle and namesake, Judas Thomas, who taught me how to read."

I saw Judas roll his eyes. "Yes, Dad, you've told me before. And Uncle Judas learned mathematics from Uncle Abban, and he taught you how to do your numbers too. And that's how you rose to become Herod Antipas's steward."

Joses continued, "And sure, I was a tough boy and leader of a gang of young thugs, and we could have all gotten prime jobs in the army if we had wanted to become soldiers. But it was reading, writing and arithmetic that made me valuable at the palace. So you focus on that first and leave the swordplay to later."

"Yes, Dad," said Judas dutifully. "Speaking of which, I need to go finish reading the Law and Prophets before the sun goes down. It's a lot more difficult reading by a lamp." With that, he started to walk out of the room.

"When I was your age, we were lucky to even get a lamp," Joses called out. "I had to read under the light of the full moon." But Judas had already gotten through the door, and he made no reply to acknowledge whether he had heard the last remark.

I left Joses alone in silence for a moment before saying, "You ride the boy too hard."

"He's not a boy," Joses almost shouted. "He's almost reached his twelfth year, and other lads his age already have to work in the fields and learn to do their fathers' work. I want him prepared to work toward taking over my position if anything happens to me, and his skills with letters and numbers will be far more important than sword fighting."

Stating the obvious, as usual. But men just had to have the last word, even if it was the same word they had said moments earlier.

"I agree with you on that point," I said, drawing the syllables out slowly. "He comes from two great families, yours and mine. He must train to be a leader at the palace, but he may also need to know how to lead people in the countryside. They might also look to him to defend them from the Romans, and to lead them to the Father like his uncle James at the Temple. Our boy will face many expectations in his lifetime."

PRISCILA

Well, he did not take long to fulfill my prophecy. Despite my constant warnings, despite my patient coaching, despite my schooling him on the protocol of actions and the delicate language of diplomacy, Paul blurted out everything that was on his mind when he appeared before the emperor's magistrate. He told of the magical powers of his Christos, how this god was greater than any god that the people of the empire had ever known — including Caesar himself — and how anyone who did not believe in his Christos would spend eternity burning in flames, but anyone who did believe would live forever in bliss.

The magistrate, rather than try to sort through the man's ravings, arrested him and put him in chains. Paul now sat in a cell behind bars in the Tullianum, on the northeastern side of the Capitoline Hill. Officially, the Romans referred to this as detention while awaiting trial. But most of the knowledgeable people in the city knew of it in much more blunt terms. Though the prison had stood on this spot for hundreds of years, the authorities had never modified it to accommodate long-term incarceration. It was usually just a prisoner's final resting place before execution.

But at least his guards allowed Aquila and me to visit Paul in the prison. And they allowed us to bring him long scrolls of blank parchment and a stylus and a jar of ink. Paul had long taken labors to write letters to communities of followers we had visited in our years of travels together, and now he was determined to write even more from his prison cell here. He continued to cheerfully greet us when we came each morning, convinced that his jailing was part of a divine plan that would glorify himself and the Christos before all the world.

"I have written to Thessalonica of the joy I found among the people there. And I have written to Galatia, and to Corinth," Paul said, his eyes sparking as if he could see his Christos just over our shoulders.

Aquila almost appeared as if he would glance over his shoulder to see what Paul was looking at, but I made eye contact with my husband and told him with just a brief twitch of my eyebrow to do no such thing.

"And I am nearly finished with a letter to the faithful here in Rome," Paul continued.

I tried hard not to show any emotion on my face. Paul projected ecstasy in his voice, but I felt little more than a deep depression. All my dreams had collapsed in doom. I had thought I would use Paul to draw crowds to hear him speak. That while he told wild tales of this new god that was greater than all of his listeners' household gods, I could work the crowd, finding out which ones possessed wealth, which ones would make good and steady customers.

But now Paul was reduced to writing letters instead of delivering impassioned speeches at the Forum. What could I ever build on top of that?

"Please," he said, reaching between the bars of his cell to clutch my hands. "I must beg a favor. Timothy has been traveling with us for many months now, and I think he fully understands my thinking. Please send Timothy to me here to help write more letters. I want to write a letter to Philippi, and more letters to Corinth and Colossae. Timothy earned his living as a scribe before he came to follow us, so he can complete the letters faster than I can alone."

Aquila spoke up. "I think that you do need help to write as many letters as you can, Paul. I will certainly send for Timothy as soon as I can."

I guess my husband could see in my face the sudden twinge of irritation I felt, because he quickly turned to me. "We need to get Paul's words out to everyone who can read. Not only will we send letters to all the churches we have established, but we will have some trusted scribes create copies to send far and wide. The time may be short, because the Day of the Lord could come at any moment." After that last remark, he gave such a minor jerk of his head toward Paul that no one else would have ever seen it if they were not looking for it. But I saw it. I had known Aquila for as many years as Moses led the Hebrews in the desert, so we needed no words to communicate. I understood him immediately.

In a flash I realized Aquila had hit upon a moment of absolute brilliance! Yes, we would make Paul's final letters from prison so famous that people we had never met would clamor just to touch the hems of our robes as we passed when we came to visit their cities. The Apostle Paul, as he called himself, would grow in fame as the martyr who sacrificed himself for the Christos.

And Priscilla's and Aquila's fame would grow just as great — the traveling survivors of the great persecution, the purveyors of the word, and also of various other goods necessary to every household of any stature in any corner of the empire.

Yes, we would bring Timothy to help write letters. In fact, I might even write a letter myself. I was thinking about the Hebrews following Moses through the desert a moment ago. Yes, I should address a letter to the Hebrews, tell them of the new Moses they should follow.

And then later, I would visit them to see how well they had absorbed the message. And if they wished to follow our new Moses through the desert, they would need tents and whatever other supplies I might have available for them.

Yes, I could make this work. Despite Paul's blunder, I would come out of this well.

REBECCA

"Becca, Rabbi James said he'd like to see you up at the Temple this afternoon," Rachel said as she limped into the kitchen, leaning on her staff. I looked to make sure she was standing steadily on her feet, because she had fallen several times in the past number of weeks. I kept her bed here on the ground floor and I had a cot for myself in the same room. I wanted to be nearby if she needed anything in the night.

It had been a long time now since Rachel was last able to climb the stairs to attend to Rabbi James. I carried the food and drink upstairs. And when he had visitors — which wasn't as often now as it used to be — I would carry a pail of water with towels for them to wash their feet. I took care of them both. But I never forgot that James's mother said Rachel was in charge. Jesus, the King, had said the same thing, the men told me. So I took my orders from her.

But this one worried me.

"I've never gone up to see him at the Temple before. I'm only a serving woman. Will they even let me in to see him? And besides, who will take care of you here at the house while I'm away?"

Rachel waved her hand at me like she was swatting a fly. "Don't you worry none about me. Now, when you get to the Court of the Women, you find yourself some man in a Temple robe standing near the Treasury and you tell him the Rabbi James asked you to see him. That person will go fetch him for you."

I nodded but told her I still doubted whether I could force a man to follow through if he resisted.

Rachel wagged her finger at me. "If any of those pipsqueaks up there don't do what you say, you tell them Rachel will come kick their skinny little butts. And tell them they'll be lucky if that's all I do."

"Yes, Ma'am," I said with a grin. I didn't really think Rachel could ever climb the steps to the Temple, and I doubted that she could kick her leg high enough anymore to actually connect her foot to the shin of a man's leg, let alone his hind side. But the name Rachel still struck fear in many men's hearts up on the hill, so I guessed that this would be enough. After she sat down and made herself comfortable, I set off.

I followed her instructions and went to the Court of the Women. I stepped in front of the first Temple man I saw and told him Rachel had sent me to see the Rabbi James. The man went in search of James immediately without question. Yes, that proved the point! Rachel's name still carried a lot of weight up here in God's House.

When James came out of a building, he motioned me over to a bench. As we sat down, other folks continued about their business all around us. None paid us any attention.

"Rebecca, I have a very important job for you, if you are willing to do it for me," he said, looking intently into my eyes. "This favor will not just benefit me, but I hope will help out hundreds of people. Can I count on you?"

"Of course, Rabbi," I said. "I'll do whatever you need."

"Good." He glanced around, as if checking whether anyone else was listening. "I have written a letter to the community at Pella. The Poor, I believe you call them. And I also have some other scrolls and precious items I want them to store in their synagogue there. I was hoping, if I assign some men to drive a wagon for you and guard it on the road, that you would take these precious items and deliver them directly to the rabbi of the synagogue on my behalf."

I looked across the courtyard, watching people go to and fro. They did not seem to act as if anything had changed in their day-to-day lives. Everything seemed to go on as it always had. No big upheavals.

But this! The Righteous One wanted me — me? — to deliver precious items to the Poor in his name? Of course, I felt honored that he thought of me. But I had too many questions in my head at the moment.

"Why me, Rabbi? Surely you have dozens of priests or scribes who could go in your place, people who would know how to speak for you, what kinds of words to use, what issues would be important and which would not. And what are these items you want delivered? If they are very valuable, surely it would be better to send them in a heavily guarded caravan. And who will take care of you and Rachel while I am gone? No, this does not sound possible to me, Rabbi."

I will always remember the tender look on his face, the half-smile that showed through what must have been the double measure of worry and stress he was feeling. I did not fully grasp what was going on at the time, but something in my gut told me that something was worrying him. Why else would he pursue such an unusual path?

"Rebecca, my brother Jesus once taught me that if you don't want anyone to pay attention to what you are doing, then do it out in the open for all to see. Act as if you have nothing to hide, and nobody will take much interest. But if you do act as if you have something to hide, no one will rest until they find out what it is. That's why I am asking you to perform this task, because no one will suspect you. They will think that if I were sending something important and valuable, I would have a dozen armed Temple guards riding along, just as you suggested. But you have friends and perhaps even kinsmen among the Poor, so no one will give it much thought that you are traveling there to see them."

He paused for a moment, seemingly watching the people go by as I had been doing moments earlier. But he did not really seem to focus on any of the people.

"As for what I am sending to Pella, there are several things. The most important, as I mentioned, is the letter I have written to their community. You touched me deeply when you first told me about the Poor, how they felt poor in spirit but wanted desperately to preserve their faith in the Father. I hope that this letter will tell them how to stay strong and how to thrive as a shining beacon of righteousness. I hope they will read parts of the letter in their synagogue every Saturday along with their readings of the Law and the Prophets. If they do that, then I will know my service to the Father is complete."

I had been nodding along in understanding, but that last comment startled me. "Are you in danger, Rabbi? Why are you talking about your life being complete?"

He moved his head from side to side, apparently telling me no.

"In addition to my letter, you will be taking them several chests of very old scrolls of the Law and the Prophets as well as a number of important writings by scholars who have been studying the scrolls for many years. I want the Poor to have their own library so they do not have to come to Jerusalem for learning. After all, Pella is at the north end of Perea, not far from my family's home in the Galilee, so I know it is a very long journey."

It all seemed reasonable, but I still had that nagging notion. "Rabbi, are you moving these scrolls out of the city to keep them safe?"

His smile did not project happiness but resignation. "I cannot hide this from you, but I must ask you to keep it just between us." Although the other people in the courtyard were scurrying about their business and not paying any attention to us, James leaned closer to me and lowered his voice. He placed one hand over mine, in comfort only, not intimacy.

"When you first told me about the Poor, you said they were withdrawing to Pella because Jerusalem no longer seemed safe. What you said is true. The Zealots caused enough trouble in their day, but now a harsher group has split off from the Zealots. These people are called Sicarii, the Dagger Men. They mix into large crowds and stab Roman soldiers, and they even stab Judeans who they think are collaborating with the empire."

"But Rabbi, certainly they would not try to assassinate you. You have never collaborated with the Romans. In fact, you have preached that we should love our enemies and focus on the Father rather than earthly concerns."

Again, that grim smile. Though he was taking me into his confidence, I felt that he was not telling me all his fears. "No, I do not expect the Sicarii to attack me. But they will try to force other men in powerful positions to challenge the empire. The wrath of Rome could fall upon this city. That is why I would feel much better if you rejoined your community in their new home, Pella. No matter what happens here in Jerusalem, we absolutely must preserve all the knowledge we have learned about our lives with the Father, and those of our ancestors. Pella is one of the Ten Cities, and I think it will remain the safest."

I wanted to cry, but I knew I should not. "But Rabbi, shouldn't you and Rachel come too? I feel like you are asking me to abandon you both."

He patted my hand. "I have spoken to Rachel, and she agrees that you should go. But Rachel is too old to travel, and she does not want to try to start a new life in a strange place. I will not leave because I have devoted my entire life to the Temple. And Rachel will not go because — " and here he seemed to choke up — "Rachel has devoted the entire second half of her life to me. Whatever happens, she and I will face it together.

"Also, and this you must keep quiet, because it has not become general knowledge in the city, the new governor has fallen ill. If Porcius Festus succumbs, I expect there will be a power struggle. It may not be safe for anyone in Judea, especially here in the city. That is why I would like you to take these items beyond the Jordan, where they may be kept safe."

He was trying to convince me that he was worried about the safety of the scrolls. But I sensed the real danger would be for people. Probably James himself. And if there was danger for James, then there was danger for Rachel too.

Now I could not hold it back any longer. I sobbed as quietly as I could so that no one would hear and take notice, but tears flowed freely down my cheeks.

MARY

I could not stay here any longer. In the years since Judas Thomas's death, I had closed myself off to the people around me. I remained closed to Sarah and Lazarus, but I avoided the villagers, and I no longer cared to speak with the priests and deacons whom Lazarus had trained and sent out to establish worship centers throughout southern Gaul. My daughter and my brother kept the people away as much as they were able, and Sarah handled most of the people's needs for communion with the Father. Sarah had completely replaced me as the spiritual head of all the faithful in this country, and that pleased me greatly. I stayed in my room and would sometimes watch out the window while she preached to the crowds outside. Yes, she preached! I had never said much more than to tell the people to hold hands before we prayed directly to the Father, but my girl took time to tell the people how to treat their neighbors in such ways that the Father's kingdom would be known here on earth. The growing crowds of people seemed enthralled by her words. I know that I certainly was.

"But what of the next life?" one man called out once. "Travelers from Rome have told us there are many Christos there in the city, and that they endure suffering with the hope of a better life after the resurrection. They say the kingdom is not in this world."

The Black Madonna. That's what they called my girl. And when that man called out that question, I felt my own heart rise as the Black Madonna raised her arms above her shoulders to encompass the entire crowd. "Look around you," she called out in a strong voice. "You see your neighbors living in peace with each other, with enough food and drink to sustain their families. You see them living in the Father's light and sharing stories about what his son Jesus did among the people of Judea. You see them raising their children with love for themselves and their neighbors. Yes, you will fully know the glory of the kingdom after your death and resurrection. But do not wait until then — the kingdom is all around you. Open your eyes, open your hearts, open your arms and embrace it!"

Yes, the people flocked to Sarah now. But I still felt the call of their demands, and I was too weary to do anything for them. I could not stay.

Lazarus knew of my concern. After all, we had grown up together, brother and sister, and often either of us did not need to speak out loud for the other to understand what was on our mind.

Knowing my desire, Lazarus had spoken to a number of farmers in the countryside to the north, and he told me what he had learned. Within a walk of two days from here, a deep cavern had been etched into the side of a rocky hill. A stream ran nearby the cavern, and there was a small patch of land at the foot of the hill large enough to grow a small bit of fruit and grain. Two farms bordered each other near the hill, so the location was not completely isolated from human contact. But people would be close enough for me to call on in an emergency.

The cave sounded like heaven to me. I loved my brother and my daughter, but a part of me died when Thomas took his last breath. I needed to live out my days alone.

I would tell Sarah of my plans. And then I would prepare for the move to my final home.

SUSANNA

"Rani, the Brahmins are threatening violence," Abban said with a tone of urgency. "You must prevail upon your brother to show greater respect for our people's customs."

I almost laughed. Even my own husband was calling me the princess now. My nickname had caught on so strongly because I had long since lost my patience for fools and would not hesitate to bark orders when needed. Many of our workers and the townsfolk in the cities where we had built our synagogues learned early on not to give me nonsensical excuses for tasks not performed correctly nor for actions not taken. I was never harsh, but the men of this land had come to respect the power of Judean women's eyes. Or at least mine.

But I did not laugh, because Abban was broaching a very serious subject. Though many of the wealthy members of the upper class had learned to tolerate Thomas because he brought them into direct contact with the Father, we had heard plenty of warnings that he faced danger if he persisted in elevating the lower castes. His doctrine that all of us stood equal before God contradicted what had long been accepted as the normal course of human affairs here. The Brahmins said that they owned the wealth and the power to direct the affairs of others, and the various classes below the Brahmins must satisfy themselves with their permanent place in the world. And the lowest caste — a respectable person must not even touch one of them. That's the way it had always been, and that's the way it would stay.

Jesus Thomas, of course, would have none of that.

"I will warn him," I said, trying to divert Abban from a hopeless cause. Thomas would not change. "Tell me, how are things progressing with the seven synagogues?"

Abban sat down and took his sandals off. He took a clean towel and dipped it into the bowl of water I kept here for this purpose and massaged his toes and soles with the wet cloth. "I have always loved your custom of washing the feet. It brings so much relaxation to the body and mind," he said. "As for the synagogues, they are thriving. We only get new people joining during special times like the planting in the spring and harvesting during the autumn, but the membership remains stable during the rest of the year. The people contribute enough of their crops, labor and money to sustain the ministries that they provide."

As Abban wrung out the towel and hung it to dry, Thomas entered the room. He had a light in his eyes that caused me to inwardly groan. Whenever I saw that expression on his face, it usually meant he had dreamt up some wild idea that was going to make my increasingly pale hair turn whiter.

He sat down, the three of us forming a small circle around the table. I waited for a moment for him to offer a reason for the grin on his face but finally lost my patience. "Well, what is it?"

"Abban, my brother," he started, his teeth shining white against his dark complexion, "what can you tell me about Vedapuri?"

Abban seemed startled by the question. As for myself, I didn't know if the name referred to a food, a person, a place or one of the many philosophies that the people of this land followed. I had never heard the word before, and I could see by Thomas's face that he had probably only heard of the term a short while before he asked Abban.

My husband, for his part, rolled his eyes back in his head as if searching his childhood memories. "Vedapuri is located on the other side of this land, near the eastern ocean. The Cholas rule there. A wise man named Valluvar came from Vedapuri. In fact, if I remember correctly, his writings reflect a philosophy similar to yours, in that he did not believe the people should be separated by classes. From what I have heard from our trading partners, Vedapuri also does a great deal of business with ships from Rome. The Romans bring gold in exchange for pepper and beautiful cloth. Why do you ask?"

Thomas took a moment to absorb the information. I did not know what he was thinking, but I feared the worst.

"A man I met today suggested I go to Vedapuri. He said I would hear the sound of peacocks calling out, for a great many of the colorful birds gather there. And as you said, many people there have come to accept that there should be no caste system of separating the rich from the poor."

I was about to object but Abban spoke first. "Perhaps many people have come to believe so. But many more will cling to the ancient ways, and you may bring danger upon yourself if you oppose them."

He should have known by now, but Abban had walked right into the trap. Warning my brother of impending danger was almost the same as promising him great success if he would just take the dare. I knew now what Thomas would say even before he opened his mouth to reply.

"Nevertheless, I think I should go."

PRISCILLA

Aquila helped the boys sort the various letters into stacks so they would be ready for transport. I had hired several scribes to make a dozen copies of each letter. Riders would take copies to the major cities where we had established a following. Antioch, of course, and Corinth, Colossae, and Athens. I would send one of each to Galatia, Philippi, and Thessalonica. I had heard there was a growing community in Alexandria but that they had their own book about the Christos, and it was written by someone from Jerusalem. Therefore, I would send two copies of each of our letters so that the Egyptians would have a greater volume of material from Paul. I wanted them to adopt our vision of the Good News, not the backward meanderings of the Judeans. I was sending two copies in case someone had the good sense to place one of each in Alexandria's library. That would assure us not only of credibility but also long life — it was the greatest library in the world and would never falter.

The remaining three copies of each would remain with me here in Rome. One complete set would remain wrapped in the same room where I kept my jewelry and other valuables. One set would be used at the gatherings of the faithful here in the city. I would instruct priests to read from the sacred letters each week, so that the people would remember our ways.

And I would keep one set of the letters available to loan to important people. I would maintain strict rules, of course. Only leaders of proper faith groups from other cities would be allowed to borrow them while they were visiting here. They could borrow only one letter at a time and must read and return it to me within a day. I would not allow anyone, no matter how important, to transport any of the borrowed copies out of the city. They could hire our scribes to copy them if they wanted to carry letters home for their own communities. I would insist on reviewing each new copy before it was released, to ensure the scribes made no errors or misinterpretations.

We must maintain control of the new movement. And by we, I meant I.

"Are you certain there will not be any more letters?" Aquila asked, as he brushed off his hands. He had sent the two boys off to get water for themselves and us. Fortunately, this villa had its own well, so they would not have to wait in line with the peasants.

"I am fairly certain Paul is finished," I sighed. "He has already said everything he can and has said it in as many ways as he can. And I've heard from my friends that the magistrate has reached his final decision. Our Paul will not remain with us in this world much longer."

Aquila looked up at me as if in shock. "You think they will execute Paul?"

It had always seemed so clear to me ever since Paul's arrest that I wasn't sure whether my husband was feigning surprise or genuinely had not suspected the obvious outcome. Paul openly claimed his Good News was greater than Caesar. And he did not make his point in a friendly, persuasive manner. No, he browbeat his listeners and said anyone who disagreed with him would burn for eternity.

No, our Paul had sealed his own fate. If the decision rested on my own shoulders and I had the empire's authority to condemn him, I would probably do no differently than what the Romans would do. The only remaining questions in my own mind was how much time we had left, and whether it would be a public, drawn-out crucifixion or a quick beheading within the Praetorian camp.

REBECCA

Many Judeans lived here in Pella, but some neighborhoods of the town contained foreigners. Most of the Judeans had somewhat dark complexions, but they appeared light compared to some of the other people here. Others, however had skin so pale that I wondered how they survived in the glare of the hot sun. Our people spoke Aramaic but most of the foreigners communicated among themselves in their own languages. Every group had several men who knew Greek well enough to communicate with their counterparts in the other groups and then translate to their own folks.

But the groups pretty much stayed out of each other's way, so communication with outsiders became less important on a personal, one-to-one level.

Soon after arriving and settling into a house for widows where I had been offered a place to stay, I learned that the Poor did not comprise a single group here. The two largest segments, as near as I could tell, were the Ebionites, who mostly came from southern Judea, and the Nazoreans, who were Nazarites who might have come from any part of Judea, Galilee or the Decapolis, though I gathered that a large number of them had spent time in the wilderness settlement of the Essenes near the salty sea at the southern end of the Jordan. Despite the differences in their origins, both groups devoted themselves strongly to James, the Righteous One, and his brother Jesus, the King.

The house of widows received some alms from the treasury of the synagogue, but we also had to work to earn our keep. The oldest and longest serving woman at the house, Esther, assigned me to wait on the synagogue's rabbi. It seems he had requested me because of the scrolls and other relics I had delivered from Jerusalem, and my friendship with James.

"Rebecca, do you think James would approve of this arrangement of the scrolls?" asked Symmachus, the rabbi, indicating a jumble of scrolls he had piled in no particular order on a table against the front wall. The man clearly did not need my advice — his knowledge of ancient Hebrew and Greek, in addition to his command of all the Law and the Prophets, placed him above all others in this part of the country. But I think he gave deference to me because none other than the Righteous One himself had sent me here. At first I tried to downplay my status. Later, however, I learned that the local people's perception that I was somehow holy had in turn lent new status to Pella. This town was now home to an apostle sent out by James and Jesus, and therefore it had won renown as a holy place. I could not allow myself to harm the city's new reputation through my own sense of modesty.

But I did not know enough about the scriptures to give Symmachus a good opinion on their display, or at least not in regard to their literary or spiritual importance. Instead, I looked at his display with an outside observer's eye. The faded discoloration on some of them showed me which of the scrolls was the oldest. That gave me an idea. Judging their ages by their shades of coloration, I tried ordering them from right to left, oldest to newest. A few looked almost identical, so I guessed which of them to place before the other. After I had lined them up thusly, I turned to the rabbi and asked his opinion.

"Hmm, now why would you place those two next to each other?" he mused, peering down at a pair of them. "Oh, I see your reasoning now. The themes follow each other even if they do not follow chronologically. Brilliant! And following that logic, it would make sense for this one to follow that one, and then this," he said, pointing at other scrolls moving leftward down the line. Then he came to the two with identical coloration. "Ah, but here I think I disagree. These two should switch order."

I made a show of examining the two in question. "Yes, Rabbi, I believe you are correct. You have good judgment in these matters. I think even James would agree with your decision"

Beaming with pride, Symmachus switched the two scrolls in question. And then he bowed his head slightly toward me in thanks for my assistance.

I did not fully understand what had just happened. But after that day, many of the Judean men of Pella bowed their heads when they passed me on the street. Even Esther treated me kindly when we women gathered for our evening meals.

Rabbi Symmachus must have said something. People listened, and the word about me had spread fast.

PRISCILLA

"I will present my body as a pure and holy sacrifice to the Lord," Paul exclaimed, his smile wide and his eyes wild. "Like an unblemished lamb, I will be delivered to the fleshly powers of this earth and raised up as a beacon of hope for the nations."

I tried to hide my frustration. "Yes, Paul, but I need you to focus on this now. Here is the wording for letters of introduction for Aquila and me," I said, showing him a draft I had written out on a piece of papyrus. "I just need you to copy this in your own hand onto these blank sheets so that we can carry on your important missionary work."

The cell we sat in was not large, but at least it only held this single prisoner. I suspected that any other prisoners might have begged their guards to put them into other, more crowded cells just to get them away from Paul. Having traveled extensively with the man over the past several years, I saw the effect he had on those who might have been impressed at their first meeting but were forced to endure repeated contact. Every city we had visited, Paul would immediately stir up trouble by starting arguments with the local Judeans, telling them they would burn in hell if they did not accept his "gospel," as he called it. After the Judeans made a show of throwing him out of the synagogue and threatening bodily violence against him, Paul would play the martyr before the Greeks and thus gain the latter as listeners. It was a routine that had served us well over the past number of years, and we had converted a large number of Gentiles into followers of the Christos by perfecting his performance of this drama.

But I was the stage manager, not the audience. I didn't need to listen to Paul recite his lines here in his solitary confinement. I had serious business to line up for the future, and I only had a short time to make use of Paul in preparing the way.

Paul glanced at my draft and set it aside dismissively.

"These letters of introduction may not even be necessary," he said. "The Day of the Lord may come at any moment. In fact, I would guess that he will come down from the clouds even as I am being raised up and am about to breathe my last. Yes, the Christos will burst onto the earth in a blaze of glory at that very moment, rescuing me from mortal death and lifting me to eternal life. So the end will come before you have even left Rome, let alone have reached any of the cities where we have followers."

"You don't know that." I had made this argument dozens of times, but Paul had convinced himself the world as we knew it would end very soon. He did not see the need to prepare for the future because, to his way of thinking, we would have no "concerns of the flesh" in the future.

"If we don't need it, so much the better," I continued. "But write the letters anyway, just in case. And write one for Timothy too."

Paul rolled his eyes to show he thought the request inane, but he moved the papyrus back in front of himself. "All right, then, if it will put your heart at ease. Do you want just a single letter for yourself to carry with you, or do you require separate letters addressed to the churches in each of the cities?"

He got to work, and I remained silent so I would not break his concentration.

SUSANNA

The travel overland to Vedapuri did not take as long as I feared it might. We started on the western shore of this land and walked to the eastern shore. Based on the number of days it took when we walked from Galilee to Jerusalem during all the early years of my life, I calculated that this journey was about six times as far. But compared to the distance we had traveled from the Galilee to Malabar, this trip seemed short and leisurely.

And the people we met along the way! Back home in Galilee, and even in Judea, most people seemed the same. Maybe I thought they were all alike because I grew up around them and had grown accustomed to their ways, but I usually could predict what even strangers in my homeland believed about God and their neighbors and how they would act. Here, I never knew what to expect. From what I could gather through my limited understanding of their language and the bits of lore that members of our party would translate, some of these people believed their current life circumstances were either rewards or punishment for actions they had taken in previous lives. Some others among them believed that only by completely emptying themselves could they find fulfillment — and I found the irony of that statement amusing. And all of them seemed to accept that those born into the lower classes could do nothing to redeem themselves in this life, and conversely, that nothing could ever debase those born of the highest classes. The damned and the blessed walked the same earth, but they would never stand in the same place together.

But when Jesus Thomas crossed their separate paths, those divisions disappeared, or at least temporarily. Thomas would do that thing of his, making everyone around him intensely aware of the immediate presence of the Father. At moments like these, the Brahmins would attempt to claim him as their own. He would nod to them but then turn to open his hands to the laborers and even the beggars as well, and for a brief time all classes would coexist. I suspect that they would probably immediately turn away from each other again as soon as we passed.

On the second morning of our journey, after breaking our fast but before setting out on the road, I felt sick to my stomach. This surprised me because I very seldom got sick. I had to kneel next to a tree and vomit.

Apparently, the sound of my sickness was less discreet than I had hoped to keep it. Abban and Thomas both ran quickly to my side.

"It is nothing," I said, wiping the corner of my mouth with the back of my hand. "I'm sure it was just something I ate."

Abban clutched my hands with worry. But Thomas laid his hands on my head for a moment and closed his eyes. When he opened them again, his teeth shone white against his dark skin.

"Abban, my brother," Thomas said, "my mother is going to become a grandmother again. I am going to become an uncle. But of more immediate concern, you are going to become a father. Congratulations! Now," he added in a jocular tone, "it may be necessary for me to school you on the proper upbringing of a Judean baby. I do not think your own childhood should serve as an example."

After he said it, I came to realize that it must be true. I could not yet say that I felt the baby within me, but I had been told about the symptoms by countless women in my lifetime. Despite the age I had reached, I was going to be a mother!

After packing up the camp where we had spent the night, we continued on the road toward the eastern shoreline. I noticed that Abban almost seemed to be skipping part of the way. Thomas had a new spring to his step as well.

The peasants could not afford to follow us along the way, because they all had to work to feed themselves and their families. But apparently, they had their own ways to spread news faster than we traveled, because crowds of peasants would greet us when we entered each new town. Thomas would shout out his blessings and would lead them in a simple prayer to help them feel the Father's presence in all their doings. Then he would move among them, laying his hands on the sick and elderly, and openly touching the workers.

This touching of the peasants especially scandalized the Brahmins, but they apparently feared to say anything in front of others.

On one occasion Thomas saw a wealthy man shaking his head in disgust at the touching of the peasants. With a blank expression on his face, my brother walked to the man and merely stood in front of him, gazing intently into his eyes but saying nothing. The man's face seemed to go through a full range of emotions — raging anger, indignation and accusation toward Thomas, righteous pleading in defense of himself, denial of any wrongdoing or ill intent, and finally sorrow and a plea for forgiveness. All of this passed without words. I can't remember if it took several long minutes or only a few short seconds, but I felt like I had watched the man's whole life pass before my eyes. In the end Thomas stepped forward and locked forearms with the man in brotherly greeting, thus touching him with the same hands that had touched the peasants just moments earlier.

I knew Thomas could handle one-on-one confrontations like this. But what would happen if his enemies swarmed at him from all sides, as the Romans had done at the Temple? I shuddered at the thought.

SARAH

Mary, my mother, seemed comfortable. The cave sheltered her from the weather, but its face was wide and looked out over the countryside. Judging by the lack of waste or gnawed bones, it did not appear that any large wild animals used this cave. Uncle Lazarus had made arrangements for farmers to deliver food to her each week when they came to her Sabbath prayer meetings.

Meanwhile, I had taken her place leading the meetings in town here near the southern coast.

I had grown up expecting to remain unmarried, because of the dark skin I inherited from my father Judas Thomas. The people of Gaul had skin so pale that I stood out as an oddity among them, and my uncle confided that many parents warned their sons to avoid coming within an arm's length of me.

So it came as a surprise to me when Maximin approached me one Sunday after prayer.

I would preach to the people about the Law and Prophets and things my uncle Jesus had said, as recorded in the book my father had compiled before his death. But for the most part, we would all sit quietly with our eyes closed, meditating. We would often choose just a short phrase, or perhaps a single line from a song, and chant it over and over again. The chanting did not distract us — rather, once the words and tones had become automatic and required no thought, it would allow our minds to roam more freely over whatever topic I had discussed in my sermon. Each person communed directly with the Father, without interference from me.

Maximin clutched his hands and wrung them together in front of his waist when he approached me. He looked at my face for a moment before looking down at the ground. Then he peered up at me again. "I liked what you said today, Miss Sarah."

"Just call me Sarah. 'Miss' sounds like you're afraid of me."

He grinned sheepishly. "Well, maybe I am."

"Please don't be," I said. "Is there something I can help you with?"

"Um," Maximin stammered, looking down again, "I was wondering if you would like to join me and my family for supper this afternoon. We live not too far away, and I'd make sure you got home before dark."

Like I said, this came as a surprise. "Why, I don't know. I ordinarily prepare supper for my Uncle Lazarus. He has so many responsibilities organizing the churches in the country, I worry that he would forget to feed himself if I weren't there to put a plate of food in front of him."

"Oh, I f-forgot to s-say something." Maximin was stuttering now. I hoped he would recover soon. My mother had told me stories about how my father had stuttered terribly when he was a boy. It took him years to gain enough confidence in himself to speak plainly. "I was hoping your uncle would come to supper too. My parents think very highly of him."

Well, I thought to myself. Isn't that precious?

REBECCA

Rabbi Symmachus sounded almost on the edge of tears. Worse, he seemed almost afraid to speak to me.

"What is it?" I asked.

He started to speak but choked for a moment. He raised his hands halfway as if awaiting help, and then dropped them again. Then he just blurted his message out as quickly as he could, to get it over with.

"The Righteous One is dead. I just received word from Jerusalem."

"Dead?" The news left me gasping, so I could only get one word out at a time. "How? When? Why?"

The rabbi sat down and buried his face in his hands. Muttering between his fingers, he moaned, "His enemies stirred up a mob. They stoned him and threw his body down from the wall."

Rabbi Symmachus looked up in misery. "God's Righteous One is dead. What will become of our nation?"

I grasped his hands in desperation. "Rabbi, what of his household. An elderly woman named Rachel cared for him. Did you hear whether she got away?"

He shook his head from side to side. "All dead. They told me that when women brought the news to Rachel, she tried to climb the steps to the Temple so she could hit Annas with her cane. The other women helped her up the steps. But when she reached the outer courtyard and saw the High Priest, she screamed at him and raised her cane to strike him. His guards stepped in front of her to block the way. She fell down and her head struck against the stone floor. She died shortly afterward."

I clutched my chest and felt my heart beating rapidly. Rachel. So many of us servant women in Jerusalem looked up to her almost like she was our mother. Gone. But though my heart ached, it also swelled with pride at the manner of her passing. She died defending her boy, the Righteous One of Israel.

"What will we do now?" The rabbi asked the very question that I was about to utter myself. But since he asked it first, I realized that he did not have an answer. So rather than ask the question again, I decided I must prop him up in his misery, give him courage and confidence to play the role that clearly was his to play.

"Rabbi Symmachus, the Righteous One sent me here with his personal letter to the community here, and with those scrolls, for a reason. He prophesied that this day might come, and he sent me here with his library of scriptures so that our people's knowledge of the Father and the King would live on. He was counting on you to carry on for him."

"Me?" He looked aghast at my suggestion. "What can I do. I am nothing. I am only a man."

I would not let up. "Rabbi James was only a man. His brother Jesus, the King, was only a man. In fact, people throughout Judea and Galilee say the King never died, or if he did, he came back to life. They were men just like you, and now they are calling on you to carry on their work. It is for this that you were born and received all your training in the Law and the Prophets. The Father has raised you up for this very purpose. Rabbi, your nation depends on you."

Rabbi Symmachus looked dazedly into the space before him. I could not tell whether he was searching for a way to escape or considering how to begin his new tasks.

Finally, he spoke.

"Rebecca, I will need your help."

PRISCILLA

"Aquila, I have received word from Phoebe that she needs twelve blankets of hide for the church in Cenchrea. They have opened a dormitory for travelers arriving at the port on their way to Corinth." I looked through her letter to see if she sent any news of importance.

My husband looked up from his bench with a tired expression. "All right, but I miss Paul. I could do this work in half the time if he were here to help."

I laughed. "I think it is just barely possible that the two of you might have been able to finish the task at all if you didn't waste so much time talking. Actually, I think you go twice as fast now that Paul is gone. Yes, I miss him too. But don't pretend to me that he made your work go any faster."

As soon as the words were out of my mouth, I realized Aquila might angrily defend Paul. But no, he joined me in laughing. "I miss his talk most, I suppose." He said nostalgically.

The Romans had killed Paul two years earlier. He had hoped for a public crucifixion on a cross atop one of the seven hills of Rome. I think he wanted everyone see him on the hilltop as he martyred himself for the Christos. Secretly, though I'm sure he would never admit it out loud to anyone but Aquila and me, I believe that he also thought the Day of the Lord would explode in bright light as he hung there, and all eyes would turn and see him on the cross. The world as we knew it would end at that moment, and Paul would triumphantly come down from the cross to lead us himself into the next life.

Alas, it did not turn out that way for our dear Paul. My friends in the emperor's court told me a much grimmer story. Exasperated by the sound of his never-quiet voice, the guards finally strangled Paul in his cell one night when they feared his date of execution might be delayed by stormy weather. I'm told the other prisoners applauded.

Yes, we missed him even though he was often a tax on our patience. As he mentioned in a few of his letters, some people had a gift for making impassioned, inspiring public speeches. Paul had that gift, and we made good use of it. We had not found a single individual to fill that void since Paul's death, but no matter. We had his letters, and several other letters that some of us had written in his name.

Paul had the gift of preaching, and I had the gift of administration. I had a network of churches in the eastern empire, and I maintained control to ensure that they would not stray from our strict regimen. In addition to distributing copies of Paul's epistles, I sent the churches letters each month telling them what topics they should discuss in their sermons and which subjects they should avoid. The people at those churches had the gift of teaching, and I wanted them to pass on Paul's gospel to future generations.

Aquila stood up from his work bench. "We should go soon. You have to address your group in a little while."

"You're right, we should leave now." I picked out a shawl made of fine cloth and wrapped it around my shoulders. Unlike presentations before Judeans, here it would not be necessary for me to keep my head covered. After pulling both sides of the shawl to make it hold tightly, I walked to the door.

Women could not speak at the Forum without creating a scandal, so I would make no attempt to address my audience at that august site. But I knew a merchant who lived in a large home not far from the Forum, and he allowed me to hold gatherings there. He only had enough room for about a dozen listeners at each meeting, but that was enough. I gave instructions for each of the twelve to go out after the meeting and repeat what they had heard me say to a dozen of their friends, who in turn would tell even more people.

"My friends," I said as I stood at the front of the room this afternoon. "You have read what Paul said about the Christos. In the shrines in your own homes, you have a god who can make the grapes produce a sweet wine, but the Christos can turn mere water into wine instantly. You have another god who can bring rain, but the Christos can cause a storm to cease and can even walk across the water. And you have a god who was the son of a union of two of the lesser gods, but the Christos was born of a virgin who merely received the favor of the One God, with no sexual union."

I looked out at them as they realized the power I was describing. "This Christos that Paul described to you is equal with the One God. Your household gods are inferior. If we are to stand tall within the empire, we must have the greatest god in the empire. Join me in spreading the word about the Christos."

The twelve clapped in appreciation, and then they came forward for individual instructions.

SARAH

My child will have lighter skin than I, just as my own skin was slightly lighter than my father's. Marrying pale-skinned mates would almost always lighten the pigment of the offspring, though I had heard the story countless times about how my father Judas and his brother Jesus inherited their dark complexions from an ancient African princess. I'm sure their father Joseph must have suspected at one time or another that his wife Miriam had been unfaithful, but he kept faith in her and raised the boys along with James, Simon, Joanna and Susanna, all of whom were as pale as he and Miriam. His good stewardship of the children had brought great leaders to the nation — four men of consequence and two strong women as well.

The people here in Gaul called me the Black Madonna. My daughter (or perhaps my son?) would not be black because her father was not. If she chose to follow in my footsteps as a minister of the new faith, what would they call her? The Lady of the Dusk? The Brown Mystic? Well, I said silently as I massaged my swollen abdomen, it doesn't matter what they call you, my little one. If you choose to, you will continue to teach them about the Anointed Ones of our family. And the Father will protect you all your days.

Maximin had seen me rubbing my belly. "Are you in pain? Should I call the midwives?" he asked. Silly man — if the baby were causing me enough pain to require the midwives, it would not be necessary for him to summon them. I would scream so loudly that the entire village would know my hour had come.

"Do not worry about me," I told my husband aloud. "Tell me, have we received any word from my mother?"

"Her health is good," Maximin replied. "And she sent word that she is praying for Lazarus's health as well. The messengers said her face literally glowed in the cavern when she said this, so confident was she in her brother's recovery."

I merely smiled. If Mom said Uncle Lazarus would recover from his severe illness, then there was nothing more to say. He would recover.

"Speaking of Lazarus," I said, "though he will continue as the overseer for all the churches of Gaul for as many years as the Father gives him, I want you to assist him. And I don't mean just carrying heavy loads or giving him a boost onto a horse's back. I want you to learn about the churches in every village and town in Gaul. I want you to get to know all the people he knows, understand all their hopes and dreams as he understands them, and grasp all their challenges even as he does."

Maximin realized where I was leading. "You want me to take over for him?"

"Not yet. But I want you to be ready when the time comes."

He nodded in silence, apparently absorbing the implications. Lazarus led the many dozens of churches in southern Gaul. When I say led, perhaps that is too strong of a word. He gave general direction but left it up to the local priests to lead their congregations on their own discretion. As a lifelong close companion of my paternal uncles, James the Righteous One and Jesus the King, he knew their styles of leadership intimately and trusted the Father to maintain control. Lazarus did not consider it necessary to tell priests what they should or should not say.

Maximin pointed at my belly. "How about yourself? Have you chosen someone to take over the weekly meditations when you give birth?"

I tilted my head and scolded him like a teenager who had just uttered nonsense. "I am a woman. My grandmother gave birth to a family of six holy children. My own mother gave birth to me in a strange village while fleeing Roman authorities who wanted to execute her husband. Then she carried me across a desert to Egypt, and later across the sea here to Gaul. My baby will come to the meditations with me and may even help lead them when she or he is old enough to speak. It is our family's way."

My husband smiled sheepishly. "Yes, dear."

PRISCILLA

The women sat expectantly, waiting to hear how to become part of my new movement. I let the suspense build for as long as I could before moving forward to stand in front of them. I heard them gossiping among themselves, each claiming to be more knowledgeable than the other. From where I stood hidden in the recesses, I overheard several women loudly claim to have known Paul when he went from city to city preaching the word. I looked at their faces and recognized not one of them. I actually *had* traveled with Paul, so I would probably know by sight anyone who had been present at more than one of his appearances. These false or exaggerated boasts happened often and I had grown used to it — people (of both genders) trying to increase their own importance by claiming acquaintance with a celebrity. It usually did not cause any harm, so I let it pass.

However, one woman in this crowd took it too far. I heard her whispering to her neighbor that she had even slept with Paul once when her husband had traveled to other parts, and she boasted of Paul's sexual prowess. Hah! I would have to embarrass her later by divulging some private details about Paul. He certainly would never have had sex with a married woman. I don't believe he ever had sex with even an *un*married woman in his lifetime. I do not have any knowledge whether he had sex with anyone of his own gender. I assume that if he ever found sexual release, he did so alone.

The building of anticipation in the room had clearly gone on long enough. With a flourish and a swish of the fine material of my robe, I swept into the room and took my place at the front.

"Ladies, welcome!" I tried to make my smile stretch almost as widely as I stretched my arms our to each side. "We are here today because it is up to us women to bring order to the empire. Our husbands fight wars and conquer land and capture slaves, but it is we wives who make it all work as it is supposed to. Am I right?"

A number of them gave little cheers, while several others just nodded in amused agreement.

"Very well. Before we go further, how many of you have read Paul's letters?" A few hands shot up immediately. Then some of the other women, seeing their friends raising their hands, raised their own as well, however tentatively. After a long pause, almost every woman in the room was claiming to have read the epistles.

This, too, followed the usual pattern. No matter — I wasn't going to test them on their knowledge.

"Excellent," I exclaimed. "Then all of you know that we will have eternal life. And if we handle our husbands and families correctly, they will join us in eternal bliss too. Now, I know that all of you wish to have your children with you in heaven, so it is essential that you follow our instructions closely on how to worship the Christos and maintain a prayerful community."

A loud rustling noise stopped me from going further. I peered toward the back of the room and saw a very stout woman struggling to her feet. I thought to myself, gads, she has the girth of three women. If she were a soldier and I was her general leading the army into battle, I would place her like a phalanx on the front line to shield a platoon of archers behind her. But I would let her wear the huge necklace that now spread across her ample bosom, because the sight of that much gold would probably distract the attention of the enemy soldiers.

"I have heard," she said, "that this Christos arose among the Judeans."

"Yes, he did," I answered simply.

She wagged a fat finger in the air. "I have heard tales about the Judeans' Law, and how strict they are in its observance. What sorts of actions are you going to require of us to become followers of this Christos of yours?" The two women seated on either side of her nodded in agreement, but neither of them dared speak.

I waited a moment for the chatter to die down. "As you will recall from your reading of Paul's letters," I began. Hah, let them try to mount an argument now, after having falsely claimed to have studied his writings! "You will remember that Paul said repeatedly that you can ignore the Law. No good works are required from you. In fact, if you try to justify yourself by good works, you will fail and might bring condemnation down on yourself. You only need faith in the Christos. Nothing more."

"Are you certain?" asked the woman. I sensed that she would welcome an excuse to sit down again as soon as she could. Carrying that much weight on her two legs must be causing a huge strain.

"My husband and I traveled with Paul for many years, and he spoke of this often. I know his mind when it comes to the question of faith versus works."

The fat lady surprised me by suddenly singing "Hallelujah" in a loud, melodious voice. Then she sat down. It was over.

REBECCA

The synagogue's benches filled as the men filed in. From where I sat with Rabbi Symmachus at the front of the room, I saw the assembly from a new angle. Even back in Jerusalem, and certainly in the several weeks since my arrival here in Pella, I had always sat with the women in the back of the synagogue, and I never paid any attention to the men taking their seats. But here I could not help but notice that very few of them voluntarily came to sit on the benches in the very front. Instead, they crowded the back of the men's section, only moving to benches ahead as those in the rear filled up. It looked as if they wanted to be in a position to flee if the rabbi called for volunteers. Or perhaps they just wanted to leave as soon as possible when it was over. In fact, now that I thought of it, I remembered a time when I was much younger, when a man sitting near the rear of the synagogue would sometimes begin snoring loudly during the readings from the Prophets. So maybe that was why the men tried to avoid the benches near the front.

Though most of them were concentrating on squeezing onto benches as close to the exit as they could, a few took the time to glance toward the ark at the front of the room. That's when they noticed me — a woman! — sitting in a place of honor next to the rabbi in the front of the room. I pretended not to notice them looking at me in astonishment. But as they nudged their fellows next to them and pointed, I could feel the heat of their glares. I held my silence and kept my eyes turned downward.

Finally, the benches filled and all the congregation stopped shuffling. As silence fell, the rabbi stood and held his palms forward, his fingers splayed.

"Before we begin," he said, looking at the men, "I have important news. Rabbi James of Jerusalem, the Righteous One, has been killed."

Shocked gasps exploded among the men in the front of the room, and a few shrieks sounded from among the women in the rear. Rabbi Symmachus held up his hand for silence.

"As you know, Rebecca here was a close confidant of James and served in his household," he said, extending his hand toward me. "I have asked her to say a few words before our prayers."

Despite the men's shock at the news about James and the rabbi's explanation for my presence, I still sensed hostility as I stood before the assembly. Perhaps I only imagined it. Perhaps I and other women had grown so accustomed to letting men stand in front of us, letting men decide whom we should marry and where we should live and when we should speak and when we should remain silent — perhaps I just assumed that the men took offense at me standing here before them as if I were important.

But then I recalled how my association with James not only gave me greater status in their eyes but also swelled their pride in Pella's importance to our people. After all, the Righteous One himself had sent his emissary here. I must not let them down.

"Dear people of Pella. When I told James that the Poor were gathering here east of the Jordan, he told me that you were explicitly following the will of the Father. He foresaw catastrophe in Jerusalem. Not only this current turmoil, which has claimed his own life and that of my kinswoman Rachel — " several women cried out at the news of Rachel's death " — but he also warned me of a war coming. That is why he sent me here with his library of ancient scrolls of the Law and the Prophets, and many of them were the oldest copies to be found anywhere in the holy city. They are written in the ancient language of our ancestors, not these Greek translations in common use today.

"He also sent a letter that he wrote directly to you, the Poor. James expects the Poor to preserve mankind's friendship with the Father and thus save the world from destroying itself. James is counting on you, the very people in this room."

Silence followed. I did not know whether they were still in shock at James's death or at the news that he had singled them out to preserve the ancient writings and save the earth from destruction. Whatever the cause, I spoke again before the silence could grow awkward.

"In our people's history the Father has anointed a number of heroes to lead us forward. He anointed David, who united Judea and Israel into a single kingdom. He anointed Judas the Hammer to free us from the Greeks who ruled over us. And in the time of our own lives, he anointed Jesus the King to bring us back to the Father, and he anointed James the Righteous One to strengthen our bond with the Eternal One.

"And now," I continued, "Jesus has risen from the dead after the Romans tried to kill him, and his spirit gives us strength. And James has passed his mantle to us, even as Elijah passed his mantle to Elisha. We, the Poor, must carry on for the two Anointed Ones."

Rabbi Symmachus raised his hand to ask for my attention. "Tell us, did James give any message before he sent you to us? What was the last urgent matter on his mind, if you are aware?"

I stopped to think. Though I was not part of the many disputes and arguments that had engulfed James in the past few years, one topic came up repeatedly. Even Rachel had strong opinions, and Rachel almost never injected herself into Temple affairs. That topic? Paul. At that moment, one heated conversation flooded back in my memory.

"You may hear some people tell you that you only need faith in Jesus the King to win salvation," I told them. "These people will tell you to forget the Law and perform no good works because they are insufficient in the Father's eyes.

"But James said this. What does it profit a man if he says he has faith but has no good works? If you see one of the Poor cold and naked, starving on the street, and you say, go forth and be clothed and warm and well-fed but you do not give that person any clothes or food, what good is that? Faith without works is dead."

I paused and looked down at the ground for a long moment. When I raised my face to look at the crowd again, I put steel in my voice. "Hearken to the Prophets. And obey the Law to the fullest. We depend on it. The world depends on it."

SUSANNA

Knowing the customs of this land better than I, Abban made the funeral arrangements and kept them as simple as possible. For one thing, there would not be a chorus of women wailing. I did not mind that detail, because I never cared for the wailing women at funerals anyway. To tell the truth, in my lifetime I had attended funerals for some powerful but not well-loved men associated with the tetrarch in Sepphoris. I learned that the women wailing at their burials were hired to make it look like masses of people were heartbroken at the men's deaths. In reality, though, many of the women paid to weep had probably never met the deceased men in their lifetimes or, if they had, felt no sorrow at their passing.

For Jesus Thomas's burial, there would be no shortage of sorrowful women and men. But they would remain silent.

When Thomas and our party had set out on the path for Vedapuri, word spread quickly that a holy man was making the pilgrimage and hundreds of peasants — even those whom the Brahmans said must never be touched — lined the road to pay homage. Thomas would stop for a moment in front of each group and bless them. I myself did not feel the presence of the Father in these instances as I had on so many other occasions, but I gathered that the peasants did because of the light that suddenly shined in their eyes. Some of them excitedly stood up and then clapped their hands to their mouths to stop themselves from shouting. As we passed, I would look back and see many of them hugging each other in silence.

As we approached Vedapuri, I could again smell the ocean in the air. Gulls flew overhead, squawking as if in greeting. Just a little farther, and then we could rest. But about twenty men stood blocking the road in front of us, all dressed in the same drab material and wearing swords strapped to their hips. Their leader, a tall man with a neatly trimmed beard and moustache, stepped forward and confronted Thomas.

"You are the man who is telling our people that all are equal?"

Thomas merely nodded. "It is God's way."

Rage filled the man's face. "It is not our way!" With that, he quickly drew his sword and plunged it into Thomas's chest. Standing slightly behind my brother, I screamed as I saw the blade erupt from his back, crimson with blood. Abban held me back as I screamed, fearful that I would rush forward into danger myself.

Without another word, the man withdrew his blade. He and the other men turned on their heels and walked back up the road.

Jesus Thomas lay on his back, his chest rising and falling with short, shallow breaths. Abban and I knelt on either side of him and raised him to a sitting position. He gave a choking cough, and blood dribbled out of his mouth onto his beard.

My brother's eyes looked up into mine, and I think he smiled. His body suddenly went rigid, and he only had the strength to utter two final words.

"Carry on."

That was three days earlier. A local farmer had loaned us a simple wagon and a bull to pull it. We piled hay on the wagon and covered it with white silk, and lay Thomas's white-robed body on it with his hands clasped over his chest, his stiff fingers interwoven. Mourners knelt as the wagon passed on its path to a hill overlooking the city. This region did not have burial caves like back home, where I would have placed Thomas's anointed body on a stone shelf and returned a year later to put his bones in a box. So we buried his body in the ground and marked the spot with a small boulder. Abban etched Jesus Thomas's name onto the rock.

As I turned from the grave, a sea of faces looked up at me. It seemed they expected me to speak. As I stood there, I suddenly felt filled with my brother's spirit, as if he were holding my hand and telling me what to say.

"Many thousands of people in my homeland call Jesus the Anointed One. In other lands many more thousands of people call him by the Greek word for the Anointed One, the Christos. Those people would say that he alone was empowered to speak for God the Father. They would say that only he could approach the Father and ask his blessing and forgiveness for the rest of us.

"But you yourselves know better than that. You yourselves have felt the Father's presence in your lives. You yourselves have the power to approach the Father and ask his blessing and forgiveness for others.

"My brother Thomas, whom we bury here today, has shown us the way. He would say this to you: Each one of us is an Anointed One. Now go out and do what the Father asks you to do in service to your neighbors."

With that, I said no more. Abban held my hand as we walked down the hill to begin our journey home.

* * *

Also by Patrick W. Andersen

Second Born Series
Second Born
Acts of the Women

Standalone
The Ambassador